Beyond the Broken

To John —

Here is to life beyond
the broken!

[signature]

Beyond *the Broken*

A Novel

Sharisse Kimbro

OPEN BOOK
EDITIONS
A Berrett–Koehler Partner

iUniverse, Inc.
Bloomington

Beyond the Broken

iUniverse books may be ordered through booksellers or by contacting:

iUniverse
1663 Liberty Drive
Bloomington, IN 47403
www.iuniverse.com
1-800-Authors (1-800-288-4677)

Cover design by Cecilia Loftus

ISBN: 978-1-4759-6276-5 (sc)
ISBN: 978-1-4759-6275-8 (hc)
ISBN: 978-1-4759-6283-3 (e)

Library of Congress Control Number: 2012921772

Printed in the United States of America

iUniverse rev. date: 2/12/2013

To Noah and Asher,
the two very best reasons
in the whole wide world
to go beyond the broken
and become whole.

Hold fast to dreams
For if dreams die
Life is a broken-winged bird
That cannot fly.

—Langston Hughes

Acknowledgments

WRITING IS A VERY SOLITARY endeavor; however, no one arrives at this moment alone. I stand on many shoulders and am buttressed by the support and encouragement of countless others to find myself wondrously here.

To the "early investors" who read the manuscript once, twice, even three times (Erin) and counting: Stacey, Ken, Mia, Nancy, Tracey M., Cindy, and Robert, your constructive feedback, honest insight, and editorial notes were invaluable.

I am grateful to those whose generous contribution of time, talent, and treasure helped make my dream a reality, including: my mother, Cecilia, Tracey, and Kaitlin.

To everyone who saw something in me that I did not yet see in myself, it was your faith that kept me going, kept me writing, and kept me believing: my brother, my father, Stacey, Nikki, Gina, Rich, DeeDee, Colleen D., Colleen C., Suzi, Dawn, Bambi, and Susan.

Thank you, Marcos, for speaking the title of this book into my life and for being my friend until it manifested.

I am perhaps most appreciative for the situations and circumstances that sought to break me into a million little pieces but instead caused me to come together in ways I could have never imagined. I am thankful for the rough and ragged road that led me here.

Neva

NEVA PRESSED HER CHOCOLATE HANDS against the brown-and-white marble in the double shower when a familiar heaviness halted her breath. *Breathe*, she told herself as she instinctively put her hand on her chest as if she could keep her heart from leaping out. *Breathe.*

She inhaled, slow and deep, shaking her head as she tried to focus on her breathing.

"Mommy!"

The sharp sound of her son's scream surprised her. Neva jumped a little and pressed her hand even harder into her chest, bending over in the shower, now unable to stand. There was plenty of room for her slightly taller-than-average frame to fit doubled-over.

"Mommy!"

The water peppered her back as Ellington continued to yell from his bedroom down the hall.

I hope he doesn't wake his father, she thought as her heart continued to beat faster and harder while her son kept screaming louder and longer. *Stand up. Breathe.*

"Mom-my! Come here! Now! It's a me-mergency!" he shouted. "Mom-my! Where are you?" Neva knew that Ellington was persistent and would not stop until she appeared. *Stand up.*

Neva struggled to straighten and placed her hands against the slippery walls to steady herself as she turned off the water. She gingerly stepped out of the shower, removed the shower cap from her dark, shoulder-length hair, and wrapped a towel around her cocoa-colored torso, not bothering to dry off. Fearing the consequences if Ellington screamed once more, she walked as fast as she could toward her five-year-old's room, trying not to slip down the hall. She knew that the pain in her chest would only worsen if she didn't quiet him down before his father woke up. *Thank goodness he's a heavy sleeper.*

Ellington had wet his bed again. Instead of getting up and taking off his own soiled pajamas, he just lay there screaming for her.

"Mom-my! I was waiting for you!"

"Shh! Be quiet, baby. I'm here now," Neva whispered. "C'mon, you can take off your own pj's."

"But they're all wet. Can't you do it?"

"Please try. That way Mommy can get dressed and we can be on time for school."

"I need your help, p-lease!" Ellington whined.

Neva sighed as she dutifully helped him peel off the heavy flannel bottoms and stripped the damp sheets off the bed, while struggling to keep hold of the towel that protected her from his increasingly curious five-year-old eyes.

"There, I helped you. Now take off your shirt, so I can run you a warm bath, okay?"

"Okay, Mommy," he replied sweetly as Neva dashed into the Jack and Jill bathroom; the bedroom on the other side was the one unfurnished room in the house. Neva wanted to make it a second office, a space of her own, kind of like what Claire Huxtable had in that episode of *The Cosby Show* when Cliff turned one room in their house into her own private space where no children were allowed. Neva chuckled as she remembered how everyone was trying to get in that room during that episode, but Claire was unflappable. It was funny.

It would not be funny if we were late, she thought. *I hate to start my week that way. Once I start out behind, it feels like I can never catch up.* On the way back to check on Ellington, she noticed that tiny puddles of water spotted the hallway. The thought of Dante's potential response made her forget about being late. Neva carefully got down on her knees, took the edge of the towel, and gently patted the tiny pools one by one—soaking in all the liquid to avoid any damage to the new hardwood floors he recently installed. The other ones were too dark, he said.

Neva's husband, Dante, dictated what colors went on which walls, approved every piece of tile that was purchased, selected every knickknack, and inspected each detail of, well, everything. The result was an entire house that looked like him, all beige and brown. Neva's favorite color was pink.

She had silently hoped that Ellington would have been a girl, so she would have had her chance to sneak in a hint of femininity. The bedding was all picked out, but she never got to buy it. Instead, Ellington's safari-themed nursery seamlessly assimilated into the home's decidedly neutral décor, just as her husband wanted.

All the water gone, Neva let a small sigh of relief escape from her lips as she walked back into Ellington's room and found him jumping on the naked bed, wearing nothing but a smile. Neva tightened the towel around her chest, gathered him up, and put him in the tub. He splashed around loudly.

"Honey, hurry up," she said as she turned her back to him and leaned forward with her elbows against the vanity, which was directly opposite the tub. Almost instinctively, her head fell into her hands. As she mentally resigned herself to another day of covering her body in sweats and stuffing her uncombed hair under a baseball cap, she took some solace in the fact that at least she had taken a shower. *Some accomplishment.*

Neva sighed and shook her head as she caught a glimpse of herself in the mirror. The emptiness behind her eyes startled and saddened her. She wanted to look away, but found herself drawn into her own spacious stare. She kept looking, trying in vain to find the self she once knew, the person for whom a shower could no more pass as an achievement than earning a B. The deeper she searched, the louder Ellington splashed. And splashed. Water was getting everywhere, including on Neva.

"Ellington!" she yelled as she turned away from the mirror to scold him. As she turned back to try to find herself again, a single tear escaped down her cheek when it became clear she could not.

Heather

HEATHER'S STOMACH CHURNED AS SHE waited in one of the black leather Le Corbusier chairs that casually lined the reception area of the law firm offices of the chairman of the board of trustees for the Oakland Fine Arts Museum. The invitation was highly unusual, and she didn't know quite what to make of it. She got the call Monday morning to come in that same afternoon. *What a way to start my week,* she thought. *I'm glad I was able to push it back a day. I needed a minute.*

The older African American woman who manned the reception desk looked over at her every once in a while and smiled, which only made Heather more nervous. She was glad she had decided to wear her reliable red interview suit, even if it was out of style, but as she fidgeted in her chair, she wished she had worn something a little more comfortable.

The receptionist cleared her throat and awakened Heather out of her internal style dialogue in time for her to notice the chairman's secretary standing behind an open glass door. She was a short, robust white woman with gray hair, who always seemed annoyed whenever Heather called. She didn't look any happier to see Heather in person.

"You can come in now," the secretary curtly advised as Heather rose from her perch and feigned a confident stride past the reception desk and through the door the secretary was holding. Heather could have sworn she heard a faint "Good luck." Heather turned her head as she rounded the corner and noticed the receptionist still smiling at her.

"Ms. Neale, come in. Have a seat," Mr. Chamberlain's voice boomed from behind a desk way too large for the size of the room. *I wonder what he is overcompensating for?* she thought as she nervously complied.

"So glad you were able to come in today, and on such short notice."

"Well, of course, I—"

Before she could finish, he interrupted, "Ms. Neale, I, along with all the board members, considered it quite a coup to steal you away from the DuSable Museum in Chicago. We were all quite impressed with your credentials and experience. I mean, you are a Stanford undergraduate and have a doctorate from the University of Michigan—all very impressive."

"Yes, I—"

"But we are beginning to feel that, well, maybe we were a tad overconfident. You know, a lot of people have invested a great deal in this museum, and it means so much to this city and the people of Oakland."

"I know, and that's why—"

"And everyone knows that I'm all for community and doing things, you know, to help 'our people,' but we want to have a world-class institution here at the Oakland Fine Arts Museum. Only the very best, which is why we sought you. But perhaps we were mistaken. It seems that you have gotten a bit off vision with your latest endeavor. Now, maybe after we get established and some time has passed, this idea of yours, this community arts project, will have some, um—what's the word?—context in which to be properly perceived, but right now, we feel that it's just too soon. Am I making sense here?"

Now that he was finally asking her to speak, she had nothing to say, she was so shocked by what he had said.

"I will take your silence as agreement and trust that you will put forth no more of the museum's precious, and might I add, rare resources toward this effort and get back to the business of doing the job we hired you for—to build this institution and make it a gem in this city's crown. I'm so glad that we had this little heart-to-heart. We should do this more often."

"I'm sorry," Heather shook her head, stunned, as she stood from her seat, "I think there's been a huge misunderstanding."

"Why—what do you mean?"

"I was very clear about my vision of the way institutions should be integral to, and reflective of, the communities in which they exist. I told you when I interviewed months ago that I was committed to community art and arts education and working to elevate the environment as much as reflect it. I must have been mistaken in thinking that this was the precise vision you and the board wanted for this institution and that, in this way, we would make a name for the Oakland Fine Arts Museum and do something that would really set it apart."

He rose as he rebutted. "Well, priorities change, visions have to be malleable, and leaders must be flexible." He stepped from behind his mammoth desk and stood directly in front of Heather, but she held her ground.

"I don't think I can be flexible on this issue. It's central to who I am as an artist."

His voice elevated as he moved in closer, "Well, you need to do some yoga or something else to get more flexible, because let me speak plainly: we aren't running a 'ghetto museum' filled with so-called 'street art.' You understand me? The name on the door says '*Fine* Arts.' Got it?"

"Yeah, I think I finally do 'get it.'"

"Good. It's essential that you do. Frankly, your job depends on it."

"Oh, I'm crystal clear."

"Good."

"I quit." Heather couldn't have stopped the words from flying out of her mouth if she had wanted to. She could tolerate a lot of things, but disregard for her artistic vision was not one of them. She didn't care if it had been her dream job—director and chief curator at an emerging institution. She thought there was room for innovation and change because they weren't so bogged down in tradition. Even in the art world, she felt like a misfit of sorts; her ideas had always been risky and unproven, and therefore, in her previous positions, deemed unworthy of implementation. This, she thought, was finally a chance to create her vision, it, to finally be able to express herself, to be herself. How disappointing to discover that really, it wasn't.

Annette

THE MORNING LIGHT FILTERED THROUGH the sheer curtains of the tenth-floor window of the Mandarin Oriental Hotel. Annette loved coming to DC. She led the government relations practice at Horne, Sterne & Woode, a large international law firm headquartered in Chicago. Once Barack Obama was elected president, the cachet of all things Chicago increased considerably in the nation's capital. The ever-ambitious Annette was intent on riding the current political wave as far as it would carry her.

She developed a crush on the law when she worked for HSW as a paralegal the year after her graduation from college. Her love grew deeper during her first year at Harvard, and she was head over heels by the time she returned to HSW for a summer associate position her first and second summers. She did well, so it was no surprise when they offered her a job in the early fall of her third year.

HSW was the only place Annette had ever worked. Even with the office politics and constant pressure to perform, it still felt like home. As the firm's only black equity partner and one of the few females in leadership, she far exceeded what her husband earned as the dean of students at one of Chicago's elite private schools. He always reminded her that he was not driven by money, as if that somehow made him better. How much he earned didn't matter to her, and as much as he championed his own altruistic career motivations, he never seemed to shy away from the benefits of her considerable salary, including: a four-bedroom row house in one of Chicago's priciest neighborhood, the S-Class Mercedes to celebrate his fortieth birthday, and a second home in Michigan. She always thought that her generous contribution to the household income would satiate his desire for children, but it never did. He said all he really wanted was a family. *Don't the two of us make a family?* Annette often wondered.

She delicately opened the sheets, grabbed the thermometer from the nightstand, and discreetly slipped out of bed, careful not to make too much noise. On her way to the bathroom, she tiptoed over her skirt and jacket crumpled in a heap on the floor and almost tripped when her foot caught in the armhole of her custom-fit bra, which had been expertly removed the night before.

Safely arriving at the bathroom mirror, she stuck the digital thermometer in her mouth and swept her long auburn bangs from across her forehead. She hoped that by taking her temperature in the bathroom, she hadn't thrown it off too much, but surely she could not take it in the bed this morning. She rapped her carefully manicured fingers on the countertop while she waited for the thermometer to beep. Casting her light brown eyes down on the silver plastic stick, she wondered why she bothered. Charting her ovulation hadn't worked yet. Maybe she was doing something wrong. Math never was her forte, but still, people with a lot less on the ball got pregnant every day by mistake. She couldn't even do the damn thing on purpose. It didn't make sense to her. Here she was with all the resources to care for a child and she couldn't make it happen, while every teenager in America seemed to be able to get pregnant by just looking at a penis.

The thermometer beeped, and she dutifully recorded the numbers on the chart. Annette closed her eyes and shook her head in disbelief. Of course, she was ovulating when she was here and her husband was back home. *We can't seem to get this thing right no matter what we do,* she thought as she threw the chart and the thermometer on the vanity in frustration. She quickly recovered, took a deep breath, and splashed tepid water on her face while she forced a positive thought: *I will get pregnant.*

Catching her reflection in the mirror as she gently patted her face dry, she thought she needed a little something, so she lightly applied some bronzer to her honey-colored skin and a touch of nude lip gloss to look more "naturally" refreshed. As she examined her work in the mirror, something still seemed "off." She squinted as she tried to decide if she was finally starting to show her age or if it was something else.

She washed her hands and tried to forget about it, as if that were possible. She had a lot of other things to focus on, but the whole baby situation made her feel inadequate for the first time that she could remember. And she could have sworn that her husband looked at her funny when she left for this trip. She kept staring at the mirror, trying to see what he saw, and found no answers. *Humph*, she grunted. Drying her hands, she concluded that there was nothing wrong with her. And she was going to prove it.

Her red-toed feet stepped lightly but purposefully back into the expansive hotel room. She picked up her bra, placed it on a chair, and reached for her BlackBerry, where it was charging on the desk. She moved her thumbs adeptly as she sent her assistant an e-mail, asking her to call Tamara's office to get a referral to a fertility specialist and book the first available appointment, preferably by Friday. It didn't matter that it was 7:00 a.m. on Wednesday in Chicago; her assistant responded right away. Annette was used to getting what she wanted when she wanted it, and this baby would be no different.

Tamara

TAMARA CAREFULLY LIFTED THE BABY from the mother's womb and gently handed the tiny boy to the waiting nurse, who quickly cleaned and examined him before delivering him into the hands of the nervous new father, who was crying so much he was shaking. Tamara could barely look at him. He was so ... doting. Throughout the entire surgery, he hadn't stopped stroking the hair of his pregnant wife. And he looked at her so lovingly. It made Tamara sick. She was glad this case was over. They were just too perfect.

Like most couples, they wanted a natural childbirth, but with the mother's preeclampsia, Tamara had to perform an emergency C-section. She had given the speech a million times before, it seemed. "I know you prefer to deliver your baby naturally, but you should be prepared for a C-section, given the complications of _____ (fill in the blank with whatever the condition of that particular mother). It really is the best way to ensure your health and the health of your baby." This couple was particularly resistant to the idea that things weren't going to go as planned. It was clear from the beginning that they were the kind of folks for whom things typically happened according to plan, perfectly. *Well, not this time*, Tamara smirked.

Tamara hurried out of the operating room and peeled off her scrubs. A quick stop by the waiting area to inform the newly minted grandparents that all went well, and she could finally leave. Two sets of grandparents and maybe an aunt and uncle rose from their seats when Tamara approached them. They looked nervous, so Tamara forced a smile, which immediately seemed to make them relax.

"Everything went well. We have a healthy baby boy."

They erupted in hugs and kisses. Tamara turned and quickly walked away before anyone grabbed her. She always felt a little out of place in the jubilation that followed the birth of a child. "Another happy customer," she said to herself as she entered the doctors' locker room. She silently and quickly changed into her winter running gear, not bothering to make small talk with the other doctors, who were changing as well. She laced her shoes, tuned on her iPod, and raced out the door.

Tamara turned onto the path alongside Lake Shore Drive and started to pick up speed. Running after a long night of deliveries always seemed to clear her head. Her creamy cheeks flushed pink as the freezing air whipped around her face. Tamara started running during her freshmen year at Stanford. It was a useful way to manage the "freshman fifteen." And running out there was a great way to enjoy the usually perfect weather. Running along the lakefront in Chicago in the dead of winter was another matter entirely.

A dark shroud of clouds hung over Lake Michigan, reluctant to give way to the sliver of pink light that was trying to claim its place in the sky. As she took the curve near Lake Point Tower and ran speedily by Millennium Park, then Grant Park and Buckingham Fountain, she turned up the classic Jill Scott song "Golden," trying desperately to find some inspiration somewhere.

As the pink started to break through the gray, a feisty orange tried to barge its way into the sky. This colorful battle was not altogether lost on Tamara. The fact that the sun was trying to shine on a cold February morning was a gift that even she could not ignore. About this time every year, Tamara questioned her decision to ever leave sunny California to come back home. Chicago winters were the worst. Weeks could go by without the sun making any appearance. It would be day after day of dismal gray—and then it would snow. And snow. And snow. And then it would get even colder.

When Tamara reached Museum Campus, she turned around and turned her attention from the sky to the lake. Lake Michigan was one of Chicago's most exquisite features, although the word "lake" always seemed too diminutive. When Tamara was a little girl, she thought it was the ocean because it was so vast. It looked like it could go on forever. She remembered fantasizing as a teenager about getting married at the South Shore Cultural Center in a room overlooking the lake. She imagined that the love she would declare to her husband would be as unending as the water. That recollection almost made Tamara laugh out loud as she ran even faster, speeding up toward Northwestern Memorial Hospital, her long, black ponytail swinging as her strong legs raced her to her second home, where she could finally wash the smell of new life off her body. It wasn't like she had any reason to rush home.

Another Thursday with no weekend plans to look forward to. Dating was no longer worth her effort or energy. Tamara found that most black men who were worth anything were already taken, and the ones who weren't were either gay (or on the down low), uneducated, or underemployed; those who weren't any of those things had arrogantly internalized the oft-quoted statistics about the high number of unmarried black women over thirty, so they felt (and acted) like they were a precious commodity and let women do the pursuing.

Tamara was not about to become the aggressor in any relationship and could not be bothered with anyone who could not conjugate a verb, or who felt uncomfortable because she was a doctor and probably made more money than he did, or who thought that she should accept, even appreciate, the fact that he was with her tonight, and ask no questions about where he would be or who he would be with tomorrow. All she wanted was an attractive, intelligent, secure, kind, employed black man with no criminal record who didn't live with his momma or have a bunch of kids. *Why is that so difficult to find?*

Lauren

Lauren reached over on the nightstand and grabbed the box of cookies she hadn't finished the night before. She was so hungry when she got home from China. She could barely eat a thing the entire trip. Chinese food in China is way different than the Chinese food she was used to. When she got home from the airport, everyone was already asleep and she was too tired to cook, so she just headed upstairs, where the cookies were waiting in her nightstand, ever faithful. It was nice, but having some company would have made it even nicer.

A few crumbs in the bed never hurt anyone, she thought as she stuffed three of the thin cookies into her mouth at once, while skimming her hand over the neatly made side of the bed her husband used to sleep on. *How long has it been since we shared a bed? Probably not since little Kyle was born, which was almost three years now.*

As if on cue, there was a soft rapping at her bedroom door. *Why isn't Kyle with Zoe, the au pair?* Lauren wondered as she sighed and glanced at the clock. It was seven thirty on Saturday, Zoe's only day to sleep in, but she knew Lauren had just gotten back in town. Maybe she was busy getting the twins ready for piano or dance. Lauren stayed in bed but didn't move. *If I don't answer, maybe he'll find Zoe.* Kyle knocked on the door again. *He's persistent,* she thought; *maybe he really needs something.*

"Who is it?" she called.

"It's me!" Kyle answered loudly.

"Me who?" Lauren teased.

"Me, Kyle," he responded.

Lauren laughed in spite of her exhaustion.

"You may come in 'me, Kyle,'" Lauren said reluctantly as she opened the locked bedroom door.

"Mommy!" Kyle jumped into his mother's ample arms without being invited there and held on tightly.

"Oh my goodness," Lauren said with a startled voice, "good morning to you too!"

"I missed you, Mommy!" he said as he planted a big kiss on Lauren's cheek.

"Mommy missed you too, baby. Did you have a good week?"

"Uh-huh."

"Well, what did you do?"

"I dunno."

Lauren laughed, although she didn't find it a bit funny.

"Did you go to school?"

"Uh-huh."

"Did you learn something?"

"Uh-huh."

"What did you learn? Tell me one thing."

"Ummm …"

"C'mon, you can tell me one thing you learned this week, can't you?"

"Well …"

"Oh, Kyle, really?"

"I'm sorry, Mommy. I can't remember one thing."

"That's okay, baby. What are you and Zoe going to do today?"

"I dunno."

"Well, you can do whatever you want, anything, just name it."

"Really? Anything?"

"Yes, anything. Just tell Zoe, and she will do it. The zoo, the park …"

"Swimming! I want to go swimming!"

"Well, you can do anything besides that. It's too cold, and we haven't opened the pool yet. It's the middle of winter, you know."

"Oh," Kyle scrunched up his little forehead to think about his other options.

As he was in deep contemplation, there was a rapid knock at the door.

"Come in," Lauren called.

"Lauren, I'm so sorry. I was getting the twins breakfast and I thought he was right there, then I turned around and he was gone. I have been looking for him all over the house," Zoe apologized.

"It's okay; we had a nice visit."

"I'll be heading off to karate now. Kyle, c'mon with me," Zoe said as she reached over to take Kyle out of his mother's arms and into her own.

"I wanna stay with Mommy!" Kyle clung tightly to his mother's neck.

"Ah, yes, karate. I couldn't remember what they had this morning. These kids have so much going on. Kyle, go with Zoe. We will do something fun tomorrow, on Zoe's day off," Lauren said, while unhinging Kyle's arms from her neck and his legs from her waist. Kyle took Zoe's hand with mild reluctance as Lauren got back in the bed.

"Shut the door, please," Lauren shouted after them as they headed downstairs. *Just a little more sleep will get me back on track.* It seemed that her work travel schedule had increased instead of lightened as she had more children. She didn't know whether it was the kids or her age or what, but one thing was certain, she couldn't manage the jet lag so easily anymore. As she closed her eyes for a second time, there was another rap on the door.

"Ugh! Who is it?" Lauren asked in a perturbed, elevated voice.

Her husband, Prescott, peeked his head in. "Did I wake you?"

Lauren sat up and ran her fingers through her wavy hair. "Oh, no, of course not. Come in, you don't have to knock, you know, it is still your room."

He walked into the room slowly, leaned over, and gave Lauren a spacious hug and a polite kiss on the cheek but remained standing beside the bed. "Well, I didn't want to disturb you; I know you got in late. Welcome home, by the way. Sorry I didn't get a chance to see you last night. How was your trip?"

"Good, busy but good. I'm exhausted. I can't hang like I used to with these business trips."

"Well, it's good that they continue to give you so much responsibility, isn't it? I mean, that's why you worked so hard to get that promotion."

"I'm not complaining. I'm just saying I'm tired, that's all."

"Well, I'm sure it's a lot. Thank God for Zoe, huh? Speaking of Zoe, I'm going to take Kyle off her hands for a few hours today to give her a break."

"Aren't you going in to the office? And a break? I mean, why does Zoe need a break? That's what we pay her for—to watch our children."

"It's cool. I only have to work for a little while. He can play on my secretary's computer for a bit, and then we can get some ice cream or go to the park or something. I like spending time with him."

"Of course you like spending time with him, you're his father, but I mean, why am I wasting my money having an au pair if you are going to do her job for her? Besides, ice cream? It's the middle of February."

"I didn't know you could only eat ice cream at certain times of the year. You're obviously really tired. You should get some rest. You know we have the black-tie tonight."

"How could I forget? I arranged my trip to come home so I could attend. I'll get myself together by then, don't worry."

"You're already together, honey," he sweetly replied with a smile. "See you later." He leaned over and gave her a light peck on the forehead and walked out the door.

Gone seven days, and all I get is a kiss on the cheek and a peck on the forehead? Lauren reached past the cookies and opened the nightstand drawer to grab her little purple friend. After checking to be sure it still had batteries, she leaned back in the bed, put her hand between her legs, closed her eyes, and let the whirring send her into ecstasy, artificial as it was.

Neva

NEVA MANAGED TO GET ELLINGTON bathed and dressed for school, cook breakfast, and put some clothes on herself in enough time so they wouldn't be too late for school. *This week is getting off to a good start,* she thought. *I even got a load of laundry started.* It seemed that Neva was incessantly washing clothes. Having everything neatly folded in nice little stacks was sometimes the only sense of accomplishment she enjoyed on a given day, but even that was fleeting because no matter how many neat piles of clean clothes she created, more dirty ones continued to fill the hamper. Still, she relished in the temporary feeling that she had actually done something right that day.

As Ellington sat at the breakfast bar happily eating his oatmeal and playfully kicking his feet against the counter, Neva looked at him in disbelief. He managed to stay so happy somehow. She was grateful for that—grateful that her mood didn't seem to impact him one bit.

There were moments, like this one, when it still surprised her a bit that he was her child, that she had a child at all. She had never felt sure that she wanted one or could manage to have one. Still, at her husband's insistence, here he was. She could never tell Dante how she really felt. He would have never married her. He wanted a family more than anything.

Too late for regret now. Ellington was most definitely here, she thought as she cupped her morning coffee and kept staring at him. She remembered how the nurses brought him over minutes after he was born and placed him on her breast. Feeling completely drained after a long delivery, she thought, *What do you expect me to do with this?* He, however, needed no instructions. When his tiny mouth grappled onto her nipple, she wanted to scream, but she didn't have the strength.

Nursing soon became what Neva liked to call one of motherhood's greatest conspiracies. Before she had Ellington, Neva watched women nurse and thought of how beautiful and peaceful they looked. It seemed to be the most natural thing in the world. *After all, it's what breasts were created for, right?* She used to think with self-righteous indignation that women who didn't nurse were selfish, but now she knew why they didn't—it hurt!

As Ellington continued to suckle, a few tears seeped out that Neva hid with a smile. Dante and the nurses thought she was overcome with joy, and she didn't tell them any differently. She didn't ask for help or inquire whether she was doing it right. She pressed the pain way down and kept on giving Ellington what he needed, until she almost forgot she ever felt it. Little did she know that it would become a strategy that she would have the opportunity to perfect over the next five years.

Heather

THE LIQUOR FROM THE TEQUILA burned Heather's throat as her long tawny legs stuck to the hard wooden floor. The ebony slat of the bottom edge of the platform bed pressed through her worn Stanford T-shirt and into her lower back as her hands carefully encircled the glass bottle of Patrón. She lifted it slowly, being as careful as her wobbly hand would allow, and poured another. She successfully avoided spilling any on her journal, which was open on the floor beside her, but a drop of the clear liquid landed on her leg.

She leaned over, bent down, and licked her leg, whisking away the wasted spirit. Heather peered out the window as she rose from the floor to catch a glimpse of the sky in between the two buildings immediately outside her bedroom window. It was still so dark and quiet. She turned and had to squint to see the clock, which read five o'clock, but she wasn't sure if it was day or night. Heather sighed as she thought about the job she had lost and the future that was now permanently beyond her grasp.

"Here's to failure," she said out loud before opening her throat wide and swallowing the tequila effortlessly. She looked up on her nightstand and saw the picture of herself with her best friends from college: Tamara, Neva, Lauren, and Annette. The eager smiles from their shiny faces mocked Heather as she slammed down the shot glass and looked at them with their taunting, toothy grins. *They are all living their dreams, doing what they love, except me. Tamara is a big-time doctor, like she always wanted. Neva is a mother and a wife. Lauren has it all—a career and a family. Annette is a partner at a law firm. And I am … unemployed. This is not supposed to happen.*

Heather gave them the finger as she reached up on the nightstand. Then she turned them on their youthful faces with a force that left a small crack in the glass of the frame. *I don't want them looking down on me,* she thought as she climbed back into bed, her head reverberating with the remembrance of all she once wanted to become. It didn't seem like twenty years ago that she was eighteen years old sitting in the hallway of Stern Hall with Tamara.

"You have to have some idea of what you want to major in," Tamara urged.

"No, not really. Not yet. I have time, though, don't I?" Heather quietly responded.

"Well, don't take too long. I mean, you don't want to waste your time taking a bunch of classes you don't need. If you mess around too long, you'll end up being here for five or even six years."

"Well, that wouldn't be so bad, would it?"

"Oh my God, yes! I am four years, in and out. My parents would kill me if I didn't finish on time."

"My mom is happy I'm here. I don't think she would care how long it took. Do you think financial aid runs out after four years?"

"I have no idea, but it should. Don't you think? I mean, if you can't get it done in four years, maybe you shouldn't be here at all."

"Damn, that's harsh."

"If you say so, but think about it. No one got here without being focused and smart. I don't see any good reason why someone at Stanford can't graduate in four years."

"Well, not everyone is like you."

She remembered that conversation. They always wanted her to be "more grounded" or "focused." *All I wanted was to be myself,* Heather thought as she fell asleep.

Sometime later, her growling stomach woke her. It was three o'clock in the afternoon on Monday. It had been almost one week since she quit her job. *The past week has flown by and crawled along at the same time. Maybe I should eat something.* Opening her mouth and actually chewing seemed like too much work at the moment. Rubbing her hand over the hollowed cave of her abdomen, she supposed that was how her mother felt at the end. She remembered the hospice nurse saying that you can't make anyone sleep or eat. Heather had never been able to make her mother do anything.

Tamara had been nagging Heather to be sure her mother got regular mammograms, but she couldn't be bothered. Instead, her mother was always organizing some protest, participating in some rally, or distributing flyers for some worthy cause. She was so preoccupied that she always seemed to "forget" to do her monthly self-exams, so by the time the doctor discovered the lump in her right breast, the cancer was already at Stage 3. She remained ever the Berkeley activist, always fighting "the power." Heather's mother was a revolutionary to her core. When her parents threatened to disown her because she got pregnant by a black man, she didn't care. She proceeded with the pregnancy, had Heather, and married Heather's father, regardless of what she stood to lose, which was much more than her parents' approval.

Heather never knew her grandparents. Once her mom made her decision, they never spoke to her again. Funny, it never seemed to bother Heather's mom. She was an expert at being exactly who she was and defiantly refused to let anyone change her into someone else. Heather wasn't like her mother, bold and confident.

The doctors recommended an aggressive treatment protocol, which included a double mastectomy, radiation, and chemotherapy, but the words alone seemed to break her mother's spirit. They eventually compromised. Heather's mother had the surgery but opted for an alternative approach, which included a strict vegan dietary regimen, acupuncture, yoga, and meditation. Tamara tried to change their minds and urged Heather to insist on the more conventional treatment, but Heather's mother was never one for convention.

Initially, she felt better, so Heather foolishly hoped that maybe her mother's condition would completely reverse. But they were too late. The cancer metastasized to her brain, and she died of an inoperable brain tumor six months later.

That time went by so fast. Heather wanted a little of it back. Her mother would know how to make her feel better. She always knew exactly what to do. Her mother believed that Heather could do anything, and she gave Heather the space to try everything. She was the one who first nurtured Heather's interest in art, after noticing Heather's talent and eye for color. She even converted one of the closets in their tiny Berkeley home into a makeshift studio and had one of her artist friends give Heather lessons every Tuesday. Heather would rush home after school, put on the oversize shirt she imagined had once been her father's, and paint or sketch before the lesson even started. Her teacher joked that he should have been taking lessons from her. She never felt more at home than in those hours after school in her studio. If only she had learned to keep that feeling.

Her mother had a little art show in their house once and invited all of her friends. Heather sold every painting, but she knew it wasn't real. She knew that her mother made her friends promise to buy stuff, but it still felt good to be seen.

As she ran her tongue across the two-day-old film on her teeth, she took a whiff under her armpit, and the smell almost made her own stomach turn. *Maybe I should get up after all.* Her legs were a little wobbly as she placed her feet on the hard dark floor and stood up. She stumbled, almost missing the two steps leading into the bathroom, but managed to catch herself before she fell. She stood in front of the mirror contemplating whether to shower or brush her teeth and decided the former was most pressing. She turned on the hot water, took off her faded T-shirt, opened the clear glass door, and stepped in. Her long curly hair was tangled, nearly approaching the matted state, so she stuck her head under the water too. She searched for shampoo and found none, which, she decided, was just as well. She stood there with her head under the water for a long, long time. *I don't think I can do this anymore*, she sighed to herself as her fingers started to pucker.

She reached for a towel and realized there wasn't one. She got out dripping wet, placed her elbows on the gray soapstone vanity in front of her, and leaned forward to rest her head in her hands. It felt as if her brain were expanding to the edge of her skull and her bones were pressing together to keep it contained. She kept one hand on the sink while she used the other to open the medicine cabinet. She found some Vicodin. *That should help.* Then she noticed an old bottle of Zoloft. "Hmmm," Heather said in a hushed whisper, as if someone could hear, "these always made me feel better."

As she continued searching, her fingers touched a bottle of Prozac that she never finished, and then she came across some Xanax samples that she had gotten from her old doctor. *Maybe some of these too. I am so tired of hurting.*

Neva

As Neva pressed her foot on the accelerator and backed out of the circular driveway on her way to run some errands before picking up Ellington from school, her mind ran down her Tuesday to-do list: *Cleaners, call repairman for the washer, drugstore, pick up Ellington, soccer practice—soccer practice!* She slammed her hand to her forehead and her foot to the brakes as she realized he forgot his cleats. *At least I didn't get too far,* she told herself as she proceeded back up the driveway. *I still have time,* she thought as she drove back into the garage, closed the garage door, and ran into the house, leaving the service door open. As she grabbed the cleats from the mudroom, the phone rang.

Neva paused to look at the phone, but since she didn't recognize the number on the caller ID, she let it ring. She tried to turn toward the service door, but her feet felt like they had been cast in cement and her usually nimble legs seemed frozen. There wasn't a minute to spare before she would be late for the pickup line, but there was an urgency in the ring that made it hard to ignore. As Neva stood in the mudroom listening to the phone ring, she could taste bile building in her mouth and felt her stomach strangely churning. She didn't know how she knew, but way deep down, she was certain that this call was nothing good. *I can't deal with whatever it is right now. I gotta go,* she thought as she willed herself to walk back to the garage. Finally, the phone silenced.

Neva exhaled a sigh of relief as she settled into the tan interior of her white Range Rover, a Valentine's Day present from Dante. She thought it was too much—too big, too expensive; it was clearly something that suited him and was not at all like her. But that's the way it always went:

he would blow up at her, then give her a great present, treat her to an expensive dinner, or some such thing to help her forget what had just happened. She sighed as she remembered their fight the year before at Christmas. She didn't set the table right or she forgot a side dish he wanted or something—she couldn't even remember what now—but what she could never forget was the way he got in her face, pointed his finger at her nose, and cursed at her—in front of Ellington, her parents, and everyone. Every time she put the key in the ignition, she heard his harsh voice and biting words. Every time the engine turned, she felt the same fear that consumed her on that Christmas day and never really left. *If he would curse me out in front of my own family* ... she shuddered as she considered what he would do, what he could do next—but what he did was buy her this fancy car for Valentine's Day.

As she backed out of the garage and around the circular driveway for the second time, her cell phone rang, shaking her from the unpleasant memory. *Where is my phone?* She dug around in her purse to find it at the very bottom of the large hobo bag. It kept ringing as she rummaged around the console for her earpiece with one hand while trying to navigate the curvy streets of her Oakland Hills neighborhood with the other.

"Hello?" she answered frantically once she placed the recovered Bluetooth in her ear.

"Neva! Neva!" Carmen's heavily accented voice sounded more frenetic than her own. "Neva! You must come!"

"Carmen ...?" Carmen had been her housekeeper for years. It was the one indulgence Dante allowed. He always argued that she should be able to maintain the house by herself, especially since she didn't work, but Carmen did such a good job when Neva was pregnant, he agreed she should stay. He liked a clean house. When Heather moved back to the Bay area, Neva referred Carmen to Heather.

"Yes, it's me! You have to come—right now!" she responded anxiously.

"Where are you? Are you all right? What's wrong?" Neva fired off the questions before Carmen could answer them.

"It's Heather, she ..." Carmen broke into sobs, unable to finish.

"Carmen, calm down so that I can understand what you're saying." Neva tried to temper her voice, as if by example. "Just breathe, and tell me what's going on."

Carmen inhaled and exhaled loudly into the phone before starting again, speaking slowly and methodically. "I come to clean at Heather's, like I do every Tuesday. I pass the bedroom to get to the bathroom, and I notice that she is lying on the bed. I say 'Good morning!' as I pass by. She does not answer; she does not move. I go in, and that's when I know that she's not sleeping; she just lay there. Not moving. Breathing, I don't know. I call 9-1-1, and then I call you. I don't know what to do," Carmen exhaled as she finished.

Neva heard the cars honking, but the squawks could not make the neurotransmitters in her eyes tell her brain that the light had turned green, so her brain was unable to communicate to her foot to press the gas pedal. The deafening cacophony grew louder, and it was only after the light turned yellow and then red again that Neva stepped on the gas, running the red light, nearly striking an oncoming car. She pulled over for a moment to collect herself and to process what Carmen had just said. It seemed she was destined to be a few minutes late today.

"Carmen, you wait for the ambulance to come." Neva poured her best calm mother voice into the phone. "I can't get there in time. You will have to ride with Heather and let me know where they take her. I'll meet you at the hospital."

Neva sat completely still in her car on the side of Thorndale Road for a while. Her mind was quiet for only a moment before the thoughts started racing, *What if Heather dies before I get there? What if she's already dead? I really should be the one riding in the ambulance with Heather, not some random cleaning person.* Her frustration, mixed with the fear she was trying to ignore, bubbled to the surface in loud, choking sobs as she raced to join the Hillside Academy pickup line.

She turned her head and noticed the cleats on the floor of the passenger seat, and her mind flashed to Ellington. *How can I get to the hospital and take him to soccer practice at the same time? Maybe I can call one of his friends' moms to grab him for me? Maybe he can miss practice. Or what if I can reach the sitter to meet me back at the house? I can pick him up and then drop him back home and then go to the hospital.* She hated the incessant coordination of logistics required for any deviation from her well-orchestrated schedule.

"Aargh!" she released her frustration as she slammed her hands on the steering wheel. Thankfully, she pulled right behind the nanny of one of Ellington's friends and teammates, who agreed to take Ellington to practice and then home with her afterward, so Neva could rush right over to the hospital.

Carmen was sitting in the far corner of the already-crowded waiting area of the emergency room of Alta Vista Hospital when Neva arrived. Her dark head was bowed, and two caramel hands rested purposefully on her ample lap, with thick fingers intertwined. Her torso swayed back and forth ever so slightly as she sat. Carmen's lips were slightly parted but barely moving, as if she were whispering with her heart. Carmen rose to greet Neva. "Neva, Neva, I didn't know what to do," Carmen sighed and sobbed in Neva's arms.

"It's okay, Carmen, it's okay," Neva comforted. "You did fine." Carmen stepped back. "I'm going to talk to the doctors," Neva reassured her before crossing the room slowly but with determination, pulling at the bottom of her white sweat jacket, as if shoring herself up for whatever news she might receive.

"Excuse me," she interrupted the intake clerk, who was sitting behind a desk writing on a clipboard. "I'm looking for Heather Neale."

"Are you her next of kin?" the clerk impatiently inquired without raising his eyes.

"Yes," Neva white-lied. She was the closest thing to family that Heather had and she was her emergency contact, so it was sort of true.

"Okay, then, let me check." The clerk flipped some pages on his clipboard and rolled to a stack of charts sitting on a nearby desk, looked at the top one, furrowed his brows, pursed his lips, and told Neva to have a seat and a doctor would be out to talk to her soon. "Can I just see her?" Neva pleaded.

"Miss, her doctor will be right out. He'll be able to give you more information." The clerk's tone softened as he pointed to the waiting room. "Please."

Neva shuffled to Carmen and sat down beside her. "He couldn't or wouldn't tell me anything," Neva informed her. Carmen only responded by returning to her swaying and praying, even more fervently than before. The news seemed to make her more determined, while it only deflated Neva. Neva alternatively held her head in her hands and turned to look at Carmen, who kept on moving her body and her lips back and forth without making a sound. Neva felt bad that Carmen was involved in this at all. She was sure she had work to do. "Carmen, you can leave. I'll call you and let you know what's going on once I find something out."

"Ay, no!" Carmen exclaimed. "I have to stay here and pray," Carmen emphatically replied, not moving from her seat.

Neva considered calling Annette or Tamara to let them know what happened but then thought better of it since she couldn't really tell them anything. They would probably ask a lot of questions for which she had no answers. Maybe she should join Carmen and say a prayer. Neva didn't even know where to start. Her faith had abandoned her long ago.

What is taking them so long? Neva wondered, trying not to get annoyed. *This is ridiculous!* She started out to demand some answers when a tall man, with skin the color of burnt cinnamon and footsteps as hushed as a whisper, approached her. Neva rose to meet him.

"You are …"

"Heather Neale's next of kin," Neva confirmed.

The doctor nodded as he continued, "I am Dr. Chandra." Dr. Chandra looked over at Carmen, who had stopped praying and stood next to Neva.

"If you will follow me," Dr. Chandra said as he extended his hand, pointing the way to a small room off the waiting area. Carmen lagged behind Neva, who turned and motioned with her head to follow. *She was the one who found her, after all. Besides, I don't want to hear it alone.* They sat in the sparsely furnished room around a tiny, round table.

"It seems that Ms. Neale took a large and dangerous combination of medications, including antidepressants and sleeping pills. Whoever found her got there just in time," Dr. Chandra soberly reported.

Neva and Carmen both released audible sighs of relief. A few tears escaped from Carmen's eyes.

"But she is definitely not out of the woods yet. We were able to pump her stomach to eliminate as much of the toxins as we could, and we've started trying to neutralize the drugs she's already absorbed, but she is still unconscious," he continued.

"What does that mean?" Neva asked. "When is she going to regain consciousness? It's just a matter of time, isn't it? I mean, this was just an accident; Heather has always been a little spacey. She probably got mixed up and took too many of something. She'll be fine soon, right?" Neva anxiously questioned.

"Miss …" Dr. Chandra continued.

"Neva, you can call me Neva."

"Neva, it's important that you understand that it does not at all appear that Ms. Neale got 'a little mixed up.' The amount of medication she took was far too great to indicate an accidental overdose. Her actions appear to have been intentional. I know this is hard to hear, so let me be absolutely clear—she is in a coma, and there is a very good chance that she will never come out. We can only wait and see," Dr. Chandra stated gently but firmly.

Carmen closed her eyes and started praying again, not so silently this time. Tiny little whispers escaped from her lips that instead of calming Neva made her even more anxious. "Carmen, do you mind?" Neva sharply requested in a louder-than-normal tone. Carmen's brown eyes opened wide. "I'm sorry, Carmen. I'm so ... so ..." Neva started to cry before she could finish.

Carmen patted Neva's hand. "Shh, shh."

"I'm sorry," Neva sniffled, trying to stop her tears.

Then she turned to Dr. Chandra. "Can we see her now?"

"Of course. We just transferred Ms. Neale to the ICU. You can see her up there," Dr. Chandra responded to Neva. Then he looked at Carmen and said, "Don't stop praying."

Nothing could have prepared Neva for what she encountered. Heather's normally sun-kissed skin now seemed almost translucent. Her eyes were closed, and her respirator-induced breathing was shallow and forced. A clear IV tube stuck out of her arm. Another tube passed through her nose. Large, circular electrode pads were stuck to her chest to monitor her heart rate; another monitor was connected to her forehead with smaller circles.

Neva was there, but she wasn't there. She saw her friend lying so still, but somehow, as if by some protective measure, her mind could not fully comprehend what it was that she saw or what it really meant. *Who is this motionless girl?* Her feet were heavy as she moved closer to see for herself who it could be. Neva looked down at the blank pale face. *I don't know her at all. This isn't the girl who cleaned up after me when I got sick during a friendly game of quarters freshman year. Certainly the woman who boldly accepted a ride, for both of us, from three handsome Italian men as we walked home from school during the quarter we studied in Florence is not lying in that bed. The hands that lie flaccid are not the same ones that made pew decorations for my wedding. The eyes that flutter under the thin lids can't be the person who took Ellington to museums, did craft projects, and showed him all that is beautiful in the world.* It couldn't be her, but somehow it was. *Why did she do this?* Neva wondered. And the more perplexing question quickly followed, *If things were that bad, why didn't I know? If anyone should have known, I should have known. How could I have let this happen?* She couldn't stop the tears from rolling down her face as Dr. Chandra came in to check the monitor readings.

"I'm sorry," Neva instinctively apologized while using the back of her hands as tissue.

"No apology necessary," he graciously replied as he reached for the box of Kleenex on the table next to Heather's bed and offered her one. "I know this is difficult, but it's important to remain positive. There is significant research indicating that people in comas can not only hear the voices of those on the outside but can also perceive the emotional atmosphere around them. Hope is powerful medicine," he stated as he turned and started to walk out the door. "Still, if there are people to be contacted, you should call."

Neva raised her eyebrows as he left. He seemed a little strange to her. She made a mental note to Google him later. She turned from Heather's bedside and walked back into the waiting room so that Carmen could come in. She wasn't related or anything, so technically she wasn't allowed, but if Carmen hadn't found her, well, she didn't want to think about the alternate outcome if today hadn't been Tuesday. *What if Heather tried to kill herself yesterday?* Neva wondered grimly.

Annette

ANNETTE'S BLACKBERRY KEPT BUZZING DURING her meeting, which made it hard for her to focus, but she had to focus—this bond deal was major, and they were getting so close to cementing the details. *Why won't the phone be quiet!* She needed to concentrate. She had made big promises when Obama was elected about her ability to deliver Washington; now it was time for her to make good.

She glanced down for a moment and noticed that it was Neva. It was odd for her to call her during the middle of the workday, and she never did so repeatedly. *I wonder what's going on?* She couldn't wait until the meeting was over to see. Finally, the conference call was over. After giving the associates their marching orders, Annette rushed into an empty office to call Neva back.

"Neva, what's up? Why did you keep calling me?" Annette asked sharply, not hiding her annoyance.

Annette's questions were met with silence.

"Neva? Are you still there? I am at work, you know. I don't have time for this."

Neva spoke slowly, as if pushing the words out one by one. "Heather tried to kill herself, I mean, apparently, I guess, well, anyway, she's in a coma. They don't know ... they aren't sure ..." Neva couldn't finish before Annette interrupted.

"Wait a minute, wait a minute ... what?"

"Heather overdosed, and now she's in a coma," Neva responded more quickly this time. "I know you're really busy, but can ... you ... come?"

"Whoa, whoa, wait a minute. How did this happen?"

"She took some pills, I guess. The cleaning lady found her." Neva's explanation was halted by tears.

"Neva, slow down. I need to understand what exactly is going on. Where are you? Where is Heather now?"

A few deep breaths, and Neva was able to continue. "I'm at Bayside Hospital. I just talked to the doctor. He told me if there was anyone to call, I should call, so … I'm … calling …" Neva's tears carried the rest of the sentence away.

"Okay, okay, just calm down. I'm coming, and we'll get to the bottom of this. I have to clear my calendar, but I'll be there. Of course, I'll be there. Where else would I be? I'll call you once I've made the arrangements. I'm in DC, so …"

"I don't understand how this could have happened," Neva interrupted. "I should have known—I …" Once again, Neva was unable to finish speaking before all Annette could hear were sobs.

"It's not your fault. Hold on. I'll get there as soon as I can." Neva's sobs turned to heaves, a vain attempt to stop herself from crying. "I won't get off the phone until you stop crying," Annette said as she turned to the computer and sent her assistant Cathy an e-mail instructing her to arrange a flight from DC to San Francisco as soon as possible and telling her to cancel or reschedule all of her appointments for the rest of the week.

Neva was still crying.

"Honey, calm down. Take a few deep breaths. I'll get on the next plane, and together, we'll figure this out, like we always have. Don't worry. Everything will be fine."

Neva released a few half-sobs before she was able to breathe deeply into the phone. Once, then twice.

Finally, after a long pause, she was able to reply with the rote response, "I'm fine."

"Are you sure?"

"Yeah, sorry."

"You don't need to apologize. Just hang tight. I'll be there as soon as I can," Annette replied as she hung up the phone. She remembered she had better let her husband know that she would not be coming home as planned. He was not going to be happy. She had been in Washington for over a week now, opting to stay over the weekend. She would call him later, or maybe her assistant could deal with him too. She didn't have time for his questions right now. Her head was still spinning with the news she had just received when her phone rang again. It was Lauren.

"I just talked to Neva, can you believe it?" Lauren asked before she even said hello. "This is crazy. I mean, this is not something that 'we' do, you know what I mean?"

"What are you talking about?"

"You know, black women don't commit suicide. I guess that's her white side coming through. I don't get it. What could be that bad? I mean, really. And if it was that bad, why didn't Heather say something? Or Neva? Didn't she know Heather was about to go off the deep end? I bet she feels horrible."

"Lauren," Annette interrupted, "do you hear yourself? I can't believe you're trying to blame Neva. And what are you talking about? 'Black women don't commit suicide'? You sound crazy. What's wrong with you? Stop gossiping with me, get your ass on a plane, and we'll see what's what once we all get out there." Annette did not have the energy to hide her irritation. Out of all of her college friends, Lauren worked Annette's nerves the most.

"Don't snap at me. I didn't know if you had any inside information," Lauren retorted.

"Look, I got the same call from Neva that you did. I didn't know anything was going on with Heather either. And don't you dare blame Neva. No one could have seen this coming."

"You're right, I guess. Well, let me hang up so I can get going," Lauren said. "I've got a lot of rescheduling to do if I'm getting on a plane tonight. I have a full workweek planned. I hope they still have first-class seats available; there is no way I am flying all the way to California in coach."

"Lauren, I don't have time for this, good-bye." Annette hung up the phone abruptly.

Just then, her husband, Thomas, called. "Hey, baby, what's this last-minute trip to California all about?" he asked.

"Didn't Cathy tell you? I don't have time to go over it all. Heather's in a coma." The taste of what she said was so foul in Annette's mouth that she threw the words up more than she spoke them.

"She told me, but I wanted to talk to you about it. I mean, that's awful and all, but do you really have to go? I mean, if she's in a coma, is there really anything that you can do? Can't Neva handle that? I mean, she's already in California. You have been in DC for a while, and now you'll be gone even longer? I miss you," he cooed.

"No, Neva can't handle it, and yes, I really have to go. I can't even believe you're questioning this. Heather is one of my oldest and dearest friends from college, and she could be dying. How can I not be there?" Annette said with increasing annoyance.

"Well, then, I guess it's okay. I understand you want to be there. I guess I'll have to manage without you for a little while longer," Thomas said sweetly. "Just call me with the details once you get them, you know, your flight information and how long you'll be gone and where you're staying, and of course, keep me posted on how Heather's doing," he meekly requested.

"Did I just hear you give me permission? Is that what I heard?" The heat of Annette's anger flushed her peaches-and-cream cheeks.

"No, honey, that's not what I meant at all. You know that. I agree that you should go; that's all I was trying to say."

"Oh, whatever!" Annette curtly cut him off and hung up the phone, her emotions already elevated. She sat at the empty desk of the borrowed office, holding her head in her hands. Her brassy bangs fell over her hands like a curtain. She wished she could rewind the past thirty minutes, and go back to the way things were before. Before she got the call from Neva. Before Heather tried to kill herself. Just before.

Tamara

TAMARA WISHED THAT ANNETTE HADN'T been in DC so they could have traveled together. She didn't like flying alone. When they were in college, they would always travel back and forth to school together. The fact that Stanford was all the way in California was almost a deal breaker for Tamara. She could have just as easily gone to the University of Chicago, which was basically in her backyard. Annette convinced her that being away from home would be more fun, and besides, it was California! It turned out Annette was right. Stanford was a great place to go to college, but no matter how many times she had to do it, Tamara still didn't like to fly.

She lowered the blind, leaned her head against the window, and closed her eyes in a vain attempt to get some sleep. She certainly wouldn't get much once she arrived. Neva seemed a little uncertain about Heather's doctor, so she had to talk to him first thing. She needed to be sure Heather was being taken care of properly. She still couldn't believe that Heather overdosed. *What was she thinking?* Tamara remembered that Heather lost her job recently but couldn't recall whether she was fired or if she quit. They didn't get to finish their conversation. *Either way, people lose their jobs every day and don't kill themselves. My goodness. And to think, the cleaning lady found her. If that doesn't shout "spinster" to the world, what does?*

I wonder how it would go down if something ever happened to me? I could have a heart attack or something. I live alone too, like Heather. Who would find me? Tamara thought for a moment and surmised, *Someone from my practice would track me down before too long, so I guess I don't have to worry that I would rot in my condo or something equally awful. But who wants to be discovered because a patient needed a Pap smear or wanted a birth-control prescription refilled? Then again, my parents don't let too many days pass before they call "just to say hello." Who had been calling to check on Heather?*

As hard as she tried, sleep evaded her. Images of Heather bombarded her mind—first she pictured Heather sprawled out on her bed at home; then saw her in the hospital bed, connected to an EEG machine to monitor brain activity, with nasogastric tubes for feeding going through her nose. In her vision, the soft whirring sound of the breathing machine mechanically inflated and deflated Heather's chest. She could not breathe on her own anymore. Tamara saw Heather, usually so vibrant and colorful, now almost dead. Tamara opened her eyes to try to clear the images from her mind, but it was no use. They were seared into her imagination.

Tamara sighed as she looked out the window over the clouds and the blue sky and remembered the countless times she and Heather sat side by side on a plane and looked over the same blue sky, heading someplace warm or exotic. They would chat in excited expectation about the adventures that awaited them. They would bemoan the absence of their married girlfriends but relish in their respective freedom, having no husbands or children to tie them down. They tried to get Lauren or Annette to join them, but they never did—too busy juggling family and demanding work schedules. They didn't even ask Neva. Once she got married, she was never able to do anything, it seemed.

They missed their friends on those trips, but Tamara and Heather had enough fun without them. Tamara chuckled as the trips rolled through her mind: Jamaica, Costa Rica, Greece, Brazil … Heather would find some crazy adventure she was determined to take Tamara on—ziplining or scuba diving or climbing some mountain somewhere. Heather never wanted to do the standard tours; they would always venture off on their own, over Tamara's objections. She would always have a good time in the end. Tamara thought that it would always be the two of them. The empty seat beside her reminded Tamara that the two of them might never be together again.

Neva, Tamara, Lauren, and Heather

TAMARA WAS THE FIRST TO arrive. She told Neva she wanted to go straight to the hospital—no need to freshen up after the red-eye. When they got to the ICU, Dr. Chandra was checking Heather's vital signs and having a muted conversation with the nurse. Tamara engaged her long stride, causing her long dark ponytail to swing slightly, and crossed the room in only a few steps. She interrupted his conversation, extended her hand, and introduced herself.

"Hello, I'm Dr. Hurston. I just arrived from Chicago. What's Heather's status?" Tamara said professionally but with enough edge to let him know that he needed to take her very seriously.

As he prepared to respond, Lauren burst into the room, pulling one large piece of luggage in one hand, negotiating a large tote bag on the other shoulder, while carrying an oversize purse in her other hand and unsuccessfully checking her texts. She looked up from her phone in a fluster and announced, "All right, I'm here, what's going on? Can someone help me with these bags? We have to coordinate better next time, because there really is no elegant way to get from SFO to Oakland. I should have flown into Oakland like Tamara, so at least Neva could have picked me up too, but don't worry, girl, I understand you can't be two places at once. Whew! I am tired. How is Heather?" Lauren announced breathlessly as she stood in the doorway.

Dr. Chandra, Tamara, Neva, and the nurse simultaneously turned and looked, with eyes wide-open in disbelief, before anyone responded. Dr. Chandra nodded to the nurse, who informed Lauren that only two visitors were allowed at a time. "I just got off a plane from Atlanta to be at my friend's bedside, and that is where I intend to be!" Lauren protested loudly.

Neva walked over, gave Lauren a big hug, and calmly assured her. "You can stay. I need to check and see if Annette's flight is arriving on time, and I'll take care of your bags." Neva hoisted the tote bag on her left shoulder and took the handle of the suitcase in her right hand, opened the door to Heather's room, and started to navigate the narrow hospital doorway. Lauren politely stepped to the side to allow Neva's passage but did not venture near Heather's bed.

"Thank you. I mean, my goodness, I have come all this way," Lauren replied, ostensibly under her breath but loud enough for the others to hear. She adjusted her leather jacket, ran a hand through her cropped wavy hair, but remained in the doorway. Dr. Chandra and Tamara looked at her expectantly. Finally, Tamara rolled her eyes and said, "Lauren, she's over here," while beckoning her to come closer.

"Of course," Lauren said, taking slow but deliberate steps toward the bed.

Tamara let out a sigh of exasperation and met her halfway and put a gentle arm around her shoulder. "Come on, girl, it'll be okay," she said as she escorted her to the side of Heather's bed.

As Lauren approached Heather and saw her with all the tubes coming and going and the monitors beeping, she cried, "Oh my God, oh my God."

Tamara patted Lauren's shoulder tentatively to try to calm her. Her hand was stiff around Lauren's shoulder, and she didn't seem to have enough warmth to quell the shivers that accompanied Lauren's sobs.

"Shhhh," Tamara hushed her. When Lauren's cries would not relent, Tamara reluctantly pulled Lauren in closer and said, "I know this is a lot, but you have got to try to keep it together."

Lauren's shoulders heaved, and she sniffled loudly in an effort to stifle her cries. "O-kay," she eked out.

Dr. Chandra was still standing on the other side of Heather's bed, alternately checking the intracranial pressure monitor and watching the interaction between the women. He walked over to Lauren and handed her a tissue. "Dr. Hurston is correct; staying positive is very important. I know it is hard to see your friend this way, but I know you can do it."

Lauren closed her eyes, took a deep, cleansing breath, held it for a moment, and slowly exhaled, opening her eyes when all the air was released from her lungs. She moved away from Tamara and mustered up the strength to take Heather's hand. "Is it true that she can hear me?" Lauren asked Dr. Chandra between sniffles.

"Well, some studies indicate that it is possible …" Tamara started before Dr. Chandra interrupted.

"Yes, she can hear you," he confidently asserted.

"Heather, it's me, Lauren." She spoke in a lilting staccato, trying to force an upbeat sound. "I know I haven't talked with you in a while, but you know how it is, girl. The calendar gets full, the days all run together, and before you can blink, months have passed. I'm not making excuses; I'm just so sorry …" Lauren's voice started to break under the weight of her regret, so she turned abruptly and walked out of the room, dabbing her eyes with the tissue Dr. Chandra had given her earlier.

Now only Dr. Chandra and Tamara remained—one on either side of Heather.

"Dr. Chandra," Tamara started as she moved away toward the foot of Heather's bed. "Now that we have a moment without untrained ears, honestly, what is her prognosis?"

"Dr. Hurston, her situation is extremely dire. She ingested a large quantity of toxins. We did as comprehensive a detox as possible before too much absorption occurred. But we have no way of knowing how effective we were. Unfortunately, we will have to wait and see, but I am more hopeful, especially now that more of her friends are here to surround her with love."

"Are you serious?" Tamara responded with a chuckle.

"I am not sure I understand."

"You can't really believe that the atmosphere or environment or whatever can impact a patient's prognosis."

"Yes, Dr. Hurston, I do believe that because it is true," Dr. Chandra admitted with a tentative smile. "I'm sure you are aware of the studies indicating that the environment of comatose patients has a tremendous impact on their recovery, and I've seen it happen in my own patients. I know that your presence here will only be positive for Heather, don't you?" Without waiting for her response, he answered his own question. "Of course you do, or else why would you have come?" He broadened his smile as he put Heather's chart back in its holder and left Tamara alone.

Annette

ANNETTE WAS FIELDING PHONE CALLS, responding to "emergency" e-mails, and reviewing documents up to the very last minute before she had to leave HSW's office on K Street to get to Reagan Airport. Thankfully, she was a first-class preferred flyer, so she didn't have to wait in those long lines.

As she settled into her leather seat and cradled the glass of Cabernet in her hands, she tried to put aside thoughts of the deal she left with its guts still on the table. She did not feel comfortable leaving so suddenly, but Annette left her assistant strict instructions to call her if anything went wrong and told an associate in DC to give her daily updates via e-mail. *It has to come together. I can't afford for it not to, but I couldn't afford not to come and see about Heather, especially if, well, I don't want to think about that.*

She took a long sip of wine and tried to come up with a rational explanation for why Heather would want to kill herself. Of course it was a futile exercise; suicide was not a rational act. She took another large gulp of the wine and blew out a breath in exasperation as the plane started to taxi down the runway. *This couldn't have happened at a worse time,* Annette thought. *Hell, I have a job to keep, a baby to conceive, and a husband to manage. I really can't do this right now,* she thought as she emptied her glass.

Tamara and Annette

Tamara gladly offered to pick Annette up from the airport. She needed a moment to process everything—Heather's emotional state, which precipitated the overdose, her current physical state, and the harsh reality that she might not survive. Tamara's practical mind unwittingly floated to the question of living wills and whether Heather had given anyone a durable power of attorney. Probably Neva. What an incredible burden to place on any person you're not related to. *Thank goodness I have my family.*

She found herself repeating variations on this theme, since the more she repeated the news about Heather, the less comforting it became. One day, she knew, her parents would be gone, and then she would be alone, just like Heather. *This is not how it's supposed to be. I wanted to meet a nice man, get married, and live happily ever after, like everyone else.*

She met Parker at one of the black-tie events that Annette routinely dragged her to. "He's not going to show up at your door," she would offer, ostensibly as encouragement, while Tamara always took it as coercion. She typically was able to construct a good enough excuse for Annette to leave her alone. This time, she relented and went to the 100 Black Men Annual Awards dinner at some hotel downtown. They were sitting at the table with eight other people, but he stared at her all night.

He was a trader—tall and well built. He clearly took a great deal of care in his appearance. He was clean shaven, as if he knew he shouldn't distract from his luxurious chocolate-brown skin. The brightness of his white smile provided a striking contrast to his deep skin, so much so that it could catch you off guard. The thought of him even now made her sigh with appreciation. He was fine and he knew he was fine, but not in an arrogant way. She always found him to be more grateful for his looks than overly confident about them. It was like he hadn't always looked so good, like he had been an awkward teenager or overweight or something.

He gave her his card at the end of the evening and told her to give him a call. She took his card, knowing she would never, ever call him. But she wouldn't have to. Annette, the persistent facilitator, invited him to the opening night of *Fences*, showing at the Goodman Theater about two weeks later. Her firm was a major donor, so she always got invites to opening night. Annette made sure that their seats were next to each other. Parker and Tamara chatted easily before the play and throughout the intermission. He invited her for coffee and dessert after the show, and that was the beginning.

Their romance was everything that Tamara had been waiting for. They went to all the best places, he planned romantic weekends away, and he regularly sent her flowers, remembering her favorites were peach roses. Eventually, the time they spent together far outweighed the time they spent apart. They practically lived together, although Tamara could never *actually* live with someone—her parents would freak out, first of all, and she hoped that not "playing house" would accelerate a proposal. She had definitely internalized the old saying about the cow and the milk. Tamara was getting impatient because she didn't have time to waste if she wanted to have children. She was thirty-five years old, and no one understood the decreased chances of women over thirty-five getting pregnant better than she. She saw the frustrated women in her practice all the time.

She knew a thing or two about frustration. She and Parker dated for two full years before he finally proposed. The proposal was worth the wait. He went all out, as was his way—Valentine's Day dinner at a private dining room at the Ritz-Carlton Hotel. When they finished dinner, a carriage was waiting, and they rode along the lakefront, snuggling under blankets sipping hot cocoa. The carriage brought them back to the hotel, and Parker pretended that he left something inside. Instead of going up to the restaurant, they went to the thirtieth floor to a suite.

There were peach roses everywhere. Rose petals were strewn on the bed, and there was a drawn bubble bath and champagne on ice. He had thought of everything. As she was taking it all in, he got down on one knee (he was very traditional) and asked her to be his wife. She said yes (of course), and then got busy with wedding plans.

In retrospect, maybe the frenzy of wedding planning combined with the relief at getting married before she turned forty clouded her vision and dulled her normally acute perception to little signs she should have noticed along the way that Parker was not who he said he was. Tamara hadn't dated anyone seriously since then. She couldn't work herself up to investing the time or energy only to be hurt again.

She pulled up to the curb of the arrival section of the San Francisco International Airport and spotted Annette pacing back and forth, BlackBerry to ear, words flying, hands feverishly gesticulating. Tamara got out of the truck and helped Annette put her suitcase in the back. Annette climbed in the front seat and gave Tamara a peck on the cheek, while she continued talking louder and faster. Tamara successfully navigated the airport traffic and was getting on the 101 when Annette finally finished her call and turned to Tamara. "So, what the hell is going on?" she asked in her typical pointed manner.

"I just left the hospital ... it's bad, 'Nette, real bad."

Annette sucked her teeth and blew out a big breath. "I don't understand, T, I mean, what could make Heather do something like this? Granted, she has always been a little flaky, but suicide?"

Tamara cringed at hearing the word out loud. "I know, Annette. I don't understand it either."

"I thought she was happy now, with her new job and all. When was the last time you talked to her?"

Tamara paused as she considered it. "I'm not sure, it's been a while."

Annette shook her head as she weighed in. "How could something like this happen right in front of us without us even knowing about it? I didn't even know she was depressed."

"Well, when was the last time you spoke to her?"

"I can't remember. The only person I talk to regularly besides my husband is you."

"And that's probably because we live in the same city."

"Oh, that's not true. I'm just busy, that's all."

"We all have a lot on our plates. We can only do what we can, I guess."

"Yeah, but clearly that's not enough. We are supposed to be girls, you know, from way back in the day. How could one of our 'fold' be in such a state to want to leave the planet, and we not know about it? I mean, I know that since Heather's mother died, she is all alone, but Neva is out here, and still, we should have—I should have—made a better effort to keep up with her. I've been so busy at work and busy trying to have a baby."

"I know. I'm guilty too. We've all been busy."

"But that's no excuse," Annette said while turning her head to look out the window at the green, house-studded hills rolling on either side of the highway.

"Speaking of babies, were you able to get in to see that fertility specialist I referred to you?"

"Huh? Oh, yeah, not until April. I even dropped your name."

"What? I'll call her when we get back to see if she'll move you up for me. April is two months away, and you can't wait. The clock is a-ticking," Tamara lightly teased.

"Thanks for reminding me," Annette smirked. "When do you think we'll go back home? I mean, how long before she gets better? She's going to get better, isn't she?"

Tamara sighed as she weighed her words. "I don't know."

Tears rolled down Annette's cheeks as she turned her head toward the window again, as if there were something outside that would make her feel better.

"What can we do?"

"Right now, nothing," Tamara said with resignation.

"Well, how's her doctor? Is he any good? Because we can transfer her outta there if he's bootleg. She deserves the best."

"He seems to be all right. I don't know … he's sorta touchy-feely, not really my style, but maybe that's what Heather needs."

"How does Neva seem to be holding up?"

"It's hard to tell; I guess she's all right. I think she feels responsible."

"Yeah, well, we all do. What about Lauren? Did she make an appearance?" Annette asked snarkily.

"Yes, she's here, and in rare form, too. She hasn't changed, well, at least not on the inside. Outside, well, that's another story."

"Really? How so?"

"She's gained a lot of weight. I'm a little concerned, honestly. She had always been so thin. If she keeps going at this rate, she's going to be the next one we visit in the hospital."

"Really? That fat, huh?" Annette said with a perceptible hint of glee.

"Come on now, Annette, you have got to let it go."

"I don't care what you say; our relationship will never be the same. It was my wedding, and she missed it. I don't care what kind of last-minute work emergency she had; it was my big day. Who does that? My wedding pictures were all uneven. Thinking about it is making me mad all over again. And those damn flowers she sent me were a slap in the face."

"Well, you need to get over it, especially now. In light of, well, everything."

"You're right, but I cannot let it go. I've tried."

"Well, good thing that I don't hold a grudge."

"What do you mean?"

"Can we say Parker Samuelson?"

Annette rolled her eyes and shifted in her seat before responding, "Hmmph, that sorry-ass motha-fucka!"

"Well, you introduced me to him. Now what if I was mad at you?"

"Well, you can't blame me for not knowing he was on the down low."

"Annette, I'm not blaming you, but I could, you know. You didn't get good intel on him. You can't imagine how I felt when I found out that Parker had hit on my gay coworker at a club. I was even more surprised to learn he was a regular."

"I know, and I'm sorry, and I do feel a little responsible. And I'm glad that you were never angry with me. The most important thing is that you found out the truth."

"Yeah, but there are some things you'd rather not know, because sometimes, the truth really hurts."

Neva and Lauren

WHILE TAMARA WENT TO PICK up Annette, Neva got on the phone to start figuring out how she was going to manage her life while she was with Heather in the hospital. It was going to require a massive logistical operation to be sure that she had coverage for Ellington.

A friend from school agreed to take him home today, but Neva needed to ask Dante not to work too late in order to pick him up at a decent hour. *Did he even have the address? What about tomorrow and Friday? And next week?* She tried again to reach one of their regular babysitters to see if someone could pinch hit for her, without avail. She also tried to find substitutes for lunch and office volunteer duty at Ellington's school, but everyone seemed to be busy. They would have to make do without her. She ran down her regular schedule in her mind and was sure she was forgetting something, letting someone down, missing something important, but she could only do her best. It seemed too often that it wasn't good enough. *But today it will have to do.*

Neva sighed as she collapsed in one of the tan fake-leather chairs and resisted the urge to cry. Her eyes scanned the institutional living room and found the décor to be absurd. No matter how pale the sage-green walls were painted or how many beautiful pictures of giant redwoods were on the walls, she decided this was an ugly place.

While Neva was on the phone, Lauren had set up a workstation at a table along the far wall of the waiting room with her laptop and BlackBerry. She had been busily answering e-mails in between fielding phone calls after Dr. Chandra shooed her out of Heather's room so that they could take her for more tests. Her BlackBerry hadn't stopped buzzing since she arrived.

Neva finished the last call to the last person who finally agreed to cover for her. She leaned back in her chair, let her head rest against the wall, and closed her eyes for a moment. As Annette and Tamara came in, Neva could hear Lauren now managing her own logistics while typing furiously on the laptop.

"Zoe, listen, write it down if you have to. I don't want you to forget … ballet today, Mommy and Me music class tomorrow … and don't forget snacks for the twins' preschool class—just pick up something healthy, but nothing cheap.… Are you sure? Repeat it back to me.… Okay? Hugs and kisses all around. I'll check back in later.… Bye." Lauren ended her call, got up from her chair, and strode across the room.

"Everything okay?" Neva asked.

"Of course it is; that little French girl sees to that," answered Annette, with a well-practiced eye roll.

"Annette, really, you have no idea," Neva chastised.

"I don't understand why you all have to go through so many instructions and preparations with your kids when you both have husbands. They are intelligent, competent, grown-ass men, aren't they? Can't they just handle it?" Tamara asked.

Lauren and Neva looked at each other for a moment, paused, and simultaneously started laughing.

"I didn't come all this way to talk to you all anyway. T, take me to see Heather," Annette said as she grabbed Tamara by the elbow and walked with her out of the room.

As they left, Lauren remarked, "You can tell that neither one of them has a clue about what it takes to raise children."

"Well, that doesn't mean that there isn't some validity to what Tamara is saying. Why should we have to do everything? No one has ever given me instructions on how to handle Ellington, or arrange his schedule so that all I had to do was execute it. Just because I have a uterus doesn't mean I'm the best one to parent him. A hand now and then would be nice. I don't know how you do it with three. And you work too!"

"I simply adjusted my expectations. More help from Prescott would be nice, but I got tired of expecting something that I wasn't getting—that's why I just outsource as much of my mothering as possible. Girl, sometimes you have to help yourself."

"I guess so, but, Lauren, not everyone can have the luxury of a staff like you have. What is it up to now? Five?" Neva chuckled.

"No, I'm down to three—just a nanny, a personal chef, and a maid, but you would do well with one. Any one. You can't do it all on your own and do it well. Look," Lauren leaned in closer to lower her voice, "I know you've been up here all night, but Neva, you don't look so good. You are wearing yourself out, and for what? Do you think Ellington would care if he had someone else pick him up from school or drive him to soccer practice or whatever? Girl, I'm telling you, you need some help—and fast."

Tears started to well in Neva's eyes. "Well, I do have someone who helps me keep the house clean," she said defensively.

"Good! How often does she come?"

"Once a month," Neva said sheepishly.

"Shit, with kids, that's no help; at that point, that's disaster maintenance, and barely that."

"Oh, Lauren, really it's plenty. I'm fine. Besides, I only have one—not three like you. And I don't work like you. I just need to be more organized. Anyway, you should have seen what I went through to get Dante to agree to getting a cleaning service at all. Really, he would never go for anything more. Besides, it's expensive."

"First of all, one child is plenty of work, and from what I remember, you are plenty organized. And Dante needs to get up off the dime. Isn't he is a senior vice president at the bank? He can afford it. He manages to do whatever he wants to do; why can't he do something to help you out? Hell, tell him to play golf one less Saturday a month, and that would more than cover your housekeeper to come biweekly."

"You don't understand."

"I understand that you are running yourself ragged. You are worn out. Can you at least get a part-time babysitter, or leave Ellington with Dante every once in a while so you can get out, get a manicure, or have a girlfriends' lunch or something? Do you think you can do that?"

Neva's weak smile was her only response.

"Look, there are several national babysitting services I worked with before I found Zoe. You can find someone to help you out on a regular basis. I'm going to give you the number right now," Lauren said assertively as she dug around in her purse for her phone.

"I'm okay, really. It's fine. Let's just focus on Heather," Neva said quietly, with her eyes closed.

"I know we are here because of Heather, but Neva, I don't want what happened to her to happen to you. You just don't seem like yourself, not like the Neva I knew in school. Where is the bold, confident woman who walked across that field during freshman orientation and introduced herself to me? Where is the woman who was my emissary in the black community, so I wouldn't have to explain to everyone why the 'white girl' was at the Black Student Union meeting?"

Neva couldn't help but laugh and smile as she remembered meeting Lauren during their freshman orientation, thinking she seemed black, but could certainly "pass" for white with her light skin, hair, and eyes, but the smile quickly faded as she remarked, "That was a long time ago, and a lot has happened since then."

Lauren raised her eyebrows knowingly and replied, "Apparently, you know …" Lauren stopped short to turn in the direction of Annette's sniffle and saw her approaching them, eyes red and swollen.

Neva thought she was rescued from the uncomfortable conversation until Lauren admonished her, "We're not finished."

Lauren and Neva rushed up to meet Annette and Tamara. Annette was always the one with the quick retort, her mouth full of snappy comments. Only there was no quip on her tongue now. Dr. Chandra came into the waiting area and joined the encircled women. "I see someone else has joined you," he commented.

"Dr. Chandra, this is our other good friend, Annette, who just came in from Chicago," Neva offered.

"So, let's see, we have two from Chicago, one from Atlanta, and one local girl. Quite a group," he remarked lightly with a warm smile. "I know you are anxious to hear about how your friend is doing. Heather's condition is stable right now. All there really is to do is to wait. You all have had a full and exhausting day. Why don't you go and refresh yourselves, and we'll see you again in the morning. Neva, I have your contact information and will call you if anything changes."

"I just don't want to leave Heather alone. I don't want to leave her alone again," Neva said, her voice cracking.

"She won't be alone," Dr. Chandra gently stated. "I will stay with her."

"Really?" sniffed Neva.

"Absolutely, Neva, you were here all night. You need to rest. Go home, all of you. Have a good meal, enjoy a glass of wine, reconnect with each other—it's important for all of you to take care of yourselves in order to be truly present for Heather," advised Dr. Chandra. His compassionate gaze moved intentionally from woman to woman as he spoke.

"That is so very generous of you, Doctor. I agree with you that we should go and get some rest. All of us don't need to be spending the night here." Lauren, the executive, had spoken. The decision was made.

Annette, Neva, Lauren, and Tamara

THEY PICKED UP SOME PIZZA at Zachary's before going to Neva's house. Neva was happy to oblige Lauren's request for the pizza they used to crave after a road trip to Berkeley. When there was nothing happening on campus, the girls would crowd into Annette's red BMW and drive to Berkeley for whatever fraternity was having a party. For some reason, the boys at other schools always seemed cuter than the ones they saw every day.

As they pulled into the garage, Neva's husband appeared and greeted them in his normal gregarious manner. He shooed them inside, insisting on unloading their entire luggage from the car himself. He barely let them carry their own purses.

Neva rushed in the house, placed the pizzas on the black granite countertop in the kitchen, and went upstairs to check on Ellington. Dante hadn't bothered to bathe him and his room was a mess, but he seemed content, already asleep in his safari-jeep bed. Neva sighed as she walked down the stairs and attempted to organize the sleeping arrangements in her head. Everything happened so fast, she didn't have enough time to prepare. She had to find linen, and silently prayed there were enough clean towels.

Dante met her at the bottom of the stairs and asked in a quiet but insistent tone, "Where are we going to put all these people? Have you thought about that?"

"I'm just walking in the door; can you give me a minute?"

"Well, what am I supposed to do with all this stuff? I can't just leave it here." Neva's husband tapped his foot impatiently as he waited, luggage straps straining against his chest and arms while handles were wrapped around both hands.

"Okay, okay." Neva felt her heart beating faster and faster the longer she stood in front of him, so she walked past him and went through the kitchen and into the living room, where she found Annette and Tamara, each sitting on one of the two cream-colored couches that faced each other in the center of the room. Lauren stood near the virgin grand piano in the far corner, looking out the floor-to-ceiling windows at the magnificent view of the bay. Neither Neva nor her husband played, but he thought it looked good in the space.

The taps of Dante's feet syncopated with his huffs and sighs in a rhythm of frustration and impatience.

Neva took a big breath before she started rattling off the sleeping arrangements.

"Tamara and Annette, you could either share the guest suite upstairs, or one of you could sleep on the pullout in the media room down here. Lauren, you can take the daybed in my office if you like."

"Whatever's going to be less trouble for you, Neva. We don't mind sharing, do we, T?" Annette teased, putting Tamara on the spot. Tamara was very private and did not like to share much of anything, which made living with Heather freshman year particularly challenging.

"Just like old times," Tamara responded flatly.

"I will gladly take the office. I really do need my privacy. I hate sleeping with other people," Lauren stated definitively as she walked away from the window and joined Tamara and Annette.

"Uh, don't you sleep with your husband?" Annette asked.

"Well, actually, we have separate bedrooms," Lauren replied matter-of-factly. Annette raised her eyebrows in response, to which Lauren quickly retorted, "Look, I need my space … I can't be bothered with him every night all in my face. Besides, he snores," Lauren said as Neva walked back to the stairway, where Dante was still waiting. He had encircled himself with the luggage and was seated on the first step. His arms were folded across his chest.

"Just tell me what belongs to whom so I can take it where it needs to go," he said curtly. "It's not like you didn't have all day to figure this out."

Neva's voice remained calm as she dutifully directed Tamara's and Annette's luggage in the direction of the guest room and rolled Lauren's suitcase to the office herself. While Neva went on the hunt for clean sheets and towels, Annette, Tamara, and Lauren were making themselves at home. Everyone's shoes had come off. Annette stretched herself out on one couch, resting her head on a pillow. Tamara was now by the window appreciating the view, while Lauren searched the oversized walnut cabinets in the kitchen for dishes to set the table for dinner.

"I forgot how pretty the Bay Area is. Sometimes I actually miss it," Tamara sighed.

"You—miss it? You hightailed it away from the Bay Area as soon as you could; you couldn't wait to get back to Chi-ca-go," Lauren mocked loudly in a singsongy voice from the other room.

"Be that as it may, I still miss it sometimes. Don't you all?"

"Not really. I love Atlanta. In the South, there is tradition and history and a certain way of doing things. It's all just too alternative out here for me. Nothing seems fixed in California; everything is subject to change at a moment's notice. Just take earthquakes, for example," Lauren replied.

"Remember the big one in '89?" Annette asked as she joined Lauren in the kitchen.

"I remember that's when I decided I was leaving California forever," laughed Tamara. "I was walking down the hallway to my dorm room, and I heard all this rumbling and thought, what crazy people are running upstairs? When the rumbling didn't stop and the ground beneath me started to shake and the walls started moving, I just ran down the hall as fast as I could, trying not to fall. I remember opening the door to my room and standing in the doorway, trying to hold on to something that was still, which was impossible, because everything was moving. That was enough California for me," Tamara shared as she joined Lauren and Annette in the kitchen and joined in preparing the table, which sat in a windowed nook between the great room and the kitchen and looked out over the valleys of the Sibley Canyon Preserve.

"When I opened the door, guess who was under the desk?" Tamara continued as she carefully placed a plate before each chair on the large oval dining room table.

"Neva," all three women said in unison, laughing. Neva came down the stairs just in time to hear her name.

"What are you all laughing about?"

"We were just remembering the earthquake and how T found you hiding under the desk. You were so scared," Lauren recounted. "It is amazing that you stayed out here after that."

"It's amazing to me, too, and was never part of my plan, but you know, when I married Dante ..." Neva responded.

"When you married Dante, you forgot all about your plan," Lauren replied plainly.

"Shh, he's right upstairs," Neva replied in a shaky voice. "You didn't have to set the table; I was going to get everything out once I finished getting your rooms together."

"Neva, relax," Annette assured her and patted her on the shoulder.

"You don't have to serve us. We've known each other too long for us to act like guests." Lauren motioned for everyone to sit down.

Annette found some candles on the dining room sideboard and placed them on the kitchen table. "Ooh, let's light these. We need some ambience," she stated as she lit them before sitting down.

"We didn't know if we should set a place for Dante," Lauren said as she moved the pizza from the countertop to the table.

"Oh, no, he already ate. He doesn't usually eat with us. He won't be coming back down." Neva cast her eyes down at her plate as she took her seat. Lauren shot a knowing glance to Annette.

"I'm trying to remember the last time we were all together," Tamara stated as she looked pensively around the table.

"Hmm." Lauren paused as she opened the bottle of Barolo that Annette took out.

"I think it was at Lauren's last baby shower," responded Annette as she searched the box for the smallest piece of pizza.

"No, I missed the shower because Ellington got sick at the last minute, and I had to stay home," Neva recalled as she took a deliberate bite of her slice.

"It couldn't have been the opening of Heather's exhibit in Chicago a few years ago?" asked Tamara as she hungrily snagged several pieces from the box.

"Nope. I wasn't there for that, Prescott had a thing, or maybe I was traveling for work. I can't remember now," Lauren stated, already on her second small piece. "I can't believe we can't remember the last time we were all together."

"All of us aren't really together now," Neva said quietly, her observation hanging in the air like the early morning fog, thick and gray and cold.

Neva picked up her piece of pizza, opened her mouth to take a bite, but she couldn't and put the slice back on her plate and pushed the plate away.

"You know what I mean," Lauren retorted.

"Regardless, it shouldn't take a tragedy next time. We should at least try to get together once a year, take a trip or something. Thomas and his college friends do that every year," Annette suggested.

"That shouldn't be so hard to do," Tamara agreed.

"It's a lot easier for the two of you to pick up and go without a thought. For Neva and me, it's harder because we have responsibilities," Lauren remarked.

"I have responsibilities too, like a job and a husband," Annette commented.

"Yeah, Lauren, and it's not like ushering life into the world is any kind of major responsibility or anything. Our value should be measured by more than whether a woman is a wife and mother," Tamara replied, her irritation increasing.

"Well, of course it is," Lauren replied. "I'm just saying that I have it all—children, a husband, and a demanding job. I just don't have the time. I mean, when I do get to take some time off, Prescott wants to go somewhere or we have a family vacation scheduled. Taking a girls' weekend would require a lot of negotiation."

"Girl, just leave everything in the hands of your nanny. Give your husband a lot of good sex before you go, and c'mon. You have a weekend to spare. I know you do," Annette suggested.

"I wish it were that easy."

"Me too," Neva jumped in. "I would love a weekend away from everything, but Dante would never let me go."

"Let you go? Neva, he is your husband, not your daddy," Annette replied.

"And a weekend away, with or without us, would certainly do you some good," Lauren added.

"I'm sorry; I just don't get it," Tamara added. "I mean, Lauren, yes, you work full-time and have three kids, but you also have full-time help. And Neva, you don't work at all, and you only have one child. I'm sorry, but how hard do either one of you really have it? I mean compared to all the single mothers out there, or those families who are really struggling. I don't mean to be insensitive, but …"

"But you are being insensitive," Lauren responded.

Before Tamara could reply, Neva quietly added, "You have no idea what it's like, but I know I don't have a right to complain."

"Neva, you're not complaining; you are telling the truth, your truth. You don't have to hold your tongue, especially not around your friends," Lauren admonished.

"I'm not trying to upset anyone; I'm just being honest too. And you're right, I have no idea what it's like. It just seems to me that you, relatively speaking, have it pretty good," Tamara answered.

"Just because it looks good from the outside doesn't mean that it's good on the inside," Neva replied. "No matter how much help you have or the number of children you have, motherhood is still no joke. It is, by far, the hardest thing I've ever done. Not to be insensitive, but you just can't understand if you don't have any children of your own."

"The hardest thing you've ever done? That's really saying something. Neva, you've done some hard shit. I mean, come on, you have two engineering degrees from Stanford—now that's hard," Tamara replied.

"Yeah, and you were the youngest person in your company to ever get a patent—that's hard," Annette added.

"All that stuff seems like a lifetime ago. No one knows me as a Stanford grad or a patent holder … I'm just Ellington's mom and Dante's wife now, and those roles are, well, much harder for me to fill."

"Having children, being a mother, it seems like that should be, I don't know, natural," Tamara replied.

"Maybe it is for some women, but not for me," Neva whispered.

"I can attest to that. The things we think are natural don't always come easy," Annette echoed.

"Children or no children, married or not, I concede that we're all busy women, with multiple things competing for our time. The real question is whether we are going to let that continue to be an excuse for not coming together more often, not staying connected," Tamara answered.

"See, right there, you said it was an excuse, but my family and professional responsibilities are not an excuse, and I resent your minimalization of them. Yes, I would love to see you all more often, but dammit, I have a lot of balls in the air. Why can't we admit that our lives are just very different and respect those differences?" Lauren vehemently interjected.

"I do respect the differences. I think it's just a matter of priority, and you, Lauren, have made your priorities crystal clear," Annette responded.

"Guys, just stop, please," Neva pleaded. "How did this become about us? Heather is lying in a coma she may not come out of. While we are focused on our families and careers, Heather had no family and just lost her career, so maybe we should focus on that. We were her family. Look what happened because we weren't here for her—too busy, caught up in our own lives when she needed us …"

"It's not our fault, and it's definitely not your fault," Tamara interjected while placing her hand on Neva's. "Heather made the decision to do what she did completely on her own."

"Tamara's right. We all face challenges and go through difficult times, but none of us have tried to kill ourselves, I mean, really, we certainly can't blame ourselves for that," Lauren remarked.

"It sounds like you all are blaming Heather," Neva said strongly. "Where's your compassion? Heather is our friend, our sister, and let's face it—we let her down. How many times had she been there for us? We should have been there for her. Whatever was going on inside of her, she should have been able to tell at least one of us, and maybe we could have made a difference—at least I'd like to think so. If not, what's the point of even calling ourselves friends?" Neva pushed herself away from the table, carried the empty pizza box into the kitchen, and began busying herself with cleaning up.

Tamara rose from her seat, went into the kitchen, and stood directly in front of Neva, stopping her in her tracks. "Of course, we all wish that Heather had come to one of us—any of us, and maybe we could have prevented this horrible thing from happening. But it's not our fault that she didn't—that's all I'm saying. Besides, shouldering all the blame is not only unhealthy, it's counterproductive."

"I agree 100 percent. I refuse to take the blame for this foolishness," Annette said as she leaned back and put her feet up on the chair Neva had vacated. "Should we have known she was so close to the edge? Probably. Could we have stopped her if we knew? Who knows? Maybe we all missed it by not maintaining consistent contact with her—or one another for that matter, but what good does it do for us to sit here and blame ourselves?" Annette posited while pouring herself another glass of wine.

"Hear, hear," agreed Lauren while holding out her glass for a refill. After Annette poured the rest of the wine into her glass, Lauren got up from the table and moved into the living room.

The remains of dinner neatly discarded, Neva and Tamara followed Lauren into the living room. Neva continued the conversation as she sat down on one of the couches, careful not to spill her glass of wine. "I know that we are all doing the best we can, trying to juggle all of the balls we have up in the air, but we're not catching them. The best we usually can do is an abbreviated conversation in the car on the way to school or work, or a quick text in between patients or clients. But I think we are missing each other's real lives.

"All these years, I believed that we were so close and such good friends that if something really serious happened, we would be able to come to one another; but apparently, that's not true—at least it wasn't for Heather, and I think we would be remiss if we don't ask ourselves, 'Why?' Honestly, I'm afraid of who's going to end up on life support next if we don't answer that question."

"Neva does have a point. It would be wrong to dismiss Heather's actions as mere 'foolishness.' We should really try to figure out why she did this. There has to be a reason," Tamara, the pragmatic scientist, asserted.

"I don't think we can figure this out, really I don't," Annette added. "I mean, look, we could sit here all night and make suppositions and offer hypotheses of one kind or another, but I don't think we will ever know what was going on in her head when she took those pills. After all, how much can we know the motivations behind another person's actions when we can barely figure out why we do what we do ourselves?"

Neva understood exactly what Annette was saying. It was just over a year ago, just about this time of year, that Neva did something she still struggled to understand.

The day was unusually warm, so Neva didn't bother to bring her coat; but she was so cold. Heather gave her the sweatshirt off her own back. Neva was still shivering but was silent on the long trip there. Neva told Heather to wait in the car. She wanted to do it alone.

And so she did. It. All alone.

Neva straightened her spine by imagining a string pulling the top of her head and allowed her chin to rise just a little as she walked into the clinic. She wanted to be dignified about the whole terrible thing. She passed a lone protestor, who was silently holding a sign with a horrible picture. Neva just kept her eyes focused straight ahead; she continued walking, determined, almost as if she were being led.

Once inside, Neva still couldn't stop shivering. She had never been anyplace like this before. She was used to going to doctors' offices where the pregnant women were literally expectant. None of that here. None of these pregnant women were expecting anything, at least nothing good.

The woman at the front desk barely looked up as she handed Neva a clipboard with a stack of paperwork to complete. Neva found an empty seat beside a young girl and her boyfriend. Her arms were folded; his head was in his hands. They weren't speaking. No one was. The room was eerily quiet. Absent was the excited banter that usually punctuates a roomful of soon-to-be parents. Missing was the friendly chit-chat of "When are you due?" or "Do you know what you're having?" Only the somber silence of painstaking decisions and unwanted outcomes lingered in the room. She sighed and started in on the forms and paused at the question asking marital status. Neva looked furtively around as she quickly checked "single." If she had checked "married," she would have needed her husband's consent, and he didn't even know she was pregnant.

After what seemed like way too long, the unfriendly woman called her name to come to the back. Neva tried to be strong and forced a half-smile.

She kept Heather's sweatshirt on and only undressed from the waist down. She was still so cold. She wished she had remembered socks too, as she placed her bare feet in the familiar metal stirrups that lacked padding. They felt steelier than she ever remembered, though she must have saddled up dozens of times. She closed her eyes when she heard the whirring sound and tried to imagine something pleasant, but her mind couldn't go anywhere other than between her legs.

It hurt less than she thought, but she really didn't know what she expected to feel—except empty. Once it was quiet, she opened her eyes, and there was nothing but blood. After a few hours, she walked outside by herself and got into the car with Heather. They rode to her loft in silence for Neva to spend the night and recover, but even after all this time, she still hadn't recovered. Whenever she closed her eyes, she just kept on seeing all that blood.

"Neva, are you okay?" Annette called out to Neva, who had stopped in her tracks by the window, motionless, with her back to her friends, remembering that day. She turned to face them, tried to walk back to the couch, and found her legs lacked the strength to move forward. Her feet seemed glued to the floor, and she felt that her knees might give out beneath her. In fact, she was barely able to stand as the tears started to fall.

"Neva?" Lauren said with growing concern as she rose to her feet.

Neva did not say a word. All she could do was stand still until she could stand no more. Suddenly, her legs crumpled beneath her, and she landed in a heap on the floor.

"Oh hell, what is this?" Annette jumped from her seat, followed by Tamara and Lauren, who all crouched around her. Neva sat with her head bowed and chest heaving. Her blue-jeaned knees were bent awkwardly behind her, and her white shirt was wrinkled against the windows that covered an entire wall of the living room and looked out over the bay.

"Neva, what's wrong?" Tamara urged as she knelt down, placing her hand on Neva's forehead. Neva tried to stave off the sobs by taking punctuated deep breaths so she could answer. Lauren and Annette looked quizzically at each other, unsure of what to do or what to say. Tamara went into the kitchen to get a glass of water. Lauren shrugged her shoulders, sat down beside Neva, and took one of her hands in her own. Tamara gave the water to Neva to drink while Annette joined them on the floor. After a few sips, Neva looked at her friends and offered an embarrassed smile before she started to speak, slowly and deliberately. "I haven't been feeling very well for a while," she started.

"Neva, what's going on?" Lauren questioned.

"A little over a year ago, I started having all these crazy symptoms: heart palpitations, chest pains, dizzy spells, and headaches. At first I thought it was nothing—no big deal. Then, when they persisted, I got scared that something was seriously wrong with me. I thought I had a brain tumor or was having ministrokes or something. I didn't know what was going on. I went to my internist, who did a full workup. I had every kind of MRI, EKG, ultrasound, you name it," she continued.

"What were the results?" Tamara asked.

"Well, the scan for my brain didn't show anything, and the tests showed there was nothing wrong with my heart. The doctor ran some blood tests too. She thought maybe I was anemic or something. It turns out I wasn't anemic. I was pregnant."

"Well, that's good news, isn't it?" interjected Lauren.

"Not for me," Neva answered.

"Neva, what are you saying?" Lauren questioned.

"I know you're not supposed to say this, Lauren, and don't get me wrong, I love Ellington, but being a mother is so hard for me. Sometimes I think I should have never had children. I feel like a failure all the time, and I didn't want to make the same mistake twice."

"Neva, you are a great mother, and—" Annette interjected, but before she could finish, Lauren jumped in.

"Well, if that's how you felt about it, then you should have been using birth control. I don't think that anybody gets pregnant in this day and age unless they want to. You're a smart girl, c'mon!"

"I did use something, Lauren," Neva replied, snatching her hand out of Lauren's grasp. "I have been on the Pill since Ellington was born. But I had been losing so much weight, I guess that impacts the Pill's reliability. I don't know."

"That can happen, Neva, but why didn't you tell us you were having such a hard time?" Tamara asked.

"Who would I have told, and what could I have said? Some things are just unspeakable. Besides, it would have been insensitive to Annette, who has been trying so hard to have a baby, and I know you want a family too—what would you have thought if I told you how hard mothering is for me? You would have thought about how many of your patients try for years to have a baby and have so much trouble. You would have told me to be grateful for the healthy child I have and get over myself."

Tamara's silence was all the confirmation Neva needed to know that she was right in keeping her secret.

"So, what happened?" Lauren asked tentatively.

"I did the only thing I felt I could do," Neva said slowly.

"What exactly are you saying, Neva?" Annette interrupted.

Tears filled Neva's eyes, but she could not bring the words to fill her mouth.

"What's the problem? If you were bold enough to do it, you should be bold enough to say it!" Annette egged Neva on, unswayed by her tears.

"Annette, stop it," Tamara replied.

Annette stood up and looked down at Neva, still sitting on the floor next to Tamara. "Yeah, I know what you did. I just can't believe you did it. Not you, little miss 'I'm a virgin' all freshman year, miss 'I do everything right' …"

"In some ways, I can't believe it either," Neva whispered.

Annette started pacing around the room, a wineglass in one hand, the other arm flailing in the air. "How could you do something like that?" she screamed.

"Shh!" scolded Tamara. "Ellington's sleeping upstairs."

Annette gulped down what remained of her wine and continued talking in a lowered but still scathing tone. "Knowing how hard I have been trying to get pregnant, how could you just throw a baby away? That is the most selfish thing I have ever heard. You were right not to tell us." Annette slammed the glass down so hard on the coffee table that it shattered as she stormed out of the room.

"Annette, wait," called Tamara, who quickly followed her upstairs, leaving only Neva on the floor and Lauren sitting next to her, no longer holding her hand. Now Lauren leaned back, with arms folded, head shaking. Neva sighed as she got up from the hardwood floor of the living room of her tastefully decorated house and started cleaning up the broken pieces of glass. Through her tears, she did not notice the blood that was starting to flow from her hands.

Lauren

By six thirty the next morning, Lauren was up, dressed in Burberry from head to toe, and in the kitchen. The house was quiet, and since she was the first one up, she decided to make breakfast, something she rarely had time for at home. She got a pot of coffee going and rummaged in the refrigerator, where she found a pineapple, along with some strawberries and blueberries. One thing she did miss about California was the abundance of super-fresh, high-quality produce. Lauren rounded out the continental breakfast by setting out some yogurt, granola, and orange juice on the island. She poured herself a cup of coffee and sat down at the counter, got out her BlackBerry, and started checking e-mails.

Tamara walked sleepily into the kitchen still in her pajamas, shuffling her pink furry slippers across the hardwood floors. "Good morning, early bird," she yawned, and poured herself a cup of coffee.

"Girl, I hardly sleep anymore. My time clock is all screwed up from all the travel. I've been up since about three thirty, but I stayed in my room and got some work done before we head to the hospital. I didn't want to wake anyone."

"I don't know how you do it."

"You do what you have to do, I guess. Can you believe Neva? How's Annette doing?"

"You know Annette. I love her, but if there is anyone who can hear news like that and make it be about her, it's Annette. I know she's a little extrasensitive because of her situation, though, so I have to cut her some slack. Plus, I think we were all blown away by Neva's revelation. I mean, if it was you or Annette, it would be expected … but Neva?" Tamara half-jokingly said while putting some yogurt and granola in a bowl and then sitting down next to Lauren on one of the counter stools.

"Damn, T, thanks."

"You know what I mean. Neva just always tries so hard to do the right thing. I can't imagine how hard this must have been for her."

"I guess."

Just then, Annette walked stiffly into the kitchen. "Good morning," she said dryly, making her way toward the coffee.

"Hey," Lauren stammered, "I like those boots; did you get them at Nordstrom?"

"Huh? Oh, no." Annette looked down at her feet as if she had to remember which boots she had on. "Saks. Got a great deal."

"There is nothing better than Saks' after-Christmas sale," Lauren concurred. "Are you hungry? There's granola and fruit."

"No, thanks. I'm good with this," Annette responded, lifting her cup while leaning against the counter with her eyes closed.

Suddenly Ellington came running through the kitchen, interrupting the uncomfortable silence, wearing a Superman cape over his school clothes, holding his arms straight out in front of him as if he were flying. When he realized there was a room full of "aunties" looking at him, he stopped dead in his tracks. They laughed as they covered him in hugs and kisses and showered him with remarks about how big he had gotten and how handsome he was. Neva tiptoed in quietly behind him.

"Ellington, you have gotten *so* big! Come here and give your Aunt T a kiss!"

Ellington stood still for a moment until Neva encouraged him. "Go ahead, Ell. You remember your Aunt T, don't you?"

"Not really," Ellington answered honestly.

"Well, I remember you. I knew you before you were even born!" Tamara commented and walked over to the five-year-old and planted a kiss on him.

"Don't overwhelm him, ya'll. Sit down, baby. This is still your kitchen."

Ellington smiled a little and took a seat at the kitchen counter.

"Can I get you some breakfast, baby?" Lauren asked while patting his hand.

"Yes, please," Ellington answered politely.

"Just tell your Aunt Lauren what you want to eat."

"Oh, Lauren, you don't have to do that. I can get it," Neva responded and headed past Lauren toward the refrigerator. "I'm sorry I wasn't up sooner to have breakfast ready."

"Neva, I got it. Just sit down, girl. I made myself at home. I keep telling you—we're not guests," Lauren answered.

Neva complied by sitting on the stool next to Ellington.

"I want somma that." Ellington pointed to the fruit and granola on the counter.

"Okay, coming right up. Is juice okay too?"

Ellington nodded while Lauren poured Ellington some orange juice and made him a parfait with the yogurt, granola, and fruit. Lauren asked, "Neva, do you want some too?"

"No, thanks, I have to go and get Ellington's things together for school. A neighbor is taking him for me. Can you guys make sure he eats all of his breakfast?"

"He really has grown," Annette commented

Neva hurried out of the room and went upstairs before anyone could answer her. Once she was out of earshot, Tamara whispered to Annette, "Okay, now, you have got to apologize to her; she feels bad enough."

"What did I do? I think she should apologize to me," Annette replied bitterly.

"Come on now, what Neva did really had nothing to do with you, and she doesn't owe you anything. What you owe her as her friend is your support and understanding, not judgment," Lauren commented firmly.

"I think you came down pretty harshly on her too, Lauren. I think both of you owe her an apology," Tamara replied.

Annette exhaled deeply, resigned in her anger and disappointment.

"It's just another example that we all are capable of doing unspeakable things if we are provoked enough by our circumstances," offered Tamara quietly so Ellington could not hear. "Just like Heather. None of us thought she was capable of doing what she did. Something or some things in her life made her feel like swallowing all those pills was the only way out of the pain she was in. I'm sure Neva felt the same way."

"And, if we were honest for a moment, it's not like Neva is the only one who has had one." Lauren looked knowingly at Annette.

"Well, that was a long time ago, when I didn't have the resources to raise a child. Now, things are different," Annette replied. "I mean, it's not like she is some scared, uneducated teenage mother. She is a grown woman with the full capability to be a mother. Hell, she already is one!" Annette replied.

"Annette, enough! We don't have time for this. Let's not forget that Heather is laid up in a coma. Not everything is about you," Lauren suggested.

"Lauren, what do you know about me and my situation, with your three damn kids?" Annette fired back as she stormed out of the kitchen.

Annette and Neva

ALTHOUGH SHE WASN'T DRIVING, ANNETTE was clearly in control of the group. That was nothing new. Her commanding presence meant that she could always affect the entire emotional atmosphere no matter where she was. When she was shut down, everyone and everything around her seemed to silence as well. There was too much internal dialogue going on for her to talk anyway.

As Neva carefully navigated the twists and turns of the familiar highway, Annette could barely look at her. *All the mornings I spent with a thermometer in my mouth before I even had my beloved coffee, the times when I had obligatory sex simply because I was ovulating, the hopeful anticipation I mustered every morning followed inevitably by the sinking feeling in the pit of my stomach when my period came again. Month after month, I performed the same ritual to the same unfulfilled end. It seemed that the longer I tried, the more I wanted a baby. I can't believe that Neva callously eliminated what I had been trying so hard to obtain.*

When they finally arrived at the hospital, the doctors were running tests on Heather. Lauren again set up her makeshift workstation in the waiting room, discreetly pulling out her BlackBerry, and started checking e-mail. Annette and Tamara went to see about Heather's night, while Neva sat down on a couch in the middle of the room and flipped mindlessly through a magazine.

Dr. Chandra rounded the corner, almost walking right into Annette and Tamara.

"Well, good morning," he replied calmly. "Visiting hours aren't for a while yet."

"Well, we just wanted to get back here as quickly as possible. How was Heather's night?"

"It was a good night. She is stable. There has been no change in her condition, which is not necessarily a bad thing. If she is not doing worse, then she is doing better. As for the tests, we are just checking the electrical activity in her brain. It's standard procedure, nothing for you to be concerned about. I'll let you know as soon as she gets back so that you and your friends can see her."

"So, no more news on when … or whether … she is going to wake up? I mean, how long will we have to wait?" Annette inquired.

"Unfortunately, I do not know. It's only been one day, and only Heather knows the answer to that question. I have to check on some other patients, but as I said, I will be sure to let you know when Heather gets back to her room." Dr. Chandra touched Tamara lightly on the arm as he proceeded down the hall.

Annette looked blankly at Dr. Chandra. The meaning of his esoteric statements was still elusive to her.

"Okay, is he for real?" Annette asked as they headed back to the waiting room to join the others.

"I know he's a bit alternative, but I'm starting to think his approach is refreshing, and there's more research all the time supporting the mind-body-spirit connection."

"Well, I think it's weird."

Neva and Lauren were now sitting next to each other chatting easily about the stars' fashions in *People* magazine.

"Did you find the doctor?" Lauren asked as Annette and Tamara entered the room.

"He said her condition hasn't changed, which he said was a good thing, which I don't completely understand. Then he said something like he thinks that Heather is deciding whether she wants to wake up. I don't understand half the stuff he says," Annette replied.

"What do you think, T?" Lauren questioned.

"He is a little metaphysical, but there's all sorts of research out there about the mind-body-spirit connection, and he is obviously on that tip, so I guess we should go with it. But what do I know? I look at *coochies* all day."

Everyone laughed, except Lauren, who smirked. "Tamara, really."

"I'm just kidding," Tamara retorted. "But seriously, since he's Heather's doctor, we should respect what Dr. Chandra says. The will to live is a very powerful force, and we can't ignore the fact that Heather wanted to die. I think what Dr. Chandra was saying is that he's not sure how much will Heather has working for her at this point."

"Forget trusting his ass; I'm going to Google his behind. How do you think you spell 'Chandra'?" Lauren asked.

"Oh, Lauren, really." Neva shook her head.

"What? Nothing wrong with a little research."

"I agree." Annette leaned in to see the tiny BlackBerry screen. "Okay, found him. Says here, he went to Berkeley undergrad."

"Boo!" Tamara teased.

"Stanford Medical School … and there's some kind of fellowship he did after residency or maybe before, I can't tell," Annette continued.

"What's the name of it?" Tamara asked.

"Peabody Fellowship. Have you heard of it?"

"It sounds a little familiar. I think it's where doctors can receive a grant to study and work overseas in a developing country."

"Oh, that's where he learned the voodoo-magic doctor tricks! In some jungle somewhere," Lauren joked.

"Oh, Lauren," Tamara responded, while Annette just laughed.

"Mind-body-spirit, whatever. I just want our girl to wake up," Annette stated.

"That's what we all want," Neva added.

"Hey, has anyone given any thought to what we are going to do with Heather if she does wake up?" Annette asked.

"What do you mean, 'do with her'?" Neva questioned.

"Just to be proactive, we should probably start checking out psychiatric facilities in the area and figure out how we are going to pay for it. I'm sure Heather doesn't have insurance," Annette stated.

"Money should be the least of our concerns right now," Lauren added haughtily. "I'm sure I can handle whatever the cost will be. You know, I was thinking … are we sure there's no one else we should contact? It seems like there should be someone we can call. Does she have any friends she used to work with, or some long-lost family member that should be made aware? I just find it so hard to believe that she has no one besides us."

"Maybe someone should go to her place and look around, you know, check her answering machine, get her mail, go through her phone and address book, just to be sure," Tamara suggested.

"That's actually a good idea," Lauren stated. "Since we can't see her anyway, there's no use in sitting around here. C'mon, Tamara, let's go."

Before anyone could protest, Lauren grabbed the keys from Neva's purse, took Tamara's hand, and left Neva and Annette sitting across from each other in the waiting room.

"You don't even know where you're going," Neva called out to them.

"You have a GPS, don't you? We'll figure it out," Lauren yelled, peeking her head just outside the elevator.

Neva resumed flipping through one magazine, then another, until she had scanned them all. Finally, Annette spoke first. "Look, I know I probably hurt your feelings yesterday. I know it was hard for you to admit what you did, but your words went right through me. If you only knew how hard I have tried, and failed. How many times I saw a big, fat minus sign on the home pregnancy test. How many late periods gave me false hope. The countless humiliating conversations with Thomas, 'not this time, honey.' All I could think about was how what has been so elusive for me came so easily to you, and it seemed like you didn't even appreciate it, and that just made me mad."

Neva moved to sit in the chair next to Annette. "I'm so sorry it has been so hard for you. I had no idea. You always acted like it was another problem to figure out; you never said how it made you feel. I guess just like I never told you how I've felt all these years, being a mom, how difficult it is for me. So difficult that I didn't feel like I had a real choice. I did the only thing I could do. Having that baby would have been too much; I didn't have it in me. So, I chose to save myself, and not only for my own sake, but for the sake of the child I already have."

Annette tried to hear Neva's heart, but couldn't tune out the loudness of her own thoughts. "You know what else? You remember the abortion I had when I was in school? I have so often wondered whether my inability to have a baby now is because I aborted one before. Hearing about yours just made me mad at myself all over again, but it's much easier to yell at you," Annette chuckled.

"Oh, Annette, I am so sorry. You know that what happened before has nothing to do with your situation now. But I can understand why you feel that way. And I can only imagine how you must have felt hearing my big secret."

"We all have secrets. I guess the key is knowing when to share them and when to keep them. You were right to share yours." Annette squeezed Neva in a big hug. "At least you feel better, right? No more crazy headaches or heartaches, I hope."

"I wish that were so. They were not, apparently, a symptom of my pregnancy. The doctors could never figure out what was going on with me. Annette, to tell you the truth, most times, I can barely breathe," Neva admitted, tears welling up in her eyes.

"Oh, Neva. How did Dante take the news? I know how much he's always wanted a girl."

Neva's silence caused Annette's eyebrows to lift.

"So, you mean even your husband doesn't know?"

"If I was going to tell him, I should have done it before I did it—and I was just too scared. Telling him now would end our marriage for sure."

"Oh, Neva, surely he would understand."

"You don't know my husband."

"Even if you explained how you felt?"

Neva shook her head vehemently as she continued. "I have been trying to tell him how I feel for years, but he doesn't get it. He knows there's something wrong—he just thinks that there's something's wrong with me."

Annette sighed, "Now you are making me feel bad. I know it couldn't have been easy for you to make that decision, and even more painful to keep it a secret from your husband."

The nurse came out to the waiting room and informed them that they could see Heather. Annette and Neva rose from their seats and walked across the southwestern-style carpet that covered the waiting room floor, and continued down the cold tiled hallway to Heather's room. Their canter turned into a tiptoe as they walked in and approached her bedside. As they stood over her, they reached for each other's hands and tightened their grasp—as if to keep each other from falling. Heather looked a little paler, more drawn and fragile than the day before, but somehow, she seemed at peace.

Annette observed, "You know, she almost looks like she's just sleeping. She seems so calm. It's strange, almost like she's ..."

"Happy." Neva agreed. "I keep thinking about whether Heather wants to come back or not. I keep wondering whether I would come back if I were her. I can understand her hesitation, in a way ... she lost her job, she has no family ... she is all alone," Neva offered.

"Alone, maybe, but even alone, she is enough," Annette offered. "I wish she could have seen that. I don't know how, in all the fine education we got, no one ever taught us how inherently valuable we are—just us. No man or baby or career is necessary to define or validate ourselves; we are okay just as we are. I'm still learning that."

"Me too," Neva added.

Heather

I ALWAYS HATED THE FIRST day of school. Everyone always stared. You would think I would have gotten used to it. I never did. I wish my mother and I "matched" like everyone else. And what made it worse, she seemed oblivious to it all. She would take me to the front door of whatever school I was attending that year—didn't walk as much as march, head held high, shoulders squared, back arched. She was in protest mode all the time it seemed. It was as if she was constantly daring someone, anyone, to say something. No one ever did, at least not out loud.

I felt all the downcast eyes of embarrassment and the eye rolls of blatant disapproval as I passed by. Unlike my mother, my shoulders sank just a little bit more with each step.

Lauren and Tamara

"I WONDER IF SHE LEFT a note?" Lauren questioned as they pulled in front of Heather's building in Jack London Square in Oakland.

"I hope we find something that will help us understand why she did this," Tamara responded.

"I don't think I'll ever understand. Heather was always strange to me, and this just proves that she really needed some help, and probably has for a long time. I mean, we all have our ups and downs, and none of us have tried to kill ourselves," Lauren said as they exited the car and walked toward the main building entrance. The women used Neva's extra key to open the door and started to climb the stairs to the third floor.

"Maybe it's that attitude that made Heather do what she did. Don't you think she could tell how you felt about her? Maybe your snide remarks and sarcastic statements over the years added up."

"Certainly you aren't trying to blame this on me?" Lauren puffed as they completed one flight.

"No, of course not. But if you thought she was weird, don't you think other people did too? Can you imagine going your whole life feeling different? People absorb the way other people perceive them, and if that perception is negative, well, over time, it can start to wear you down. That's all," Tamara explained as she cleared the second flight of stairs. She turned back and found that Lauren was still on the landing between the first and second flight, holding on to the rail, breathing heavily.

"Lauren, are you okay? Come on, I'm not blaming you!" Tamara shouted down the stairwell.

"I know. I just need a minute. We don't all run marathons like you," Lauren said as she finally caught her breath. "You keep going; I'll meet you up there."

Tamara continued up the stairs and waited for Lauren. "Maybe Neva should have come instead," Tamara remarked to herself.

"Oh hell, give me the damn keys." Lauren came up behind her and took the keys from Tamara, put them in the lock, and opened the door. They both stood still in the doorway for a moment, letting their eyes move around the space before they crossed the threshold. From the entranceway, Tamara and Lauren could see all the way into the bedroom, which was elevated by a couple of steps and only partially hidden by a half-wall.

The bed was made. The kitchen was spotless. The appliances were shining, and the countertops looked like mirrors. The hardwood floors gleamed throughout. Everything was eerily in its proper place.

"This is really nice," Lauren said as she started moving through the living room looking up and down. "I don't remember Heather ever being this neat."

"I think we have the cleaning lady to thank," Tamara surmised. "She must have come back yesterday evening."

"Heather had a cleaning lady? I thought she lost her job. How could she afford that? I mean, I don't know what I would do without mine, but it's different," Lauren replied.

Tamara walked past the kitchen and up the two steps into the bedroom without responding to Lauren's speculation. She walked almost on tiptoe, not wanting to disturb anything. Lauren followed, looking around carefully as they went, trying to notice any clue that Heather might have left behind. They both sat on Heather's black platform bed. Lauren pushed the "play" button on the answering machine, which rested inside the shadow-box nightstand. There were no new messages.

How long has Heather been in the hospital? Tamara tried to calculate in her head. *Two days, and she didn't get even one call?* Tamara somberly realized how alone Heather really was.

Lauren picked up the picture of the five of them on graduation day and ran her finger across the broken glass that covered their shiny faces. As she stared at the youthful version of herself, she couldn't control the tears from gently falling down both cheeks. "You know, I remember this day, and I remember thinking it was the best day of my life," Lauren said between sniffles.

Tamara looked at the picture and said, "I think we all felt that way. I was on my way to med school and was so happy to be going back home to Chicago. You were excited about your big-time job. Heather was off to Michigan. Annette was starting her legal career, and Neva was excited about staying at Stanford for another year. We were so sure."

"And why wouldn't we be? We had the benefit of youthful arrogance—of a life untainted by disappointment. We knew we were going to become everything we wanted to be, and that the next part of our journey would be just as great as the past four years had been," Lauren sighed.

"I wish I knew how special that time was so I could have appreciated it more. I know for me, I was always rushing to get to the next thing. In high school, I was studying hard, doing all the 'right' activities so that I could get into a top college. In college, I was so focused on getting back home and starting med school. I don't know if I fully appreciated the amazing opportunities that were right there. Once I got into med school, I couldn't wait to start my practice. It's like I have never taken the time to fully experience where I was because I was always looking ahead at what was to come and the next thing was going to be the thing to make me happy. Funny thing is, no matter what I accomplished, I never stopped looking for what's next, until finally, after taking so long, I gave up trying."

"You should stop waiting for something to make yourself happy and just decide to be happy where you are, like me."

"Lauren, honestly, do you even visit the real world? I understand that in your life, everything is perfect. You have a great career. You married your knight in shining armor; you have the big fancy house; you have three beautiful, healthy kids—everything you always wanted. For the rest of us, well, not all of our dreams exactly came true.

"Annette wants a child and can't have one. Neva had a child that she didn't want. I can't find a good honest man to save my life, but at least I have work that I enjoy. Heather didn't have any of that. She lost her job, has no family to lean on, no husband to love her, and no children to care for. She has no one. She's been MIA for two whole days, and there is not one message on her answering machine." As Tamara finished her last sentence, she got up abruptly, walked into the bathroom, and started searching the medicine cabinet.

"My life is not a fairy tale," Lauren whispered almost inaudibly.

Tamara peeked her head around the corner. "Did you say something?"

"Huh, me? Oh no," Lauren quickly replied without turning to face Tamara, trying to steady her voice.

"I'm trying to find something in here, anything at all," Tamara muttered to herself while the rummaging continued.

"I'll take a better look in here," Lauren said as she sniffed down her last tears and proceeded to look through the papers and books and other miscellaneous items that filled the open-slot nightstands in Heather's platform bed. Finding nothing, she peeked into the bathroom and noticed Tamara was still occupied, so she went into the kitchen and quietly looked to see if Heather had anything to eat; that trip up the stairs wore her out, and the parfait didn't hold her long. The refrigerator only had a few eggs, a bottle of ketchup, and some hard pieces of bread inside. "Humph," Lauren grunted as she shut the door and shook her head. The pantry was next to the refrigerator. Lauren almost passed it by, certain that it would be empty, but her growling stomach insisted that she check just in case. Her assumption was correct; there were a few cans on the shelf, along with some cleaning supplies. Nothing to eat. *Tamara is going to have to stop on the way back to the hospital. I can't go all day without eating like these skinny bitches.*

Just as Lauren was closing the door, her eye caught the glimpse of something shining from behind one of the shelving units. She tried to scoot the shelf away from the wall to see what it was, but she couldn't move it at all. When she reached down and touched the corner of the piece of gold, she realized it was woven, like a canvas.

"Tamara, come in here and help me!" Lauren yelled.

Tamara bounded into the kitchen. Lauren was kneeling on the floor, tugging at the golden corner.

"What are you doing?" Tamara quizzed.

"Just come here and help me move this shelf; there's something back here," Lauren replied.

"What? Come on, Lauren, why would we go through all that trouble? It's probably nothing. You're just being nosy."

"What if it's a priceless picture that she stole from the museum? Maybe she tried to kill herself because she thought someone would find out."

"That is just ridiculous, Lauren. Come on, let's leave well enough alone."

"We need to see what this is, Tamara. Just help me move the shelf."

Tamara easily moved the shelf, using her strong legs, and when she did, an entire large black portfolio fell to the floor and exposed scads of paintings and drawings, including the one with the gold paint in the corner.

"Oh ... my ... God," Lauren said slowly while her eyes grew wide.

"Do you think these are hers? I mean, I know she used to run off to the art studio from time to time when we were in school, but I never knew she still kept up with it," Tamara stated as Lauren knelt on the floor and started flipping through the pictures one by one.

"I don't know how much you know about art, but these are really good, amazing actually," Lauren said.

"We've got to show Annette and Neva," Tamara replied.

Lauren carefully zipped up the portfolio, wrapped her carefully manicured hand around the handle, and gently set it by the door.

Heather

ANNETTE AND NEVA WERE TALKING to Dr. Chandra in the waiting room when Lauren and Tamara returned with a hemp bag full of items from Heather's house, along with a bunch of flowers Lauren insisted they stop to purchase on the way back. They left the portfolio with the paintings inside the car.

Dr. Chandra smiled broadly as they approached. "Hello, ladies. What did you discover?"

Lauren opened her mouth to respond, but Tamara shot her a "wait" look, so Lauren replied, "We were hoping to find a note, a message, or some sort of clue as to why this happened, but no luck. Anyway, we did bring some things that might help her feel comfortable, you know, more at home. That's good, right?" Lauren looked at Tamara, who was holding the bag but not taking anything out of it. Lauren looked at Dr. Chandra, who was looking at Tamara. She continued talking. "Dr. Chandra? You were saying that people in comas can sense their environments and everything, so this is good, isn't it?" Lauren repeated.

Dr. Chandra's gaze was still fixed on Tamara, so he did not respond.

Annette's gaze shifted between Tamara and Dr. Chandra. She cleared her throat, startling and embarrassing her friend and Dr. Chandra.

"Um, yes, you are absolutely right. It is good to create a peaceful environment for Heather," Dr. Chandra finally responded, blushing while bowing his head a bit.

"Ummm, Tamara, what's in the bag?" Annette finally asked.

"Oh." Tamara finally gathered herself enough to respond. "Heather's iPod, a nightgown, some toiletries, and this picture," Tamara said as she dug around in the bag until she produced the graduation picture with the cracked glass. "Remember this? Neva, you sent each one of us one. Heather still had it out. I don't even know where mine is." They all crowded around the picture and stared without speaking.

Dr. Chandra stood immediately opposite the group of women and extended his hand, seeking permission to look at the photo. Without hesitation, Neva passed the picture to him.

"You all look exactly the same," Dr. Chandra only half-teased as he reviewed the picture for a moment and then handed it back to Neva. They all laughed and chided him with comments of disbelief. "Positive images are important to have around Heather. And the music was definitely a good idea," he commented while looking directly at Tamara. "Since all of you are here now, it would be a good time to give you an update. The tests we ran earlier this morning showed that her brain activity is slowing down a bit, but it's no cause for worry, yet."

"What do you mean, 'yet'?" Lauren asked.

"I just mean that right now, she is hanging in there, and the best we can do is keep watching her and waiting. I know you want a concrete answer, but unfortunately, I cannot give you one," Dr. Chandra explained.

"Maybe I'm missing something, but that just doesn't make sense to me," Annette said, widening her stance and placing both hands on her hips.

"The reality, Annette, is that she might not wake up no matter what her brain activity is," Tamara reported somberly. "It's just not something that we can predict."

"Is that true, Dr. Chandra?" Lauren questioned nervously while fingering her pearl necklace.

"It is a definite reality that Heather may not come out of the coma, but it's not the only reality," Dr. Chandra said gently. "Why don't you go in and see her? Just don't go all at once; we don't want to overwhelm her," he suggested as he walked over to the nurses' station before disappearing down the pristine hallway.

Tamara left the others standing in a circle watching Dr. Chandra get smaller and smaller. She walked boldly into Heather's room and sat down at her bedside. "Hey, girl," she said softly as she held up the picture, "Lauren and I went to your place, and we found this. All this time when we weren't together, you kept us close, and now, we are all here, together ... for you." Tamara placed the picture on the bedside table next to the tan-and-white Kleenex box. She grabbed one and dabbed her eyes, now filled with tears. "We also found the most amazing art. All these years, I had no idea. Heather, you are so talented. Who knew? That museum job wasn't everything. You have … so much to live for …" Tamara haltingly observed.

Lauren knocked lightly and entered the room, carrying the bag with the flowers and other items. "Is it all right if I come in?"

"Of course."

Lauren walked over to Heather's bed and stood next to where Tamara was sitting. "I brought the other things. I was thinking we could set up the iPod dock and at least comb her hair and get her out of this ugly hospital gown. I cannot have my girl looking like this. I should have made you stop by Neiman Marcus so I could have picked up a Jo Malone candle or something so it won't smell so much like—"

"A hospital? Lauren, you are tripping. We can't light candles in here, but we can certainly comb her hair; just don't use any product. I'll change her clothes, though—you have to be very careful."

Lauren went to the head of the bed and started gently brushing Heather's hair, carefully smoothing her long, curly mane.

"How many times would we be walking across White Plaza and someone would hand us a flyer for an event at Casa Zapata, thinking we were Latina," Lauren recalled with a chuckle.

"I remember it getting on your nerves," Tamara replied. "Hers too."

"The stories we could tell." Lauren shook her head as she loosely secured Heather's hair with a scrunchie. Tamara retrieved the nightgown from the bag and laid it on the bed. Once Lauren finished combing Heather's hair, she set about putting the flowers in a vase while Tamara gingerly removed the hospital gown, unrolling it from Heather's shoulders, slowly moving past her waist, until it was completely off.

Tamara drew a quick breath when she noticed how gaunt Heather had become. "I suffered through four years of med school not to do nurses' work; I must really love you!" Tamara joked. She carefully gathered the nightgown into a ring and guided the gown around Heather's feet, then her legs, then her torso, and carefully placed her arms into each sleeve.

When they finished, they both stood back and saw that Heather actually looked ethereal and angelic. "Now, if I could just put on a little lip gloss," Lauren said only half-jokingly. Tamara responded with a well-developed eye roll. Annette and Neva hurried into the room.

"Carmen went back to Heather's house to clean it yesterday evening after we left," Neva reported.

"We thought so; everything was so neat when we went over there," Tamara added.

"When she was cleaning, she found this," Neva said while brandishing Heather's journal.

"Well, what does it say?" Lauren asked.

"It seems kinda weird to read it right in front of her. Shouldn't we go out to the waiting room, or wait until we go back to the house?" Neva asked the group.

Reaching consensus on where and when to read the journal was nearly impossible. Annette agreed with Lauren and wanted Neva to read it on the spot. Neva maintained that would be tacky and was sure that they should just wait. Tamara couldn't wait, so the waiting room sounded good to her. They were all talking at the same time, and their voices were getting a little elevated.

"Shhhh! I just thought of the perfect place to read the journal—the hospital chapel," Tamara announced.

"Brilliant!" exclaimed Lauren.

"You all were determined to get me in church one way or another," joked Annette.

They filed out of Heather's room. Carmen was sitting in the waiting room, in the same posture Neva found her on the day they brought Heather in. Her hands were neatly folded. She was rocking back and forth. Her lips were moving, but no sound was coming out. She was still praying.

Neva gently put her hand on Carmen's shoulder and suggested, "Why don't you go in and sit with Heather for a little while? We'll be right back."

"Are you sure?"

"Of course, Heather would like that."

"That would be nice, thank you."

"We should be the ones thanking you," said Tamara.

"It's only supposed to be family, Neva. Do you really think it's appropriate to have the cleaning lady here?" Lauren whispered discreetly to Neva as they walked down the hall.

"Are you serious? She found her, remember? She was the one who was here with me before you all came. Aargh," Neva answered as she quickened her stride.

"Lauren," Tamara admonished.

The click-clack of four pairs of heels against the hard tile announced their arrival in each wing as they wound their way through the hospital, following the signs to the chapel. They continued down this hallway and up that one, passing some empty rooms, others with a sole patient silently watching television, and still others with so many family and friends gathered that you couldn't even tell if a patient was in the room or not. They heard nervous laughter, loud guffaws, muffled crying, or sometimes just peaceful silence as they continued their way to the chapel.

"Sometimes when I was a resident, I would go to the chapel to study or even sleep," Tamara replied.

"Ooh, Tamara, God is going to get you for sleeping in church," Annette teased.

"Sometimes it was the only place I could find some peace and quiet," Tamara admitted.

The room was shaped like a pentagon, with pews neatly arranged on three sides. The stained glass windows along the two front walls framed a small, raised carpeted stage, upon which sat an altar and a small podium. Annette, Lauren, and Tamara sat down in the first pew, while Neva stood in front of them, as if giving a sermon. She nervously turned the pages of the journal to the last entry and started to read:

I don't know why, but I have never seemed to fit.

Neva's voice started to break, but she kept reading amid the others' hushed affirmations: "It's all right" and "Take your time," well-practiced encouragement from a childhood of Sundays spent in the pews of somebody's grandmother's church during testimony service.

Never black enough, certainly not white—too sensitive, too serious— too much, never enough. I've tried so hard to make myself fit, even into myself, and I just can't seem to do it. Always a square peg in a round hole.

The only time I don't feel that way is when I'm painting or around painting. I haven't been able to pick up a paintbrush since my mother died, but I have always been able to be around art even if I wasn't creating art, until now. Now, the only bit of peace I had is gone, and I don't know what to do.

I feel so all alone. No one understands what it's like for me. No one gets it, and I'm tired of trying to make them. Trying to be happy, trying to be successful, trying to be brave, trying not to be lonely, trying to be strong. I'm worn out from all the trying.

"That's it … there's nothing else … it's the last entry," Neva said as she stepped stiffly down from the platform, sat down in the pew next to Annette, and finally released the tears she had dammed just long enough to read. The women wailed in a strange symphony, until they stopped in unison, as if by some silent command.

Out of the silence peppered with sniffles, Neva started to pray, "Lord, I don't know if you can still hear me, but I'm not praying for myself. We're here concerning Heather. We're asking you to open her eyes. Bring her back to us. Help her to know that if she is tired, we can help carry her load; that she doesn't have to worry about fitting in anymore, that she will always fit in with us; help her to somehow realize how much we love her and that we are waiting here for her. Please give her a will to live and not die."

"And give her peace," Annette added. Tamara and Lauren opened their eyes when Annette chimed in. Annette, sensing they were looking at her, chirped in response, "What are you all looking at? I pray, damn!"

"Annette, really, we are in church," Lauren admonished.

Neva, Lauren, Tamara, and Annette

AFTER THE WOMEN RETURNED FROM the chapel, they were spent. Gone was the banter that was so pervasive in previous interactions. Dr. Chandra encouraged them to take a break. He was right; of course, they all needed to shift gears for a moment. They decided that the Starbucks in the hospital lobby would work. They sat on four comfortable chairs arranged in a circle with their respective drinks: Neva, a green-tea frappuccino; Annette, a doppio espresso; Lauren, a nonfat, two-pump, hazelnut cappuccino and a blueberry scone; while Tamara sipped on a regular coffee.

They sat in silence for a moment, each one not really knowing what to say after all they had just heard. Annette couldn't stand the quiet for long before she interjected, "I know we are supposed to be all somber and shit, but can I just for a moment make an observation about Dr. Chandra? For two whole days, we have been around this man, and no one has mentioned not even once how fine he is." Annette slapped her thigh for emphasis.

"Annette, really," Lauren said while rolling her eyes. Neva and Tamara just shook their heads in disbelief.

"Okay, I have to admit, I did notice, but you know, I thought under the circumstances, it wouldn't be appropriate to bring it up," Neva added.

"Because you're married?" Tamara asked.

"No! Because I didn't want to be the shallow one, thinking of how handsome Heather's doctor is, while she is, well, you know." Neva laughed before she caught herself.

"All ya'll are married, so you need to quit," Lauren admonished while pointing at Neva and Annette. "But, Tamara, feel free to appreciate."

"Have you all noticed that when he's talking to us, he really only looks at T?" Annette teased.

"Annette, I think you're right. I was starting to take it personally that he wouldn't look me in the eye, but now I see," Lauren chimed in.

Tamara shifted her weight in her seat. Color rose in her cheeks.

"Okay, stop teasing," Neva took up for Tamara.

"Oh, lighten up, Neva. Tamara knows we're just having a little fun, because we all know there could never be anything between them," Lauren stated emphatically.

"Why do you say that?" retorted Annette.

"He's not black, of course," Lauren replied. "What do y'all think he is anyway?"

"Fine. I think he's fine as hell, and fine is fine, in any color and every shade," Annette stated.

"Why do we even care? What difference does his ethnicity make? He seems like a kind and intelligent man, that's all that matters," said Neva.

"Oh, come on, you expect me to believe that any of you would actually consider a serious relationship with someone outside your race if you weren't already married? I mean, would you really want to be with someone you'd have to explain yourself to all the time? He could never really know you," Lauren said.

"There is more to me than my race, Lauren. My interests, my personality—these things are not completely formed by my ethnicity. I am not just my cultural identity. And if you were really honest with yourself, you would realize that you probably have more in common with some white people than most black folks anyway, and I'm not just talking about how you look," Tamara replied with a chuckle.

"Very funny, Tamara. I'm just saying, it's a recipe for a lot of heartache and trouble, and marriage is hard enough, without having to deal with people staring at you when you go out, or random folks making comments to you, or his family not accepting you … not to mention the confusion of the children: 'What am I? I'm not like everyone else.' Just think about what Heather wrote in her journal. Just stick to the brothas and make it easy on yourself," Lauren quipped.

"Well, it's a moot point anyway. Dr. Chandra is not paying me any special attention. If he shows me any deference at all, it's because I am a fellow physician, and he just thinks the rest of you wouldn't understand what he's talking about," Tamara joked, causing the others to giggle.

"It's good to hear you laughing," Dr. Chandra said as he surprised the women. Tamara hoped that he hadn't been there long enough to hear what they had just been talking about. He sat down on the arm of Tamara's chair, which made the other women giggle even more under their breath. In his hand, he held several brochures for residential treatment facilities in the area. As he delicately laid them on the coffee table in the center of the circle, he explained the merits of each facility briefly before heading off to check on other patients.

The women left with him and once again went in to sit with Heather, one by one, until when everything had been said, they returned to Neva's house. Once Neva pulled the Range Rover around the circular driveway and stopped the car, Annette, Tamara, and Lauren eased themselves gingerly out of the tan interior as if sore from a long and arduous workout and walked slowly to the door. Neva sat in the car for a moment with her eyes closed—and Lauren came rushing back to the car, out of breath.

"I almost forgot; I found something at Heather's apartment. I left it in the car." Lauren huffed as she opened the hatchback and pulled out the black portfolio.

"Huh, what's that?" Neva asked as she scooted out of the driver's seat and walked around back.

"Wait till you see. The most magnificent paintings and drawings—of Heather's."

"Really?" Neva furrowed her brow. "Where did you say you found these?"

"In her loft. What does it matter anyway? Come on, I can't wait to show everyone. Hurry up!" Lauren commanded as she grabbed the portfolio handle.

Neva followed Lauren into the house. Lauren rushed past Annette, who was in the kitchen already pouring herself a glass of Malbec.

"Put that glass down, girl, I have something to show you," Lauren said.

Annette ignored Lauren, finished pouring, and took a good long gulp.

"Annette! Come on!" Lauren yelled from the dining room.

Annette meandered into the dining room carrying the wine bottle in one hand and her glass in the other.

"What do you want?" Annette smirked.

Lauren laid the portfolio delicately on the dining room table, moving the vase of white tulips from the center of the table. The other women were silent as she pulled the zipper, slowly, carefully. She unveiled the first painting. "Annette, move that damn wine bottle," Lauren stated as she placed the painting gingerly on the table.

"Oh my God," Neva said.

"Wow!" Annette echoed while leaning over the table to take a better look, her red wine precariously hovering over the painting.

"Annette, please be careful," Lauren remarked.

Annette moved back from the painting as she added, "How do we know it's hers?"

"Well, she signed it," Neva commented while bending over to look carefully at the date, "It says 1988. I can't believe it. Why didn't she ever show us this stuff?" Lauren wondered aloud as she pulled another one, with darker colors, out of the portfolio and placed it on top of the first.

"Who knows?" Tamara said while leaning in closer. "What I can't figure out is why she would want to hide this kind of gift. I had no idea she was so talented," Tamara concurred.

"I'm starting to feel like I didn't know Heather at all," Neva sighed as Lauren pulled out yet another carefully crafted painting, with shades of red and orange boldly swiped across the canvas.

"Well, I guess the only thing to decide is what we should do now," Lauren observed.

"Do? What do you mean, 'do'? These don't belong to us. They're Heather's to do with whatever she wants, and obviously, she hasn't wanted to 'do' anything with them all this time. We just need to put them back where we found them. Where did you find them, by the way? You never said exactly," Neva answered.

"What difference does it make where I found them? The point is that I found them and they are amazing, and we just can't put them back in the pantry behind a shelf. Maybe if Heather hadn't been hiding this all this time, she wouldn't have tried to kill herself," Lauren replied.

"Lauren!" Tamara admonished.

"What would we do with them anyway?" Annette asked.

"They were in the pantry?" Neva asked.

"Behind a shelving unit," Tamara added.

"What exactly were you looking for in the pantry, Lauren, some Ho-Hos?" Annette exclaimed as she poured herself another drink.

"If you must know, I was hungry, and yes, I was looking for something to eat. And yes, I found them in the pantry behind a shelf. It's not like I was rifling through her stuff; I just happened upon them. What is the big deal, and why is everyone acting like I did something wrong? Here I am thinking I made a wonderful discovery, and you all are attacking me!" Lauren exclaimed.

"No one's attacking you, Lauren," Tamara responded with increasing irritation.

"Well, I—" Lauren attempted to defend herself before Annette cut her off.

"Lauren! Enough! You are not the only one with an opinion here. We can't just act like these are ours because you were being nosy!" Annette shouted.

"You know what? Forget it," Lauren responded as she started picking up the pictures one by one and returned them to the portfolio. "Like I said, I was not being nosy. If you want me to put them back, I will."

"Good idea," Annette answered.

"What are you guys so afraid of?"

"Nothing, Lauren. Can we just focus on making sure Heather gets better? Why can't we just worry about these pictures later?"

"Because there might not be a later. Heather may not get well. This may just be her legacy. And we found it. I don't think that's an accident. Call it my nosiness if you want to. We have a responsibility now that we found these."

"Okay, just for kicks, what are you suggesting?" Annette asked.

"Let's just see what could happen. What's wrong with exploring the possibilities?"

"You mean like selling them possibilities?"

"Maybe, why not?"

"They don't belong to you, for one. And maybe there was a reason Heather had them hidden. Maybe she didn't want anyone to see them."

"And maybe she did, but she was scared. Now, she doesn't have to worry about it. We can do this, for her. Don't you guys see that this is important? Finally, this is something that really matters."

"What really matters is that Heather gets better," Annette said, dismissing the idea. "I don't have the room to hold your 'big idea.' You need to put the paintings back."

"When Heather gets out of the hospital, she'll be looking for them," Neva added.

"If she gets out," Lauren responded.

Heather

I DON'T KNOW HOW I could have gotten through school and my mother's cancer without being able to paint. Tamara was always at the library, so after dinner, I would ride my bike over to the art department and just let the pain and confusion and hurt and whatever I was feeling come out of me and go onto the canvas. I always felt so much better afterward. I always tried to get back to the room before Tamara did, but sometimes she would beat me and I would have to make up some lie as to where I had been. Usually, I would just say I was at the Coffee House or CoPo or something.

I just didn't want to explain or be teased. Lauren and Annette had a funny way of making fun of what they didn't understand, and I couldn't take that on top of everything else I was going through. It was just better that they didn't know.

Besides, it was embarrassing. My stuff wasn't great or anything. It was just what I did to clear my head. It was my little hobby, no big deal. No one needed to know. It was my little secret. The only person who knew was Chris. He knew everything about me.

Neva

NEVA WAS THE LAST TO go to bed after everyone else was tucked in. She walked as quietly and as carefully as she possibly could, on tiptoe, across the dark wood floor. She silently removed her clothes, slipped on her pajamas, and slid into bed beside Dante, careful not to stir him. She was so tired, she didn't realize he was still awake and not sleeping.

"Sorry to disturb you," Neva said tentatively.

"What are you talking about? I'm still awake," he replied curtly.

"Oh, right, sorry."

He puffed before he started speaking. "I stayed up waiting for you because we need to talk."

"Oh, about what?"

"About when all these people are leaving."

"I can't believe you're asking me this. Heather is in a coma. It's only been two days, and already you're ready to throw people out?"

"You know how I feel about houseguests."

"I know; you even make my parents stay in a hotel when they come to visit."

"Just your father, not your mom. You know I can't stand him!"

"Dante, this is a special situation. I—I would like them to stay as long they like, as long as possible."

"That's not an option. One week, and that's it. You've got to figure something else out."

"What about Heather?"

"Heather is in a coma. She doesn't know if you guys are here or not. Besides, she tried to kill herself; I don't even know why you guys bother. I always thought she was a flake."

Neva started crying as she responded, "I can't believe you're saying that."

He reached over and patted her on the shoulder. "I'm sorry. I didn't mean to make you cry. I'm really tired, and you know how I need my privacy. They came so unexpectedly, and it's unnerving for me not knowing when they're leaving. Maybe I will take Ellington to my parents for the weekend. That would be good, and then we'll see where we are on Monday."

Dante rolled over and went to sleep.

The tears continued to flow down Neva's face until the pillow was soaking wet.

Heather

I REMEMBER THE FIRST TIME I saw him. He was so beautiful; I couldn't take my eyes off him. Full Moon on the Quad was a Stanford tradition. Freshmen would go to the quad to be kissed by a senior in order to become a "real" Stanford woman or man. I thought it was stupid and didn't want to go, but Tamara dragged me there.

He was standing near MemChu, and it was as if the gold from the frescos on the top of church cast a halo around him. Maybe that's a little dramatic, but I am an artist after all, and he looked like a perfect masterpiece to me. Christopher Cross took up residence in the center of my heart that night, and he still hasn't left.

He was a senior, star of the basketball team, and brilliant. I think his major was physics. Rumor was that he scored a perfect 1600 on his SATs. Stanford was full of crazy overachievers, but Chris was special, at least to me.

He was the only one who knew about my mother. I don't even know why I told him. It was probably one of those nights when I was hanging out with him in his off-campus apartment. He would ask me one question, and we would end up talking all night. I would wake up in his arms. Untouched. I felt so safe. I don't know why he never tried anything; I guess he just didn't see me that way, but I loved him from the first moment I saw him.

So, I guess in some way, it made sense that I told him and only him about my mother and the cancer. And I'm glad I did; he was so kind and understanding about it all. He was such a good friend to me. He would take me from Palo Alto to Berkeley in his little red convertible to see my mom on the weekends. We would stop at different restaurants on the way back to campus to have Sunday dinner and just talk. The Gingerbread House in Oakland was my favorite; the soul food was so warm and comforting, it went perfectly with the company. Chris was always able to hear what I was saying beneath my words. He would just sit across from me during those conversations and look at me with those big brown eyes and the perfect smile and just listen. I needed those conversations to get my mind off everything else that was going on. I guess I never told the girls because I didn't need to. Chris gave me all the support I needed.

The girls didn't understand our friendship, but they didn't know the Chris I knew. They didn't hear the kind words or gentle silences we would share. They didn't understand how he supported me, how he kept my secret. They just saw the raucous ballplayer who had women swooning all over campus—black, white, and other. Like always, they made fun of what they didn't understand. Tamara teased me for being "just another one of his hos," so I felt stupid for spending any time with him. Annette kept riding me about how we hadn't slept together and kept trying to get me to seduce him. Lauren thought he was using me. Neva was the only one who didn't say a word. She always just let me be.

She probably would have understood about my mother, but I knew it would have been hard for her to keep it a secret from the girls. She wasn't a gossip, but would have told the others, so they could have "supported" me. But I just didn't want that kind of support.

Year after year, even after he graduated, he would still take the forty-five-minute drive from the City to Palo Alto and turn right around and take me to Berkeley to see my mother. He did this consistently, until, well, until I didn't need him to anymore.

He came to my mother's funeral, of course, but soon afterward, he went to grad school out east and we kind of just lost touch. We exchanged Christmas cards and he always remembered my birthday, but that was it. I wanted to reach out so many times, but something always stopped me. I kept hearing the girls' voices in my head: "He's just playing with you." "He could have any woman on campus; why would he want you?" "I don't know why you waste your time chasing after him like a puppy dog." So every time I thought about calling him, I didn't. I never even wrote anything beyond my name in every card I sent. I heard he got married a few years ago. I didn't get a wedding invite. I would never have been able to bring myself to go. But I never stopped missing him.

Lauren and Annette

THE FRIDAY-MORNING RIDE TO THE hospital was uncharacteristically quiet. Once they arrived, Tamara went to find Dr. Chandra, leaving the others to linger in the waiting room in silence. Annette's phone rang.

"I've got to take this," she said to no one in particular as she walked toward the window to get better reception.

Lauren walked to the opposite end of the waiting room window bank and took a call as well.

Neva looked at Annette and Lauren on opposite sides of the room and chuckled. *How appropriate.* Seeing them on the phone reminded her that she should confirm the day's arrangements for Ellington. *What if the babysitter forgets to pick him up? Or what if she's late? What if he's the last one waiting in the pickup line? What if he's upset that she's not there? Will he remember that I'm not coming?* She made a short list in her head of things she needed to double-check as she walked near the elevator bank.

Tamara returned quickly to the waiting room and was left sitting alone. She had already spoken with her office early in the morning and really didn't have anyone to call.

Dr. Chandra sauntered casually into the room and sat down next to her.

"I understand you were looking for me," he said as he crossed one blue pants leg over the other.

Tamara didn't know why, but his question made her cheeks turn a coppery red.

Dr. Chandra smiled as he continued. "I'm sure you wanted to check on Heather, and unfortunately, there hasn't been any change in her condition.

I'm sorry. You don't mind relaying that to the others, do you? I have to continue with my rounds."

"Of course. Thanks for the update. I'll be sure to fill them in once they finish their 'all-important' phone calls. You know, life beckons," Tamara commented, while gesturing toward her friends, who surrounded the room with their passionate conversations, exaggerated one-handed gestures, and nervous pacing.

"Your life isn't beckoning you?" Dr. Chandra asked, leaning in to hear her answer.

Tamara thought about her life for a moment. Since her patients were covered, there would be no one expecting her call. Nothing and no one needed to be watched or looked after. *Hell, I don't even have a cat,* she thought. She briefly considered what she would be doing if she were at home. *The answer to that's easy; I would certainly be at work. It seems that I'm always either leaving or going to work. When I'm not with my patients, I think about them, strategize about solutions to their impossible situations. I get so much satisfaction when a couple whose pregnancy was labeled "high risk" holds their baby (or babies, as is often the case) for the first time. But, lately, the sweet satisfaction has turned a little bitter because it is a pleasure I'm not sure I will ever know for myself.*

"Tamara," Dr. Chandra interrupted her thoughts.

She shook her head quickly, embarrassed that his simple question was so provocative. She finally responded, "You know how it is: my patients are my life."

"Tamara, I am certain you are a good doctor—a great doctor probably—but your work, as meaningful and rewarding as it is, should not be your whole life. You deserve more—but you already know that."

She didn't know which caught her more off guard: Dr. Chandra's unwavering gaze or his acute observation, so she averted her eyes, first by looking around to see if her friends had gotten off the phone, then by digging around in her purse, searching in vain for something to rescue her.

Her very apparent discomfort did not cause any alteration in his behavior. His stare remained as intense, and instead of leaning back in his seat, he leaned in even closer.

"I don't think what you're looking for is in there," he gently challenged, adding a reassuring smile to his intense gaze.

Tamara forced a smile. "I guess you're right," Tamara said with mild irritation.

"Well, like Led Zeppelin said, 'It's never too late to change the road you're on.'"

"Led Zeppelin?" Tamara couldn't stop herself from laughing. "Really?"

"Hey, wisdom is everywhere, if you know where to find it," Dr. Chandra replied with a chuckle as he gently touched Tamara on her shoulder while standing to leave. "I'll see you later."

As Dr. Chandra left, Annette and Lauren came over toward Tamara.

"Are you okay over here? The good doctor was here for a long time," Lauren half-teased.

"Uh-huh, I saw you over here chit-chatting," Annette added.

"What-ever," Tamara replied. "There is no change in Heather's condition. Everything's the same. Is everything okay with you guys? I saw you both e-mailing and texting and talking. It's so nice that I don't have to call and check in with anyone," said Tamara. "I am a free woman, the 'master of my fate, the captain of my soul.'" She waved her hands in the air with a flourish.

"How nice for you," Lauren smirked as she sat down next to her.

"Is everything okay at work?" Annette asked. "I don't know how much longer I can stay out here. I can't really do 'unexpected trips,' you know? Things don't just stop because I'm gone."

"Yeah, I know. Unfortunately. Work can be so demanding, unnecessarily so even at times. Being out here, even under these circumstances, is actually a pleasant break, you know? Sometimes work is just so empty. I wish I could do something that really made a difference. Selling sugary carbonated beverages really isn't something that I can feel good about. So, I wasn't checking work, I was talking with the nanny to see how things are going at home. It seems that things are just fine without me—smooth as silk; no problems," reported Lauren, with a hint of disconcertment.

"That's good, isn't it?" Tamara questioned.

Before Lauren could answer, Annette chimed in. "I wish I had such good news to report." Lauren and Tamara looked earnestly at Annette as she explained, "Oh, no, things are fine at my house. I'm talking about work." Lauren and Tamara immediately shifted back in their seats, returning to only a moderately interested listening posture. "This is still important, you guys. My firm is in the middle of negotiating a major deal—my deal—and it's stalling, and with the weekend coming, I've got to stay on top of it."

"I know it's important, dear, but I'm quite sure that they can manage for a little while longer without you," Lauren responded.

"Who can manage what without whom?" Neva joined them after finishing her phone call.

"Annette was just talking about how some big deal is stuck," Lauren responded.

"I know it's taken a lot for you guys to drop everything and come out here. I'm sorry I had to call you all; I just didn't know what else to do. Maybe I should have figured out some sort of schedule, you know, so you could have come out on a rolling basis."

"You don't have to apologize, Neva. You didn't do anything wrong. Under the circumstances, you did everything right; it's just that my assistant just really stressed me out. You all don't understand the constant scrutiny I face, the pressure I'm under. Do you know how many black partners there are at my firm? Me. That's it. Everything I do is under a microscope, and it's not like when I first came out of law school; law firms are not recession-proof anymore."

"Nothing is," offered Lauren. "I feel the same way, except I have to juggle my family too. Between travel and long hours and the kids and Prescott and Zoe, I feel like there's not enough of me to go around." Lauren continued. "And I'm always wondering whether I made the right choice in continuing to work, and especially the way I've handled my child-care situation. I've given up so much, and for what? I mean, who really cares about packaged goods and marketing and brand expansion? It's all numbers and profits and shares. I've left my children in someone else's care for this? I just wonder sometimes whether it's all worth it. It's not such a good thing that things are going so seamlessly at home, you know. They are so used to my not being there, it's like I don't even matter." Lauren rested her elbows on her knees and put her head in her hands, running her fingers through her short, wavy, gold-flecked auburn hair.

"I don't understand, Lauren. I thought everything was going great," Neva speculated.

"I just can't shake the feeling that my carefully crafted house of cards is about to come tumbling down," she admitted as she lifted her head, her eyes beginning to well with tears.

Everyone's eyes widened as they leaned in with anticipation.

"I just don't know if I can take it anymore," Lauren tearfully admitted.

"Take what? What are you talking about?" Tamara asked.

"Lauren, it's okay—you can tell us," Neva said gently as she rubbed Lauren's back; she often rubbed Ellington's when he woke in the middle of the night from a nightmare.

Lauren's quiet tears turned to gentle sobs. Her hands could barely contain her head, as she shook it back and forth. "I … think … my … husband … is … having … an … affair."

"Oh, Lauren, I'm sure that's not true," Neva said in an attempt to comfort her.

"Yeah, me too," Tamara responded, with the lilt of uncertainty in her voice.

"We don't just sleep in separate bedrooms because he snores," Lauren replied dryly as she lifted her head.

Neva and Tamara shrugged as she continued. "It's been a really long time, and before then, it wasn't that often," Lauren admitted somberly as she spread out her fingers and looked at them as if she were counting.

"Like how long? A few months?" Annette asked in disbelief.

"Multiply that by, like, ten," Lauren replied.

"I'm sorry, are you saying that you and your husband haven't had sex in years?" Annette clarified.

"Yes," Lauren responded.

"Oh, hell yeah, he's definitely stepping out on you then," Annette replied.

"Wow," Tamara said under her breath, "and I thought I was having a dry spell."

"Annette, you don't know that. A lot of couples slow down, especially after children. It doesn't mean he's having an affair. I mean, how do you know? Lauren, you all seem so happy, I just can't imagine," Neva said. "I mean, even Dante and I have it on the regular. I can't imagine what he would do if we didn't."

"That doesn't sound right at all, Neva. It almost sounds like you have sex out of fear, not desire," Tamara added.

"No, I didn't mean it like that," Neva quickly replied.

"Well, what did you mean?" Annette questioned.

"Can we just focus on Lauren? How long have you felt this way?" Neva asked.

"Off and on for a while now. At first when we stopped having sex, I thought it was just because I had gained so much weight after the baby. And then, you know, with three kids and going back to work, I was exhausted, so when Prescott wanted to do it, I was just too tired to muster up any kind of desire, and then he just stopped asking. That's when I started suspecting."

"I am so sorry for you, on so many levels. How can you go for so long without having sex?"Annette wondered.

"Who has time to even think about it with my work schedule and travel schedule? Besides, being this big doesn't exactly make me feel sexy."

"You are not that big; you look fine," encouraged Tamara.

"Thanks for saying that, but I don't feel fine. And I'm not fine. Instead of having sex with my husband, I have chocolate, which only makes me fatter and more disgusted with myself and only pushes him away even further."

"Well, you shouldn't blame yourself. Sex or no sex. You are married, and he should not be having an affair," Neva stated emphatically.

"It's just not that simple, Neva," Annette said softly as she stood up and walked over to the window, folded her arms, and rested her forehead against the glass.

Neva turned her head sharply toward Annette. "Yes, it is. What do you mean?"

"Having an affair isn't always so black and white, and it isn't so far out of the realm of possibility for anyone," Annette flatly replied without turning to face them.

"What does that mean exactly?" Lauren asked.

"What do you think it means?" Annette admitted impatiently while turning to face them. They were only mildly surprised at Annette's revelation and looked at each other with raised eyebrows and clear disapproval.

"What are you all staring at? I'm just being honest. It's easy to think that things are black and white, that you always know what's right and wrong; but in reality, there's a lot of gray in these situations. Extreme marital distress can either make you the person you always were supposed to be, or it can turn you into the person you never thought you could be," Annette responded.

Immediately, Neva's face flushed, and she lowered her eyes in shame.

"I guess you fell into the latter category, huh, Annette?" Lauren said curtly.

"You guys, please, stop fussing," Tamara urged.

Annette walked over to Lauren and knelt on the floor in front of her. She took Lauren's clammy hands in hers, looked into her red swollen eyes, and tried to explain.

"You know how long we have been trying to get pregnant, right? A very long time. Well, frustration and tension have been building for a while now. I started blaming him; he started blaming me. All the while, we were having sex like rabbits—and still nothing! Sex was beginning to feel like just a means to an end. The passion was fading, the romance fleeting. It was like we were just fulfilling a duty, checking a box on the fertility calendar."

"What? Sex a duty for you? Oh, I know that didn't work," Tamara jumped in.

"Right; you all know how sexual I am. Eventually, it was doing nothing for me, so we started doing it less and less, which, of course, was contrary to our goal of getting pregnant in the first place, which only made both of us even more resentful. I don't know, maybe over time, his manhood started to feel threatened, and then some sort of situational impotence took hold, so then we couldn't do it at all anymore."

"Wow, Annette, I didn't know you were going through all that," Neva said empathetically.

"If I had known it was going to be so hard, I wouldn't have waited so long, I'll tell you that. So, now I'm getting even more frustrated and angry, because I really want to get pregnant. And I'm starting to really miss sex. And I really like sex. I tried to be understanding and loving—I suggested that we go to counseling, but he refused and started to withdraw even more.

"More time passed, and I started feeling really lonely. And I know what you're thinking, Tamara, 'How can I be lonely and married?' But I tell you, being single and lonely is one thing, because at least you have hope; you have an expectation of not being lonely one day. But when you're married and lonely, you have no hope, no expectation of anything ever being different. It feels like you're trapped in a teeny tiny black box all by yourself. I don't think there's anything worse."

"Me either," Neva whispered, barely audible.

"I missed being touched and held and looked at like I was beautiful. Thomas just seemed to look right through me anymore."

"That must have been awful, Annette. You never told me any of this," Tamara said.

"I know; how could I? How could I complain about my lonely sad marriage and struggles to have a baby to you? Anyway, that's the context when I ran into an old colleague on a business trip in DC. We went out for lunch, just to catch up, and I found myself being completely disarmed by him. A man hadn't been that attentive to me in a long time. Interaction with Thomas had become routine conversations about running our household and maintaining our social calendars. We hadn't really connected in such a long time, and in contrast, my colleague was so, I don't know, present in our conversations. He was right there for me. Listening to me. Engaging me. Looking at me like there was nothing wrong with me. It was totally compelling and completely irresistible. I accepted his offer to have drinks after work one day. Drinks turned into dinner, and honestly, I didn't want the conversation to end. I wasn't looking for it to happen; it just did."

"Wow. Just like that," Lauren responded while staring blankly at Annette. Neva and Tamara had nothing to say in response to their friend's admission.

Annette stood up. "I'm not trying to justify my actions or what your husband is doing, if, in fact, he is having an affair. All I'm saying is that you have to consider the context. As much as I didn't believe it before, what people say is really true—an affair typically is not the cause of a problem in a marriage; it happens because of problems that already exist. And if ya'll haven't had sex in years and only erratically before that—you were having problems."

"Unbelievable. No matter what, you always seem to be able to put the blame squarely on my shoulders. You know what? Forget it. I shouldn't have said anything." Lauren tried to stand up, but Neva put her hand on Lauren's shoulder and kept her in her seat.

"No one is blaming you," Neva asserted. "I know this must be just awful. Annette was only trying to help."

"I'm just keeping it real," Annette agreed.

"A little too real, but I suppose you're right. I tried for so long to make him happy by doing whatever he wanted. He wanted me to keep my job, to keep working. And I joined all the boards he suggested; I was a member of all the 'right' organizations. I thought that would be enough. But he always seemed to want something more. And I never seemed to be able to give him what he needed. As for the sex, well, I never lost the baby weight from the twins, and then when I added the Kyle-pounds, well … I'm sure whatever lingering interest he did have quickly left," Lauren sighed. "And to be completely honest, I never really understood what the big deal was about sex anyway."

"Girl, you just haven't had any real good sex if you don't know what the big deal is," Annette said emphatically, while raising her hand to high-five someone, only to find both Tamara and Neva staring at her blankly.

"Oh, come on you two, don't leave me hangin'."

"Well, it's been a while, but I guess I'll cosign with you, Annette," Tamara said as she met her hand to Annette's.

Lauren couldn't hear anyone's voice anymore; she was far away in her memory. *I loved going to the Vineyard, so much so that even when my family decided not to go that summer, I went anyway, staying with my cousins. My aunt had remarried twice already. This husband was much younger than she was. I liked that he listened to me. He treated me like a grown-up, letting me come and go as I basically pleased. It was so nice because my parents were so strict and never let me do anything.*

"Neva, I don't even want to know what your sex life is like," Annette sighed.

"It's pretty perfunctory. I don't think my pleasure even comes into Dante's mind. He just makes sure he, well, you know, and then that's it. I'm almost never satisfied."

When he called me into the office that day when everyone else was at the beach, butterflies stirred in my stomach. All he did was ask me how I was doing, and I just opened up and poured out all my little fifteen-year-old heart could hold. His hands rubbing my shoulders felt like understanding. When he pressed his lips to mine, I could taste the vodka and cranberry juice in his mouth, and it was intoxicating to me. Still, I recoiled at the unfamiliar touch of his hand to my breast until he pulled me closer and I looked into his eyes and I thought it was love.

"Girl, you sound like Celie from *The Color Purple*—'Mister lay on top of me and do his business,'" Tamara said in response to Neva's revelation. "You know it's not supposed to be that way, right?"

"Yeah, I know."

He laid me down on the worn leather sofa, raised my cover-up, moved my bikini bottom to one side, and then suddenly I felt this searing pain that caused me to howl, and so he covered my mouth with one hand while the other one he used to keep my legs open because they instinctively clenched in response to the burning that was coming from down there.

"This is some crazy shit. One married woman not having any sex. Another one might as well not be having any, and I'm having sex with someone who is not my husband." Annette almost spit the words out of her mouth.

Neva just shrugged, with her eyes downcast.

"Don't look that way, Neva, it will be all right," Tamara encouraged. "We'll figure it out for all of us. Right, Lauren?"

I didn't realize I had been holding my breath the entire time until I finally exhaled once he stood up and repositioned himself in his boxers, pulled up his shorts, ran his fingers through his curly black hair, smiled at me, and walked out of the room, leaving me splayed on the couch.

"Lauren, Lauren, have you heard anything we've said?" Tamara asked.

Tamara's question brought her out of one nightmare and right back to another.

"Lauren, are you all right? You look kinda pale," Neva asked Lauren before she could answer. "Hey, everyone, let's back up for a second. Aren't we getting ahead of ourselves? I mean, their sex life, such as it is, has been consistent. It's not like all of a sudden, they stopped doing it. They have never really done it, so maybe he's not doing anything different than what he has been doing all along," Neva added.

Annette shook her head. "Trust me; if she thinks he's having an affair, he's having one. A woman always knows."

"Well, I need to know for sure. Where do I even start? Do I hire a private investigator?" Lauren asked, coming back to the present moment.

"A private investigator? Girl, that's so old school. All you need to do is get a GPS locator and put it on his car. That way, you can find out if he's really where he says he is all the time. All those late nights working and business lunches, huh, we'll see about that. Then you check the cell phone records. Look for any repeated calls, especially around lunchtime and after work. Next, you have to start checking the credit card statements for any suspicious charges—meals, jewelry, big-ticket items, you know. And then you should check his e-mail; you all probably share passwords anyway. Did you all ever have a 'nanny cam'? That may come in handy too," Annette rattled off.

Tamara, Neva, and Lauren were speechless.

"Hey, game recognizes game. I'm just glad that my dirty dealings can at least help you out," Annette chuckled. "Fortunately, my husband trusts me completely, and I'm smart enough not to give him any reason to suspect anything. And if he did suspect anything, he'd never confront me. He has it too good."

"Annette," Lauren chided her.

"He does. I work my ass off for 'the Man,' and he gets to make a difference. Even if he did confront me, I would deny it."

"Prescott is way too honest for that. I think he would tell me if I asked him," Lauren replied.

"Or be really pissed if he's not having an affair. You have to be careful with this, Lauren; you could ruin everything," Neva warned.

"Ruin what? A sexless marriage? Lauren deserves to know the truth. And she deserves a full relationship. But I guess Neva is right; this could go either way, so you better be prepared for a wide variety of responses from him. You have to know that you are truly ready to hear his response and to deal with whatever action it requires. I want you to consider all of the possible outcomes and be very strategic about your next steps," advised Annette.

"Marital espionage. Who would have ever guessed?" Lauren replied.

"The object is to keep him guessing from this point on," Annette, the wartime consigliere, said.

"Lauren, just keep your head about you. Don't check your intelligence at the door just to stay in this relationship, like I did for so long with Parker. I mean, there were clearly signs that he was gay that I just ignored because I wanted a relationship. I wanted to be married, so I just didn't pay attention," Tamara reflected.

"And don't forget, you were sprung!" Annette added.

"Whatever."

"It's true, and there's nothing wrong with being in love. But love has its place, and for Lauren, love has got to take a backseat. You have to be cold and calculating. Get your facts straight and then decide what you're going to do. I know you're hurting just at the prospect of what may be going on, but you don't have time to hurt right now. And remember, no matter what happens; you are going to be all right." Annette reached over and patted Lauren's hand.

"Yeah, but what about you?" Lauren asked.

"Who, me? Oh, I'll be just fine," Annette nodded. "You know how I do …"

Heather

I WOULD LOOK FOR HER in her room, but she was already gone. I just couldn't stop hoping that somehow she would come back to me. I even kept the hospital bed for a while, didn't have the courage to call the company we rented it from to return it.

For a while, the phone calls and visits from friends kept her close to me, but soon they dwindled down to a trickle. Finally, the drip-drop of an unexpected visitor or an unannounced casserole stopped completely, and there I was. Alone.

Neva, Tamara, Annette, and Lauren

BACK AT NEVA'S, THE AROMA of Lauren's lemon-thyme roasted chicken along with savory root vegetables was a welcome greeting for Neva as she returned from picking up Ellington from the sitter's house just in time for her to pack his bags to head off to Dante's family's house for the weekend. Annette and Tamara had been peeking in the pots the entire time she was gone. The Sauvignon Blanc Annette, the group sommelier, selected was the perfect complement to their meal, and they all gathered around the table.

"I forgot what a good cook you were," Tamara commented as she enjoyed her first bite of Lauren's creation.

"I used to love to cook, and now I hardly ever have the time."

"Do you remember our senior year, when we lived in those dorms with kitchens, what was the name again? Anyway, we used to trick you into coming down and cooking breakfast for us," Annette added.

"The dorm was Mirielees, and do you and Tamara really think that you were tricking me? After the first time that you heifers invited me for breakfast and the ingredients were waiting for me on the countertop, I had you two figured out. I just didn't mind, that's all. I actually like cooking for people, and you two seemed to enjoy it so much, I just acted surprised all the time," Lauren replied.

"I still miss those potatoes," Tamara said while shaking her head.

"I never got any potatoes, or anything else for that matter," Neva complained.

"That's 'cause you spent most mornings at your man's house," Annette teased, making Neva blush.

"Well, at least she only had one and wasn't creeping with this one and that one and, oh yeah, the other one," Tamara teased back.

"Ha-ha, very funny."

"Not to change the subject from this banter, and I really don't know how to say this except to just say it, because someone has to say it ..."

"Just spit it out, Lauren," Annette said in between bites.

"Well, what's our game plan? How long do you expect us to stay out here, and how long are we going to let Heather stay like this?"

"What do you mean, 'how long'?" Neva asked, not wanting to believe what Lauren was suggesting.

"I mean, well, Tamara, help me out if I'm wrong, but she could be like this forever. I mean, she may not ever wake up, right? And it seems that at some point, someone has to make the hard decision, right?"

Neva threw her fork down and pushed her plate away, tears streaming down her face. "I can't believe you are even saying this! It's only been three days!"

"What? I'm just being practical. Someone has to be. We have to face the reality that Heather may never come out of the coma, Tamara, isn't that right?" Lauren looked sternly at Tamara, who had been avoiding making any comment.

"I mean, of course, there is the possibility that Heather could be comatose for weeks, even months, or longer," Tamara hesitantly responded.

"So, then, we will wait weeks or months or even longer," Neva adamantly replied.

"I didn't mean to upset you all by bringing this up, but I felt that someone had to. I mean, at some point, we have to go home. We can't move out here indefinitely to sit at her bedside and hold her hand while they monitor her and pump her with that liquid food. Has anyone even thought about whether Heather would really want to live this way?" Lauren asked.

"I don't know, but I know that Heather would want to live," Neva answered.

"Are you sure?" Lauren posited.

"All right, all right. Now it's only been a few days, and in my opinion, it's still a little premature to be having this discussion. She is showing some good brain activity, and she could improve. People wake up from comas all the time and are perfectly normal. Let's not get ahead of ourselves." Tamara inserted her words like a wedge between Lauren and Neva, hoping to keep any additional conflict at bay.

"Well, whatever. Just don't look at me later. But while we're tackling difficult subjects, I think we should resolve the issue of the paintings too," Lauren continued.

"I thought it was resolved," Annette huffed.

"I think the paintings have to be tabled for now; I mean, in the scheme of things, they really aren't that important. Heather's recovery is," Tamara stated.

"Why does it have to be 'either/or'? Why can't it be 'both/and'? I honestly don't see how you guys can fail to see the potential in Heather's work, for all of us," Lauren replied.

"Maybe it would be a good project at some point, but one that we should undertake when Heather is able to participate, you know? They are *her* paintings; it is *her* gift," Tamara replied.

"Well, sometimes people just don't know what to do with what they've got," Lauren answered.

Heather

I COULD SMELL THE CORNBREAD and collard greens wafting from Lauren's room way down the hall as I was coming back from the sculpture garden working on my Rodin paper. Lauren could cook better than any of them. Tamara, Neva, and even Annette managed to tear themselves away from their respective man du jour to come and eat. Lauren's cooking would gather them around the small table or on the couch, or even the floor. Someone would drive down El Camino, buy some wine at Safeway, and we would feast.

I liked those meals when it was just us. Especially senior year, when I knew those moments wouldn't last. I guess it made them more precious. Everyone was so focused on what was next. I was still enjoying what was right then.

Lauren was interviewing all over the place. Tamara was always studying, it seemed. Annette was frantic about the LSAT and getting into Harvard. Neva was taking a co-term year. I didn't really know what I wanted to do, so I decided I'd better stay in school. I wasn't like my friends, who had the future all planned out. I just wanted to enjoy each moment, or at least try to.

I remember that day, the smells were so strong it made my mouth water before I even realized where they were coming from. As I kept walking toward Lauren's room, the smells got more and more intense. Surprise mixed with my saliva because normally I would know if Lauren was cooking, but then again, I had been in the garden all afternoon, but still. As I opened the door, everyone was there, except me.

Lauren was at the stove finishing up. Annette was opening a bottle of white Zinfandel. Tamara was getting out the plates. Neva was sitting at the table reading a magazine. They all looked shocked to see me standing there.

"Hey, girl!" Lauren shouted, "come on in."

"You're cooking, and you didn't invite me?" I took a few steps into the apartment and stood near the green vinyl couch that separated the living space from the outside bedroom.

"No one called Heather?" Neva asked the group.

"Annette, you and Tamara drove right past me when I was walking down Campus Drive. You could have stopped."

I was trying to understand.

"We must have been on our way to the grocery store," Annette said to Tamara. She then turned to me and explained, "We didn't even see you. Do you even like soul food?" Annette chuckled.

"Have you ever had greens, you know, besides at the Black Student Union Kwanzaa celebration?" Lauren asked, half-teasing.

"I know what soul food is" was all I could say as I turned and left the apartment Lauren shared with Neva. Neva followed me and apologized. She was always the one who came after me, who tried to make it all right, but this time, she couldn't. They didn't get that I enjoyed being together as much as I enjoyed the food, whatever it was. I was used to strangers making assumptions about me because I had a white mother, but they were supposed to be my friends.

Lauren

THE TAXI STOPPED AT THE hospital first. Lauren thought it would be impolite to leave without saying good-bye, just in case what the doctors said was true and Heather really could hear her. Just in case Heather would notice she was gone.

At that hour of the morning, the room was quiet, without the usual bustling of nurses and that handsome Dr. Chandra. She stood in the doorway for a long, long time staring at her once-dear friend and tried to find something familiar in her face. She seemed so foreign now. No more California wild child inside, it seemed. Lauren laughed to herself as she remembered when she first met Heather on one of the countless sunny Palo Alto afternoons in the early weeks of her freshman year.

Lauren had just left biology class and was walking through White Plaza to the library when Heather stopped her, trying to get her to sign some petition about divesting from South Africa. Lauren wasn't interested in political causes, and she wasn't there to rock the boat. She came to college for one thing: to get a degree, in four years, period. Heather was so adamant and passionate about her cause, and well, who could be on the side of apartheid after all? So she signed the petition but declined the invitation to the protest later in the week.

Lauren eventually moved in a little closer and took the chair near Heather's bed. She haltingly placed her hand on top of Heather's just for a moment, and then she quickly drew it back. Lauren rested her hands in her own lap while her fingers deftly twirled the fringe on the cream pashmina scarf wrapped around her brown leather jacket. Even though it was California, it still could be chilly, especially in February, and especially in the morning. She remembered how when she first arrived in the Bay Area, she would change clothes three times each day: jeans or sweats for the early morning chill, shorts and a T-shirt for the midday sun, and then a jacket or sweatshirt for the cooler evenings. That routine didn't last long once she realized how much laundry it generated.

She glanced at her watch and decided she needed to leave if she was going to make her plane, but she seemed glued to the seat and sat there a little bit longer. *Maybe Heather isn't ready for me to leave,* Lauren thought to herself, then shook her head at the silliness of her idea. *What am I thinking? She doesn't know whether I'm here or not.* Still, she lacked the will to press her feet into the floor to give her thighs the momentum to raise herself from the cushiony green seat. So, she just gripped the handle of the portfolio a little tighter and remained there, at Heather's bedside.

I hope they understand that I'm doing this for her.

Neva, Tamara, and Annette

THE RICH AROMA OF THE coffee woke Neva from her slumber. She instinctively tried to get out of bed without rustling the sheets too much—until she remembered that she was alone in the bed. Dante and Ellington had gone to spend the weekend with her in-laws, who retired near Sacramento. She stretched her legs and arms wide, taking up as much of the king-size bed as possible, and smiled as she flung back the sheets and took the liberty of jumping noisily out of bed.

Happy not to have to rush to get dressed, Neva was surprised to find a basket full of freshly baked blueberry muffins on the kitchen counter. *What has gotten into Lauren, with all the cooking? She must have been up at the crack of dawn. But I'm not mad,* she concluded as she grabbed one and took a bite. They were still warm. She walked to the office and was surprised to find the daybed neatly made and the dirty sheets and towels resting on the desk. Neva opened the closet door looking for Lauren's suitcase, but it wasn't there.

When Neva returned to the kitchen, Annette was sitting at the bar in her red silk pajamas, coddling a cup of coffee and looking over the brochures from the treatment facilities.

"Have you seen Lauren this morning? Her stuff is gone," Neva asked.

"No one was in here when I came in. Maybe she just went for a walk or something," Annette suggested. "It's a beautiful morning."

"Good morning," Tamara mumbled as she staggered into the kitchen. She poured herself a cup of coffee and took a muffin from the basket as she uttered a "yummm."

"Lauren's gone missing," Annette commented.

"Really?" Tamara replied, still only half-awake.

"I don't know where she could have gone. Do you think she went to the hospital without us?" Neva asked.

"C'mon now," Tamara answered.

Annette shrugged, nursed her coffee, and waited for the caffeine to kick in. Neva continued to walk around the house, looking for Lauren. Just as she returned to the kitchen, the phone rang.

"Hello," Neva replied into the receiver.

"Neva, I'm glad it's you," Lauren whispered into the phone.

"Lauren, where are you?"

"I'm on my way home. I just didn't want you to worry."

"Of course, I'm worried. I woke up and you were gone. Did you say you were on your way home? Why are you leaving?"

There was a long pause before Lauren simply said, "I—I just can't."

"Can't what?" Neva's concern quickly turned to impatience. "What am I supposed to tell everyone?"

"I don't know what to tell them. Say my kids are sick. Tell them I was too embarrassed that my husband may be cheating on me. Tell them anything you like; I had to leave."

"Lauren, what's going on with—"

Before Neva could finish, Lauren cut her off with a quick, "I gotta go," before she hung up abruptly. Neva stood frozen for a moment with the phone in her hands.

"What's up?" Tamara asked.

"She's going home," Neva stated somberly.

"She's what?" Annette responded with fully caffeinated indignation.

"Lauren is on her way home," Neva repeated slowly.

"Unbelievable," Tamara concurred.

"I don't know why you think it's unbelievable. Lauren is a selfish, spoiled bitch. When we refused to discuss how long we were going to stay and whether and what we were going to do with Heather and when we didn't agree with her about the pictures, she 'took her ball' and went home. I, for one, am over it," Annette responded, reaching over for a muffin and taking a bite.

"Annette, come on now, I'm sure her reasons for leaving have nothing to do with any of that," Tamara replied. "Maybe something came up at work, or maybe she was humiliated after our conversation yesterday."

"T, come on. All she told us was that her husband may be having an affair—big deal!" Annette replied.

"And she admitted that their sex life was, well, lacking, and I'm sure that was hard for her," Neva added.

"Y'all are tripping. Was what she shared any more intimate than the rest of us? I mean, I admitted to actually having an affair. And what about you, Neva? You 'fessed up to having a secret abortion. So, Lauren thinks her husband may be having an affair and they don't have sex. Big deal. Her stuff is so common, it's ridiculous. So what? Her little bubble is burst? Her secret is out? We all know that her life isn't as perfect as she pretends? There's a crack in her mask? What-ever! I, for one, am glad she's gone." Annette smirked as she finished off the muffin.

Lauren

Lauren settled into the backseat of the limo and tightened the pashmina around her shoulders like a baby's swaddling. Even though it was warm and sunny even for February in Atlanta, she still couldn't stave off the Bay Area chill. She tapped rapidly on the barrier that separated her from the driver and asked him with mild annoyance to turn on the heat.

Her fingers toyed with the soft fringe as she thought about what she was going to do when she got home. *Should I confront him? Should I look into the GPS thing that Annette mentioned? Maybe I'm just imagining the whole thing. But what if I'm right?* She shook the thoughts out of her mind as she looked out the window at the red clay dirt that peeked out beneath the grass and rocks and wildflowers on the side of the road as she whizzed by. *I just couldn't spend any more time wringing my hands at Neva's house or sitting at Heather's bedside for a whole bunch of nothing. And all that gut spilling; everyone has a secret, it seems. I don't want to hear all about Neva's abortion, Annette's infidelity, and Tamara's ... well, her single misery is no secret to anyone. Anyway, I said too much as it is. Enough talking. I need to take action. Besides, they were starting to look at me funny.* She started to feel the heat blasting through the vents.

I have to know once and for all whether my suspicions are true, and if so, I need to figure out what I'm going to do about them. One thing is clear: I have to get myself together before things get so bad they can't be fixed, she thought to herself as she looked down at her wedding ring. *It is still beautiful,* she thought. A 2.5-carat solitaire from Tiffany's (she demanded not only the blue box, but also the receipt for verification). It used to look so large when her fingers were long and slender; it now seemed dwarfed by the oozing flesh the band was unable to contain. She remembered twisting it around her finger when she was nervous or unsure. Now, it fit so smugly that it was unmovable. Her finger looked like a stuffed sausage bursting out on either side of the wide platinum band. *Still, it is a beautiful ring.*

Once I get this weight off, I may have to get it resized. I can't be outdone by Annette and Tamara. They looked incredible, I have to admit. Neva was tiny too, but she just looked sick skinny, not cute skinny. I'll take any kind of skinny at this point, Lauren thought as she quickly sent her trainer a text asking if she could come back. While she waited for his response, she called her stylist. *Maybe a new look would turn his head.* As she waited for her stylist to answer, she was certain she was correct: a new haircut and color, along with a facial and massage, should freshen her up nicely. It had been a long few days, and she deserved some pampering. Looking at her hands, she decided to add a mani-pedi as well, as if putting her feet into water would make the steps ahead of her any easier.

As the driver pulled into the circular driveway of Lauren's Buckhead Georgian manor, she wondered how Prescott would respond to her early arrival. Everything happened so last-minute, she didn't have the chance to tell him she was coming home, then decided that maybe it would be better not to tell him, just to keep him on his toes and maybe catch him off guard like Annette said.

I hate playing these games, she thought to herself as she stepped into the grand white marble foyer, careful not to make too much noise. It was early, so like Heather's hospital room, the house was uncharacteristically still. She rested her luggage near the spiral staircase and walked quietly into the kitchen. She temporarily stowed the large black portfolio in the back of the hall closet. *Safe and sound with me, where they belong,* she thought as she patted the case before closing the closet door.

From a quick perusal of the formal living room to her right and on into the stately dining room with its deep red walls, she was not surprised to find everything in its proper place. Things always appeared to be right where they should be in her house. She shrugged as she continued her first-floor inspection. When she got back to the stairs, her body refused to cooperate, her feet turned away from the staircase, and her legs were too heavy to make the climb. So she repeated her path from the kitchen to the living and dining rooms, this time making a stop by the library, and then peeking in the bathroom and returning to the kitchen again.

I hope he wouldn't really be so stupid as to cheat on me with the au pair; that would be tacky and cliché, Lauren thought, *but maybe that is exactly the reason he would do it. She is gorgeous,* Lauren admitted while continuing on her odd tour, her thighs and stomach and breasts jiggling as she walked. She mentally compared her three-baby body to the untarnished-by-pregnancy frame of her nanny. *How could I have let things go this far?*

She rolled her eyes as she continued making the rounds around the first floor of her expansive home, still unable to climb the stairs to the bedroom. As she passed from the hallway to the kitchen, her eyes shifted to the family portraits and wedding pictures carefully arranged on the wall. The fixed expressions and perfect poses that used to provide her with great assurance mocked her now. She turned toward the kitchen and felt like doing something she hadn't done in a long time in this kitchen—cook. She opened the refrigerator to see if it contained the makings for breakfast. Her weekly grocery delivery order must have arrived as scheduled because everything she needed was there. She took out a dozen eggs, some roasted red peppers, and goat cheese in order to whip up a frittata.

The noise from the banging pots and utensils must have traveled upstairs and stirred her husband. Lauren couldn't tell what shocked him more: that she was there at all, or that she was in the kitchen cooking. He greeted her with an abbreviated and awkward embrace, and then rushed upstairs, muttering something about an early morning club meeting.

Lauren remained unfazed as she poured the egg, vegetable, and cheese mixture in the heavy cast-iron French omelet pan. It was a wedding gift from Prescott's sister, which Lauren took as a not-so-subtle suggestion about the appropriate role of a wife in their family. *Who spends that much money on some damn cookware?* Lauren thought to herself, remembering her feigned smile when she opened the box at her shower.

Zoe nearly stopped in her tracks when she came down the winding stairs and saw Lauren. Kyle jumped out of Zoe's arms and ran over to give Lauren a big hug. She hugged him right back and showered his face with kisses before sitting him down on one of the large gray-and-white-striped upholstered barstools.

"Lauren, I'm surprised you're back so soon!" exclaimed Zoe.

"How was everything while I was away? It looks like no one skipped a beat," Lauren responded a little too cheerfully as she carefully slid the skillet out of the Wolf oven.

"Yes, um, everything was fine." Zoe tried to sound unaffected, but Lauren wasn't convinced. "I'd better go check on the twins, so they won't be late for soccer," Zoe said as she hurried up the stairs.

Hmm, she seems a little on edge, Lauren thought to herself, *or am I just reading too much into it? Whatever.*

Maybe a shopping trip is in order. Or should I wait until I lose some weight? I could always make an appointment with the personal shopper at Neimans to help me spruce up my look just a little. I know it will take more than just a new haircut, new clothes, and a new body to get things back in order, but at least it will be some kind of a start.

Heather, Neva, Annette, and Tamara

ALTHOUGH THEY HADN'T BEEN IN the routine that long, the first visit without Lauren was awkward. Something just didn't feel right without her there; nevertheless, they continued on. Neva checked in with the duty nurse before going in to see Heather, while Annette and Tamara took their posts in the waiting room. Neva came back quickly from Heather's room, and for a moment, Annette's and Tamara's eyebrows were raised in alarm.

"Is everything okay?" Annette asked.

Neva was holding the picture of the five of them in her hands. "Everything is fine. They were on their way to take Heather to run some tests, and I couldn't stop looking at this picture. When I go home, I'm going to find mine."

"You're the one who gave them to all of us, and you don't remember where yours is?" Annette teased.

"When I get home, I'm going to find mine too. Heather had hers right on her nightstand. There were no messages on her answering machine, but we were there, well, the picture was anyway," Tamara reflected.

"I need this picture to remind me of all I thought I could be," Neva added wistfully.

"Yeah, baby, we thought we could be anything," Annette concurred.

"And do anything," Tamara added.

"The opportunities seemed endless; we seemed invincible," Neva continued.

"We thought we were the shit!" Annette smiled. "I couldn't wait to get out there in the world and kick some ass!"

Tamara and Neva chuckled at Annette's characterization.

"Yeah, I guess we were a bit cocky," Neva suggested.

"Cocky, hell, no, we weren't cocky. It was the truth. At least for me; I know I was the shit," Annette responded jokingly.

"Yeah, well, I don't think I was ever as confident as you two," Neva replied.

"C'mon, Neva, you were one of the few black women in the electrical engineering department, and then were going for a master's too? You were the bomb, too, and you knew it," Tamara reminded her.

"I certainly don't feel like the bomb now. I feel like someone dropped a bomb on me."

"Ba-by," Annette singsonged the Gap Band classic, with a chuckle. "I'm sorry, I couldn't resist. But seriously, Neva, I don't know if anything 'happened.' I think we were young and didn't know any better. We actually thought things would keep turning out as we wanted them to, like they always had. But real life doesn't work that way," Annette stated with pursed lips.

"You can say that again. My life sure as hell wasn't supposed to end up like this," Tamara suggested.

"Mine either," Annette agreed. "You don't know how many times I catch a reflection of myself in the mirror and think to myself, 'How in the fuck did I end up here?'"

"I'm surprised to hear you say that, Annette. It seems like all your dreams came true," Neva argued. "All your life, you wanted to be a big-time lawyer, and you have Thomas, a kind and gentle man, who loves you."

"Yeah, but that's not all I ever dreamed of," Annette replied softly.

"I guess none of us have it all like we thought we could," Tamara added. "But can we just get a little bit more?"

"And not feel bad for asking?" Annette questioned.

"For real. I have stopped telling anyone, even you guys, about how I wish I was married with kids. I get so sick of people looking at me crazy because they think my career should be enough. I worked damn hard to get where I am; it's not a gift, and it's certainly not the be-all and end-all. Why can't I have a family and two kids and a dog in the yard too?"

Annette and Neva looked quizzically at Tamara before wondering, "A dog?"

"You know, figuratively. Is 'it all' really out of reach?" Tamara responded.

"I don't know. Maybe we have to learn to appreciate what we've got first," Annette offered.

"But how do you do that when what you've got is so far from what you've ever wanted?" Neva countered. "Or like me, when what you thought would make you happy closes in all around you until you can barely breathe?"

"Or it seems like you've lost everything, like Heather," Tamara added quietly.

Just then, Dr. Chandra rounded the corner with Heather's chart in his hands.

"Dr. Chandra, how's Heather doing?" Neva asked impatiently.

"Good morning," Dr. Chandra greeted them cheerfully, but purposefully. "How are you all? Where is Lauren?"

"Humph," Annette grunted while sucking her teeth, crossing her legs, and folding her arms in response.

"She had to go back home," Tamara responded. "Have there been any changes in Heather's condition?"

"Unfortunately no; everything remains the same. I am sorry. I know you all are very anxious to know what is going to happen, but for now, all we can do is—"

"Wait. I know, I know. It's just so hard not being able to do anything," Neva replied.

"I know it is not easy, but it is what it is. I wish I could tell you something that would make you feel better," Dr. Chandra answered.

"But you can't," Annette responded.

"Annette," Neva admonished her. "Dr. Chandra, I know that you are doing your best, and we appreciate it, really we do. You know, I just realized that you have been here every day we have ... when is your day off?" asked Neva.

Dr. Chandra blushed a little as he replied, "I have had the past two days off."

"Then why were you here?" Tamara added.

"My life is a constant exercise in balancing what is important and what truly matters."

Dr. Chandra looked directly at Tamara as he spoke, not averting his gaze, even for a moment. Tamara met his glance, then quickly coughed into her hand and broke away from the semicircle and went over to the window. Dr. Chandra smiled again.

"I must go and check on other patients," Dr. Chandra said before he left the waiting room.

Annette could barely wait until he disappeared before making the observation, "Was it just me, or did everyone feel the heat in here? And he's bold, too—I like that. That's what you need, T, someone who isn't afraid of you," she teased.

"Whatever," Tamara remarked, brushing off Annette's comment while vainly hiding her reddening face.

Lauren

THE NEXT DAY, LAUREN SAT in the oversize black leather chair in Prescott's office and looked at Heather's pictures lined up against the cherry bookshelves that covered the wall. She arose early, as usual, even though it was Sunday, before everyone else was awake. The heavy crystal glass full of champagne and orange juice rested on the arm of the chair as she weighed what she had done and considered her next move.

She wasn't sure why she took the pictures; she only knew that she hadn't been this excited about anything in a long time. *I don't know if I've ever felt this way. It's like I had to take the pictures with me as soon as I saw them. I don't understand why I'm the only one who understands how important this is. Why can't everyone see this is our chance to make something matter? I couldn't let this opportunity go to waste. Not now. I just have to figure out the best way.*

Sell the paintings or just display them? She already knew how she could position them to her friends and club members. *"I just discovered this new hot artist that no one even knows about yet, so you should buy some pieces now while you can."* Of course, if she waited a little while to see what happened with Heather, maybe the paintings would be worth a lot more money. *What would I do with it? Heather had no family; no one would benefit from her genius, which would be a shame. I can figure out that part later. Or maybe instead of selling them, I will organize a show at a gallery instead; just put them out there and see what happens.* Thoughts of sending them back haunted her as well. Lauren just shrugged as she took another long swallow, and her eyes moved from painting to wonderful painting. Maybe she would just do nothing until whatever was or wasn't going to happen with Heather did or did not happen. And tomorrow, she was back to work.

There was time. No one seemed to be in any hurry to make any sort of decision. For whatever reason. But she had the paintings. She would go to work tomorrow. She was just going to sit back and let the dark swirls and vibrant colors speak to her and take another long sip of her mimosa.

Heather

THE FIRST TIME I SAW a Monet in person, I will never forget how it changed my life forever. The soft blue and green and pink colors of the water lilies seemed to wash over me, and I felt so much peace. I just sat there staring at it for hours. When I was in high school, my mother and I took a trip to New York, just the two of us. We spent a whole day at the Metropolitan Museum of Art, most of it with me staring at the Monet. It was so big and beautiful. I had never seen anything like it in all of my life, yet I was sure it had been in my mind all along.

Neva, Tamara, and Annette

AFTER THEY SPENT FIVE DAYS at the hospital, Dr. Chandra recommended that the ladies take a real break, if even for just an afternoon. They were reluctant, but eventually decided to follow his advice and went to one of Neva's favorite places for lunch—the Paragon. As they drove up the large hill to the pristine white building of the Claremont Resort and Spa, they felt a little guilty about the indulgence, but not guilty enough to change their minds. Walking through the hotel's elegant lobby, tastefully decorated in hues of gold and green and blue, the women were able to quickly forget Alta Vista Hospital. It was feeling so much like a girlfriends' day that they decided to sit on the patio. They could see the City and the Bay just beyond the horizon of the tennis courts. The fresh air and hyacinth-scented breeze seemed to cleanse their nostrils of the antiseptic hospital smells. Annette closed her eyes for a moment as she took a deep breath and leaned back in her seat.

"This is nice," Tamara observed, stating the obvious.

"I'm glad you all like it. Dante and I used to come here a lot for brunch, before Ellington was born. Taking him out to eat is no fun, so we hardly go anywhere anymore," Neva sighed.

"Well, you're here now, and with much better company, no offense," Annette joked.

"You know, there has been some good that has come from this. Even if it took something tragic to bring us all together, here we are. And I don't know about you all, but I needed to see you guys," Neva added while looking into her empty plate. "I feel like it could have just as easily been me lying in that hospital bed."

Tamara and Annette looked at each other, while Neva kept her eyes downcast. They remained silent. Neva shifted uncomfortably in her seat and looked around for the server. *I shouldn't have said that. I talk too much,* she thought. Annette finally spoke.

"Not me, nooooooo. That could never be me," Annette said a little too loudly as she slathered a warm sourdough roll with butter.

Tamara giggled, "Yeah, you'd be in someone else's bed."

"No, you didn't!" Annette shouted as she tore off a piece of bread and threw it across the table.

Neva and Tamara

AS THEY WALKED BACK THROUGH the doors of Alta Vista Hospital, Annette's BlackBerry buzzed again. Neva and Tamara walked ahead into the waiting room and sat on the same green couches. Annette followed not far behind, and with one ear still on her BlackBerry, she whispered, "I've gotta get on my computer for this. I'm going to find the business center." Annette quickly walked away, still talking on the phone.

Neva started to get up from the green couch to find out if they could go in to see Heather, but Tamara stopped her with a hand on her arm.

"Neva, wait a second."

"I just want to see if Hea—"

"Heather can wait a minute. I want to talk to you about what you said at lunch. I heard you," Tamara cautiously offered.

"What are you talking about?" Neva asked.

"You said that it could have been you in the hospital, that it could have been you who tried to take her own life."

"Oh, you know, I didn't mean it like that. I was just talking."

"Well, talking like that is serious."

"Heather needs to be our focus, not me."

"I think maybe that's part of the problem. You have spent so much of your life focusing on everyone else that you have forgotten yourself. Neva, the fact that you have had an abortion is one indication of how desperate things are for you. That was your first cry for help. This suicidal ideation, that's number two. I don't want there to be a third."

"Tamara, I'm fine."

Unfamiliar tears welled up in Tamara's eyes as she remembered what she had tried so desperately to forget. "Heather called a little over a week ago, and I didn't take her call. I was busy ... I ..." Her guilt would not let her finish.

"Oh, Tamara."

"I didn't talk to her. I was in the middle of a crazy day, and I didn't have time. I never called her back. I kept putting it off, waiting until later. Waiting until I wasn't so busy. There was always something else that was more important, more pressing. I wanted to wait until I had enough time to really focus on the conversation. I should have just taken her call. I should have given her my attention. Maybe I could have said something, given her some sort of warning, done something so she wouldn't be here, so we all wouldn't be here."

"I know you think that you could have made a difference, but the reality is that when you are contemplating something like that, I don't know if there is anything that anyone could say that could make you change your mind. Once I decided to get the abortion, there was nothing that anyone could have told me that would have turned me around. And the truth is, I really didn't want to hear it anyway. I wanted to do what I wanted to do, and I didn't want anyone telling me anything else."

"Well, at least I would know that I tried, that I made some attempt to give her the tiniest kernel of hope that could have possibly made her feel that she could have held on a little while longer. I didn't even try. I'm not going to let that happen again." Tamara took Neva's two hands inside hers. "I'm not going to let that happen to you."

Tamara pulled the brochures that Dr. Chandra had given them out of her purse and fanned them on the table between them. "I know we were looking at these places for Heather, for when she comes out of the coma, but I think you need to find one for yourself. They aren't all psychiatric facilities. Some are more ... amorphous, like wellness centers. I think it would do you some real good."

"Tamara, I can't. I have Ellington and Dante. There is no way."

"Neva, 'can't' is not acceptable. You have Ellington, and Dante is a discussion for another time, but do they have you? I mean, are you even in a position to be a good mother or wife if you are on the verge of falling apart? You have got to get yourself back, no matter what it takes."

"I just don't see how I can," Neva said quietly through a stream of tears.

"Dante wouldn't support you getting some help?"

Neva just shook her head, tears still streaming down her face.

"I don't believe that. Maybe if I talked to him, surely he would understand ..."

"You don't think I tried to get help before? I started going to therapy a few years ago, when Ellington was, like, one year old, and he wasn't supportive at all. I had to go on Saturday mornings, and Ellington stayed with Dante. He would complain every week, ask me if I was feeling better every Saturday when I came back, and then tell me that he didn't think it was 'working.' It was awful. I know he would never let me go away, and for a whole month? No way."

"Are you serious? Neva, I'm so sorry. We can't let him get in your way. You need help. I'm going to help you."

"How?"

"Well, I just have to come back out here and help you. I will take care of Ellington while you are taking care of yourself. I can do that."

"How can you possibly do that? You have patients, responsibilities."

"Girl, it can be done. And listen, do you know how many times I've covered for so many of my partners through maternity leaves and honeymoons and whatnot? They owe me. I've got it covered on my end. Don't worry about me. Let me do this for you. Please, Neva, let me help."

Neva immediately brushed off Tamara's offer as undoable, as if on autopilot. "Dante will never agree to it. He doesn't like strangers in the house."

"Okay, now I have held my tongue on this subject as long as I could and I hate to say it like this, but fuck him. He's part of the reason you are so damn broke down in the first place. And I'm not a stranger. I am your friend!" Tamara stated emphatically. "Neva, you can't keep downplaying how serious your situation is. You said that it could have been you in Heather's place. You were basically saying that you could have just as easily taken a handful of pills; in some way, you see that as a viable option for yourself. Honey, that's not normal.

"You slid down your mask of 'fineness' just enough to let us see what's really going on with you, and I'm not going to let you pretend anymore. No more saving face. It's time for you to save your own life. You can't let anyone stop you. Not your husband, not Ellington, no one." Tamara looked into Neva's eyes and said quietly, "Neva, you are worth saving."

Annette came into the waiting room before Neva could respond.

"Crisis avoided. I did it again!"

Tamara did not avert her gaze from Neva's eyes at Annette's entrance.

"What are ya'll talking about?" Annette continued.

Neva's only response was silence, as she kept her eyes downcast. Tamara started with, "I was just telling Neva—" when Dr. Chandra came in to the waiting room.

"I hope you ladies enjoyed your lunch. Will you join me in a conference room? I think we should talk," Dr. Chandra said gently as Annette's BlackBerry buzzed.

Neva and Tamara immediately followed him into one of the small rooms off the main waiting area while Annette lagged behind. They were all seated around the table by the time Annette finally made it in. She eased her bottom into the chair while typing feverishly with her thumbs. Everyone waited a moment for her to stop, which she didn't. Dr. Chandra politely cleared his throat, to which Annette held up a finger.

"Annette, damn, can you stop it for just a minute?" Tamara chided.

Annette finally looked up and apologized, "Oh, I'm sorry. I'm just a little … I'm … I'm sorry."

Dr. Chandra chuckled, "It's really all right, Annette. In fact, that is why we need to talk."

"What is why?" Neva questioned. "I don't understand."

Dr. Chandra chuckled again before explaining, "You all left your respective lives and came out here on a moment's notice. It will soon be one week that you have been here. I honor that, and I know that it has meant a lot to Heather. Her condition, such as it is, is stable. There doesn't appear to be any change, and she can be like this for a long, long time."

"What are you saying? There's still hope, isn't there? You always talk about hope," Neva begged.

"Of course, Neva, there is hope. There is always hope, but you cannot put your lives on hold forever. You are busy women with others who count on you, and I fear you will be unable to continue this routine indefinitely. I want to encourage you to start thinking about returning to those lives and how you want to proceed," Dr. Chandra replied somberly.

"What do you mean how we want to proceed?" Annette questioned.

Neva looked quizzically at Tamara.

"Relax, you guys. He's not saying we have to make any decisions immediately, just that we need to figure out what we're going to do in the weeks or months to come, you know, in case nothing changes," Tamara replied in a measured, calm, even voice.

Tears flowed down Neva's face as she replied, "I just don't know what to do."

Annette rubbed her back and shushed Neva while she spoke confidently. "Oh, well. That I can wrap my mind around. Next steps I can do. Give up, I'm not ready for that quite yet. Thank you, Dr. Chandra, for your candor. I think you're exactly right. We cannot hang out here in limbo for weeks on end. I have barely been able to keep everything together since last week. As I have made painfully obvious, we have to get back to life and come up with a plan."

"Actually, we already have a plan, sort of," Tamara responded.

Neva sat up straight and shot Tamara a look, which she ignored.

"What are you talking about?" Annette asked.

"Well, Neva is going to spend some time away at one of the places Dr. Chandra recommended for Heather, and I am going to help with Ellington and check on Heather."

"Wow," Annette replied, "when did you all decide that? T, you would do that? I'm shocked."

"I'm just doing what needs to be done. And thankfully, because I'm single with no kids, I can do it," Tamara replied. "I mean, I have to make all kinds of arrangements at work, but it's definitely doable. More than that, it's absolutely necessary."

"Well, I suppose I can come back out here one weekend to give you a break. It will give me some practice for if I ever get pregnant," Annette answered.

Neva reached out to hold and squeeze Tamara's and Annette's hands. "You guys are so kind to offer, but—"

"I think it's a brilliant idea, for everyone," Dr. Chandra interrupted. "I think Tamara is making a tremendously generous gift of herself, and Neva, you should simply accept it. For yourself and for Heather."

"I just don't know if I could. I mean, what would Dante say? What would people think?" Neva replied.

"You need to worry less about what others think and focus on what's best for you, because ultimately, that is what's best for the 'others' who matter in your life," Dr. Chandra interjected.

"I—I'm just not used to doing anything like this," Neva added.

"Well, you'd better start getting used to it. You can't keep yourself in last position, last priority forever," Tamara urged. "Let me help you."

Neva looked at Dr. Chandra, who nodded knowingly, and then she turned her gaze to Annette, who just raised her eyebrows. Finally her eyes settled on Tamara, who softly said, "Please, Neva. Let me help you."

Neva sighed and gave Tamara's and Annette's hands another squeeze before nodding yes.

Neva

It had been almost a week since the conversation with Tamara and Dr. Chandra about next steps. Neva tossed and turned all night every night since the decision was made; she was so nervous about telling Dante, and it was going to happen tomorrow. Tamara's comment "You are worth saving" kept resonating in her ears, and she wondered, *Am I really? Tamara's made all the arrangements. Her partners were happy to cover her patients. There's space at Bayside. Dr. Chandra pulled some strings. Annette plans to return to Chicago after they drop me off at Bayside and then return two weeks later to give Tamara a break. They rearranged their whole lives, just for me.* Neva couldn't imagine. *Although if the situation were reversed, I would not hesitate. I would move heaven and earth to be there for either one of them. I wish I could have been there for Heather.*

The familiar chest pains made her sit up in the bed as she anticipated the conversation. She always tried to not disturb Dante. *How will he respond? I can't go on like this much longer. I have to do something. Maybe this is it.*

The next morning, instead of going to the hospital, she asked Tamara and Annette to be available, though not present, when she asked, or rather, told, her husband of the plan. Surprisingly Ellington was sleeping in, so she wanted to have the conversation before he woke up.

After rehearsing what she would say one last time, she turned to leave them downstairs in the kitchen, their hands nervously wrapped around warm cups of coffee. They both sat still, as if conserving energy to steel Neva's strength.

"Are you sure that you don't want us to come with you?" Tamara asked quietly.

"No, that would make him superdefensive from the start. I'll be okay. I don't have a choice but to be."

"Remember, we're right downstairs. You're not facing him alone," Annette reiterated.

"I couldn't do this without you," Neva said as she turned and walked out of the kitchen and slowly ascended the stairs. She opened the door to their bedroom quietly and found Dante sitting in one of the two recliners in their bedroom sitting area, holding the television remote. The TV was turned to a basketball game.

"Do … do you have a minute?" Neva stuttered in a tentative, halting voice.

"Huh, what? Uh, I guess so, it's halftime. What's up now?"

"Well, I, uh, I've been talking with the girls, and, um, we think, I was thinking that, well, things have been just so hard for me lately, and, uh, I think that it would probably be a good thing that, um, I get away, to, you know, get some perspective, and uh, get my head right."

Dante turned off the TV and turned toward Neva, who was still standing beside him with her head bowed. She laced and unlaced her fingers over and over as she spoke.

"What in the world are you talking about? And why are you standing there looking so ridiculous?" He rolled his eyes as he turned his head.

Neva sighed deeply and sat down on the edge of the other chair. "Tamara thinks that it would be good for me to get away, to get some concentrated treatment."

"Treatment—for what? What kind of treatment could possibly help what's wrong with you?"

Tears started to well in Neva's eyes. "I have been having a really, really hard time ever since Ellington was born, and well, Tamara thinks that it's important for me to address what's really going on before, well, before it's too late."

Dante threw the remote on the floor and shouted, "I can't believe you are disturbing my Sunday morning with this bullshit! You are trying to blame your weaknesses on our son! You are unbelievable!"

"I'm not saying that it's Ellington's fault. I'm just saying that—"

"What are you saying? It seems to me that you've said too much already. What did you say to your friends anyway that makes them think there's something wrong with you? What did you tell them?" Dante stood up and started pacing around the room.

"Nothing. I didn't say anything to them. They are my friends, and they've known me a long time. They can just tell that I'm, well … different, not myself. They think—*I* think—that going to Bayside would be good for me."

"What do you have to go to counseling for? And why do you have to go away? I mean, therapy. We don't really do therapy, you know. Can't you just pray about it, or talk to someone about it here? I mean, this seems like a lot. And what exactly are you talking about? How much would all this cost? Where are you talking about going? And for how long? You have given me half-assed information, as usual."

"The place is called Bayside Wellness Center, and it's up in Marin, not too far, but far enough away, and I would be going for four weeks—"

"Four weeks!" Dante interrupted. "You've gotta be kidding me! Who gets to take a month's vacation from life, from responsibilities, just because things are 'hard'? Give me a break. You just need to get a grip on the reality you have created for yourself here, not try to escape it. What happened to that therapist you were seeing before? Why can't you just go back to her? Not that it did any good."

"Tamara volunteered to stay to help out with Ellington while I'm gone." Neva's voice softened, as if preparing for another verbal blow.

"This just keeps getting better and better!" Dante puffed. "You know I don't like strangers in my house."

"She's not a stranger, it's Tamara. We've known her forever. It's a generous offer. She rearranged her patients and everything."

"Well, what about me? We have commitments, social engagements we have to attend. What am I supposed to say? 'My wife's in a nuthouse for a month because she thinks I gave her such a hard life'? Unbelievable."

Neva just sat there for a long time in silence, thinking of the right words to defend her proposal, until she thought it best to simply beg.

"Dante, please, I need this … everyone thinks so."

"I don't give a damn what everyone thinks. Who is 'everyone' anyway? Your damn friends?"

"My friends know me. They care about me, and they don't want me … want me to end up like … like … Heather."

Dante rolled his eyes and sat back down.

"You are being a bit dramatic, don't you think? You know what? Fine, go! Do your little vacation, nuthouse, whatever. I don't have the patience for this anymore." He waved his hand, dismissing her, leaned over to pick up the remote off the floor, and turned the television back on.

Neva sighed in relief, got up from her seat, walked quietly out of the room, and carefully shut the door. She ran downstairs and joined Tamara and Annette. They were sitting at the kitchen counter just where she had left them. They had been given firm instructions not to come upstairs, no matter what they heard, and Neva was grateful they obliged her. She knew that Dante's voice could carry.

"Well …?" Annette said as she rose from her seat.

Neva nodded the affirmative. How she got to yes didn't matter. What did matter was that she was about to change her life forever.

Heather

I WOULD RACE HOME FROM school and try to sneak in my "studio" before my mother realized my homework wasn't done yet. I couldn't wait to put on the paint-splattered button-down shirt that hung carefully on a hook by the door. The shirt was so large, it almost reached my knees. I used to imagine that it once belonged to my father.

On good days, I used to imagine a lot of things about him as I painted. I used to wonder whether he was short or tall. Whether bright colors sometimes hurt his eyes and if I could make him laugh. I would think about whether he would like me enough to stay if he met me now. On the bad days, when I really missed him, I would be so angry, everything was all mean and dark. No matter what I painted, my mother thought all my work was beautiful. But then, she had to.

Lauren

LAUREN SLAMMED THE DOOR AS she left the first gallery she visited. She didn't even unzip the portfolio. *They are too common,* she thought to herself. *Not good enough for my Heather. I'll know it when it's "the one,"* she said to herself as she carefully placed the portfolio into the trunk of her car and prepared to go back to work for her Monday afternoon meeting. She simply told her assistant that she had an appointment out of the office.

I have time, she continued to encourage herself as she put the keys in the ignition. *Or do I? After almost two weeks, Heather could wake up any day. What would happen then?* Lauren shook her head as she wound down Peachtree Street toward her office building downtown. *I will just have to explain to her, that's all. She'll understand.*

Neva

NEVA DECIDED TO TAKE ELLINGTON to his favorite breakfast spot before school on Tuesday morning to tell him the news that she was going to be away for a while. The model trains on the walls at the Montclair Egg Shop really kept him entertained so that both of them could have a decent meal, although today Neva picked at her bowl of granola and fruit, spinning the words around in her mind.

As he stuffed a forkful of pancakes into his mouth, Neva took a deep breath and began, "Honey, you know there's been a lot going on lately, right?"

"Yeah, Aunt Heather is sick, right?" he responded, muffled.

"Yes, she is very, very sick. But the thing is, well, Mommy hasn't been feeling well either lately."

Ellington put down his fork, took a big gulp of chocolate milk, and widened his eyes. Neva forced a smile at his response. "Oh honey, it's not like that. Not as bad as Aunt Heather. I'm not going to the hospital like that," Neva backpedaled, before starting again. "I don't want to get that sick, so I have to go away for a little while to take care of myself. Do you understand?"

Ellington shook his head no and put his head in his hands. Neva reached across the table, put her hand on his arm, and pulled it down to reveal his eyes, which were filling with tears.

"Baby, don't cry. It'll be okay. I just need to take some time."

"Why can't you take some time here? Why do you have to leave?" Ellington cried.

"It just doesn't work that way, honey. I—I just have to go. It won't be long. I promise. And Aunt T will be here making sure everything goes okay."

Ellington was silent at this revelation.

"And we can still talk on the phone. It will go by so fast."

Ellington remained silent.

"I really need you to be okay with this." Neva's eyes started to fill, matching Ellington's tears. "Mommy needs to feel better."

Ellington sniffled a few times, wiped his eyes with a napkin, sat up straight in his chair, and said, "I want you to feel better, too, Mommy. I'll be a big boy for you."

The well of tears overflowed down Neva's cheeks. Ellington got up from his chair, went to the other side of the table, and put his arms around her.

"It's okay, Mommy. It's okay."

Annette, Tamara, and Neva

TAMARA WALKED ONTO THE DECK of Neva's house with a cup of coffee in her hand and was surprised to find Annette standing with her back to the house, facing the bay. As she got closer, Tamara could hear Annette on the phone speaking in an uncharacteristic syrupy voice.

"Yeah, baby, I know. It's been really hard ... I know ... me too.... I don't know when I'll be back in DC. I have to go back home.... I promised I would come back out here in a few weeks.... We all have to do what we can to help.... You don't understand ... I'm trying ... I really am.... Please try to understand."

Tamara touched Annette on the shoulder. She jumped before she turned around, and her ginger complexion turned bright red.

"I gotta go, um, yeah, me too."

"So, was that DC? 'Cause I have never heard you talk to your husband like that," Tamara stated, with eyes raised.

"Whatever." Annette reached for Neva's coffee cup and took a long sip.

"If my eyes were closed and I just heard your voice, I would've never known it was you."

"He misses me," Annette reported with an eye roll.

"What are you doing, Annette? Aren't you and Thomas still trying to have a baby? What's going on?"

"Girl, I don't know. I'm confused myself. I just can't seem to stop myself. I feel like I deserve to feel good just for a minute, even if the good I feel is wrong."

"Oh, Annette, what are we going to do with you?"

Neva joined them on the deck.

"Dante took Ellington to school today. I didn't want him here when we left."

"That's probably wise," Annette said.

"I still can't get over how well he's taking it."

"Kids are very perceptive. Maybe he knows deep down that you need this," Tamara suggested.

"Maybe. I hope he will be okay."

"The minute you decided to do something for yourself, what did he do? He lined up with that plan. He'll be fine. We'll be fine. You just take this time to be sure you will be fine," Tamara concluded.

"I know. And I can't thank you enough for rearranging your schedule, your patients, to do this for me."

"Will you stop thanking me? I am happy to do it. We should get going, no? Check-in is at noon, and Annette has to get on her flight later," Tamara replied.

"I'm ready."

The car was uncharacteristically quiet on the drive to take Neva to Bayside. The assuredness that they were doing the right thing stirred with apprehension about what lay ahead; the uncertainty seemed to make the women hold their breath in homage.

Neva wondered what Bayside was going to be like. *I don't want to spend the next four weeks talking about what I did. I can barely say the word, even to myself. And what about Ellington? Will he feel abandoned? Will he get along with Tamara? He can be so difficult to manage. How is he going to act? Can Tamara really handle everything?*

Annette was feeling badly that she didn't offer to stay as well and help out, but she couldn't. Two weeks was too long to stay away. It seemed that since she wasn't there to mother hen everyone, nothing was getting done. *This deal cannot die. Too much is riding on it. I probably stretched it by staying out here as long as I have. Besides work, I've got to get back home to Thomas and have to figure out what to do with DC.*

Tamara was thinking about the four weeks ahead of her. *My partners weren't too happy when I told them I would be out, but they really couldn't say anything about it because I did the same for them all. Between marriages and maternity leaves and illnesses, I've done my share of covering, God knows. They are just used to me always being there. My patients are all in a good place, past the difficult early stages of pregnancy, but not close to delivery. I can always get back if there's an emergency; the boy does have a father, after all. It all sorta worked out strangely. Dr. Chandra said it was a sign that it was meant to happen. I don't know about that, but I do know that Neva so desperately needs this. That's clear.*

She chuckled as she recalled the instructions she left for her partners and compared them with the exhaustive to-do lists, reminders, and schedules Neva left for her. *I mean, damn, I did go to med school. How hard can it be to take care of a five-year-old? I think I can figure it out. One thing is for sure,* she thought to herself, *that little boy is only going to one thing each week. I am not going to run him around all over town for soccer and piano and karate and whatever else, no matter what's on that damn list. That's part of the problem: Neva is running herself crazy. And those food preferences, those are going out the window too. That little fella is going to eat whatever I put in front of him.*

It took a long time to get there, but the drive was beautiful. As they made their way up and around the windy roads, higher and higher into the hills, they drove around giant redwood trees, as tall as some Chicago skyscrapers. Annette rolled down the window to smell the familiar scent of eucalyptus that permeated the air. She closed her eyes in the passenger seat and breathed deeply. *This reminds me of Stanford so much. Life was so much simpler then, before I had a husband who only wants the one thing that I can't give him or a job that seems to demand a pound of flesh for every dollar.* Annette sighed as she looked out the window and into Marin's mystical beauty, careful to notice little surprises in every direction—like a small waterfall hewn out of the side of a rock, or a giant aloe vera plant in bloom on the side of a hill. *You don't see that in Chicago,* she thought appreciatively.

The towns that sprang up along the roads contained a hodgepodge of trendy boutiques, cute coffee shops, quaint restaurants, and the errant spiritual or healing center, one of which was Bayside. A small, rough-hewn wooden sign, barely visible from the road, indicated they had arrived. Bayside seemed almost hidden in and among the giant trees and winding hills. It was as if the proprietors wanted to be sure that everyone came there on purpose. It required a climb up several flights of wooden stairs carved out of the side of an ivy-covered hill.

The three women divided Neva's bags between them and carefully proceeded to climb. They approached the large main building first. Its amber shingles blended with the bark covering of the surrounding fir and redwood trees. Tamara checked in with Neva, while Annette sat on a bench near the entrance near the car, tilted her head back, and let the sun, which had finally appeared, shine on her face for a moment.

The lobby of the main building was serene and wonderfully fragrant, with just the right blend of bergamot, frankincense, and rose. Neva relaxed a little bit just by stepping inside. It reminded her of a spa she and Dante visited in Calistoga before she was pregnant with Ellington. Their signature treatment was wonderful. First it required that you sit in a hot bath of volcanic mud to excrete the toxins in your body, and then, after a shower with natural springwater, you got swathed from head to toe in blankets and sweated miserably. Finally, when you could take no more, you were unwrapped and treated to a relaxing massage. By the time she was finished, her legs could barely hold her up. They finished the day with wine tasting in Napa. Neva didn't realize how all that mud and sweating and massaging would make the alcohol go straight through her system. She got a little bit drunk, which made Dante angry—so angry that he left her in the Brown Estate winery right in the middle of their VIP tour. He just got in the car and left. Lost and alone, she had to walk back to the quaint little bed-and-breakfast where they were staying.

I hope I will be able to walk out of here.

Lauren

It was Sunday morning again. The week went by so quickly, and before she knew it, Sunday came around again. She had been back for almost two weeks, and she hadn't gotten anything done with the paintings.

Lauren reached in the nightstand, reaching for the vibrator, no, the cookies, but for some reason, she knew that neither would satisfy her. She looked across the room and saw the new box of gym shoes under the dresser. She threw off the covers, walked over to the box, picked them up, and put them on. She dug out some exercise gear and went outside for a walk.

The sound of her feet striking the black pavement of Paces Ferry Road had become strangely comforting. Thud! Thud! Thud! *These really make a difference. I guess if I'm going to be serious about this fitness thing, I have to have the right equipment. Those Coach and Gucci gym shoes were making my feet hurt. I'm not going to be known as "the big girl" of the crew.* Tip! Tap! Crunch!

If I will ever again be considered one of the crew. No one will speak to me anymore, not even Neva. I do want to know what's going on with Heather. Well, no time to worry about that. I have enough on my plate. Work, figuring out what's going on with my husband, the kids, Heather's artwork, and now, finding time to exercise.

How did I let myself get like this? she thought as she looked down at her stomach. It practically obstructed the view of her feet moving across the pavement of Paces Ferry Road, so she had to let the sound of her feet guide her. Thud! Thud! Thud! She was moving slowly, but step-by-step, she was moving forward.

Annette

SETTLING BACK INTO THE REGULAR routine felt strangely comforting to Annette. It was Monday, and she was starting her week as she liked to, in the office early, before everyone else arrived.

DC had left several messages on her work voice mail while she was gone, each one sounding a bit more urgent than the last. She couldn't help but smile at the sound of his voice. *He is so sexy, even when he's desperate,* she thought to herself and was pleased that her unplanned trip to California yielded the unexpected benefit of increased desirability. *Men are so predictable. If you want them to come running, all you have to do is hide. It's never good to seem too available anyway,* she thought before catching herself. *What am I thinking? I'm not available at all! I'm married.* Still, the messages were so nice, she kept them. His voice was laced with passion and promise, so unlike her husband's, she thought, as she pressed "play" one more time.

She adjusted herself in her seat as she savored every word. *I am not supposed to feel this way about another man. How did this come to be? When did I become so lonely? Maybe Lauren's husband was lonely too.*

There were several messages from Lauren on her work phone. *Such a punk move. Leaving explanations on my work phone, knowing I was in the Bay Area. So typical of her.* In a flash, Annette decided to call Lauren on her cowardice and phone her back.

The phone rang several times before reaching Lauren's voice mail. *Typical.* Annette started to hang up the phone but decided instead to leave a message.

"Lauren, I wish you would have called me on my cell so we could have had an actual conversation, but it looks like you are not woman enough for that. No matter what you say, I know you are pissed that we didn't agree with you about Heather's pictures. I know you are embarrassed about the fact that your husband may be having an affair—hell, maybe you're mad at me for the advice I gave you. But the thing is, you can't keep living in a fishbowl. You can't keep pretending that everything is okay when clearly it's not. You've got to deal with reality, or else it will deal with you. Oh, yeah, and send back the pictures, bitch."

Lauren

LAUREN HEARD THE PHONE RING but had become accustomed to ignoring it. If anyone was really trying to reach her, they would call her on her cell or at work. Home phone calls were usually related to her kids, which would be handled by Zoe. She usually wasn't home at this time anyway, but she was headed in late because she had a meeting at a gallery.

She hadn't gotten a message about Heather's condition from Neva in a while. *I'm sure if anything changed, they would call me, wouldn't they? When are they going to come around to my way of thinking? No matter what, I am not going to give the pictures up without a fight. At least not until Heather wakes up, if she wakes up. Then she can decide for herself. But for now, I'm making the decisions.*

Tamara

"I MISS MY MOMMY!" ELLINGTON screamed as Tamara toweled him off after his bath.

"I know you do, Ellington. You can call her in a bit when you get your pj's on," she replied.

"I want to talk to her now!"

"You can in a bit. Okay, now let's brush your teeth."

"I don't like that toothpaste." Ellington folded his arms at the bathroom sink.

"Well, it's all you have, so you have to use it. You need to brush your teeth."

"No! Not until I talk to my mommy!"

"Ellington," Tamara's patience was waning, "come on. Let's just get ready for bed."

"Mommy." Ellington stomped his feet and held his arms fast.

Tamara grabbed his shoulders, turned him around to face her, knelt down on the hard tile floor, and looked him in the eye.

"Listen to me. This is how this is going to go. You are going to brush your teeth. Then you are going to go into your room and put on your pajamas. Then you will get to talk to your mother. Do you understand?"

Ellington stared at Tamara and Tamara stared back, undeterred. Finally, he acquiesced.

"Okay." He uncrossed his arms and brushed his teeth. When he was finished, he went into his bedroom and put on his pajamas while Tamara called Neva at Bayside.

"Oh, things are going fine. It was a good idea to have these calls scheduled in advance. You think of everything. I don't know how you do it," Tamara said into the phone.

Ellington grew visibly excited and started jumping up and down on the bed, "Mommy! Mommy!"

"Yes ... that's him ... he's right here ..."

Tamara handed him the phone and left the room for a minute.

She went down to the kitchen to clean up from dinner. She bought a fast-food-restaurant kids' meal, just to keep Ellington happy.

She went back upstairs just as Ellington was hanging up. She took the phone from his hands. He seemed placated, at least for the moment. She tucked him in bed and continued reading the story they had started the night before. He fell asleep after about a page.

Tamara walked into the guest room and fell into her chair. She was exhausted. She looked at the clock; it was 7:30 p.m., and Dante was nowhere to be found. *I wonder if this is normal or on account of my presence? No wonder Neva was so rundown. Ellington is a lot of work. And if the past week has been any indication, she was doing it all on her own. I always thought one kid was no big deal, but now I can see how hard it really can be for some women.*

I'm glad that I caught Neva before she did something else rash. I just wish I had known sooner, so I could have done something sooner and she wouldn't have had to have the abortion—or keep it a secret. When did she start feeling so overwhelmed and unhappy? What if she had gotten the help she clearly needed right after Ellington was born? Would she have been able to bear the second child? Of course, untreated postpartum depression is only part of Neva's problem. That husband of hers certainly doesn't help matters one bit. The combination of a demanding child and a controlling husband would drive any woman to despair. She shook her head as she imagined the unspeakable psychic pain that must have driven Neva to have an abortion. *How could I have been so blind not to see what was really going on?*

Women come in for their six-week checkup clearly in distress, but I cannot get them to open up and talk about what's going on. Many even refuse my referral to therapy, especially the sisters. I don't understand why the stigma of therapy is still so strong and prevalent in the black community, no matter the education level or socioeconomic status. Many of us still think that going to therapy means you're "crazy." That kind of thinking is crazy. And then there's the long-held belief that certain matters aren't discussed outside the home, "family business." Bullshit, especially when so many of us are dying because we won't admit or don't dare speak about what is killing us. Maybe that's a good research topic, the long-term effects of postpartum depression, or maybe racial differences in identification and treatment of postpartum depression. That's a good one too.

Maybe the nature of my practice adds to some women's reluctance to admit they are struggling those early weeks. Many of my high-risk moms are just so grateful to have a child; they feel guilty or ashamed for having any negative feelings at all. From now on, I am going to take extra measures to create a safe space so my patients will feel comfortable. Maybe I need to work on my bedside manner after all. I could certainly take cues from Dr. Chandra, she sighed to herself.

Heather

AT LEAST ANNETTE'S BLACK DRESSES *could be worn again, unlike Lauren's.
Those ugly pink things would certainly never see the light of day after the
wedding was over. But Lauren didn't care. She wanted what she wanted how
she wanted it. Lauren was so rigid with her rules. "Who ever heard of black
dresses at a wedding?" she complained about Annette's dress selection. Annette
didn't care, and for once I was glad. Annette just went to Saks Fifth Avenue,
found a black dress that everyone would look cute in, and ordered four of them,
insisting, "Everyone could use another little black dress."*

*And I used mine too. I wore it to my very first exhibit opening when I was
in New York. It was a special exhibition of Meta Warrick Fuller's sculptures.
It was so exciting, and I was so nervous. I really wanted my friends there, but
everyone was busy with kids and husbands and whatnot. Somehow, wearing
that dress from Annette's wedding made me feel a little less alone.*

Tamara

I THOUGHT ALL I WOULD have to do is wake him up and tell him to get dressed. Tamara sighed as she struggled to get his clothes on.

"Aunt T, these socks don't fit!" Ellington screamed and stomped his feet.

"Are you sure?" Tamara asked while bending down to look at his feet. "They look fine to me."

"Well, they hurt! Can you get me some more socks?"

"Why don't you pick out the right ones then?"

"My mommy always gets them for me," Ellington whined.

"Well, your mommy isn't here." As soon as Tamara said it, she wished she hadn't because, while true, it was mean, and Ellington's face started to screw up like he was going to cry. "I'm sorry, baby. That wasn't nice of Aunt T. Just show me the socks and I will get them for you." Tamara headed toward the sock drawer and starting pulling out pairs of white socks for Ellington's approval. "What about these?"

Ellington shook his head.

"Or these?" she asked as she produced another pair.

Ellington shook his head again.

"Okay, now these I know are the right ones," Tamara said.

"Yay! You found them. Thanks, Aunt T." Ellington took the socks from her hand, sat down on his little chair, and put them on.

Tamara sighed as she wondered, *Are all little kids this way?* Just as she started to leave the room to make oatmeal, he stopped her.

"Aunt T, my shirt is itchy; can you cut the tag out?"

"Sure, honey. Just let me find the scissors. Do you know where your mom keeps them?"

"I'm not sure."

"Okay. Why don't we get started on breakfast while I find the scissors?"

"I can't eat; it's too itchy. Can you please get the scissors first? Please?"

"Oh, okay. Do you have any idea where they could be?"

Ellington shook his head.

Tamara took a deep breath before suggesting, "I bet she keeps them downstairs; let's go down and check."

"Okay!" Ellington bounded downstairs, with Tamara following closely behind.

Tamara searched around the kitchen, opening and closing this drawer and that one, while Ellington sat at the kitchen counter and kicked his feet against the front of the counter.

"Ellington, please stop!" she yelled. Finally, Tamara found the scissors on top of the counter in a container with other kitchen utensils. "Okay, now we are in business," Tamara stated as she walked behind Ellington, reached gently for the tag, and expertly cut it off. "There. Now, breakfast."

Tamara put some oatmeal in the microwave, made some coffee for herself, leaned back against the kitchen counter, and blew out air. Once the oatmeal was finished, she added the brown sugar and butter that Ellington liked, and ran upstairs to get dressed. By the time she came back down, Ellington was finished eating and putting on his shoes, like a big boy. Tamara smiled, grabbed the keys to Neva's truck, looked at her watch, and smiled again because they were on schedule. *Maybe I am getting the hang of this after all.*

"Come on, honey. Let's go to school!"

She hadn't seen Dante all morning—again. *I wonder whether he gets up and leaves early on purpose or stays in bed in avoidance all the time? Doesn't he ever say good-bye to his kid before he leaves for school?*

After dropping Ellington at school, Tamara followed the familiar route to the hospital. She breathed in the familiar smells of the hospital and tried to relax as she walked through the doors of the intensive care unit again. She walked a little slower than usual, already exhausted at 8:30 a.m.

Tamara walked into Heather's room, pulled the chair close, and sat down. She made herself comfortable, took her shoes off, rested her feet on the edge of Heather's bed, and allowed her eyes to close for just a moment. Dr. Chandra's gentle touch on her shoulder made her jump.

"Tamara, I'm sorry to disturb you, but we have to take Heather to run some tests. Are you okay? You look exhausted," he said in a concerned voice.

"Huh? What? Oh, I'm sorry," Tamara blushed as she responded while wiping some errant saliva that escaped from her mouth as she catnapped. She didn't realize she had fallen asleep. Tomorrow. She would be better prepared tomorrow.

"No need to apologize to me. Are you sure you haven't taken on too much caring for Neva's family? I admire your willingness to do so, but be careful you aren't overextending yourself."

"I'm fine, thank you," Tamara replied curtly as she straightened herself in the chair and moved her feet. She didn't like anyone questioning her capability.

Dr. Chandra, sensing her offense, just chuckled quietly, "It is perfectly fine to admit that you're not. Taking care of a child is a great responsibility."

"Are you laughing at me?" Tamara's voice got increasingly perturbed.

"Oh, no. Please don't take it that way. Now it's my turn to apologize if I offended you."

"Didn't you say you needed to run some tests?" Tamara said dismissively.

"Yes, tests," Dr. Chandra said as he motioned for the transport nurse to take Heather. "Why don't you go and get a cup of coffee, and I'll update you on Heather's condition in a bit," he said.

I don't need any damn coffee, Tamara thought to herself as she straightened her clothes and forced herself straight in her chair. *How am I going to make it four weeks?*

Neva

NEVA DECIDED TO SKIP BREAKFAST so that she could finish the thank-you notes for the moms at school who helped with playdates and carpooling for Ellington when Heather first went into the hospital. *Did I remember to tell Tamara that Ellington had to bring snacks for his class later this week?* Neva's mind raced as she quickly jotted off one heartfelt thank-you after another. *And there's Christopher's birthday party on Saturday. Did I even RSVP? Maybe I'll send her a quick e-mail. Do I have Internet up here? She will have to buy a present; maybe I'll just tell her to get a gift card. Maybe I should write all this down so I won't forget.* Neva got out another sheet of paper and started making a list, writing "birthday party present" and then "snacks."

There was only fifteen minutes until her group therapy session, and she was not looking forward to it. She didn't like talking to strangers, especially about personal matters. She remembered Dr. Chandra's advice when she talked with him about it before she left; he encouraged her to keep an open mind. *He is so kind and understanding,* she thought. *Why couldn't I have married someone like him?* She brought her hand to her mouth as if she had spoken the words out loud and didn't want anyone else to hear them.

Lauren

LAUREN'S PALMS WERE CLAMMY AS she tried to tighten her grip on the handle of the black portfolio. She didn't understand why she was so nervous. She knew this gallery owner well, having bought several pieces from him, and she was confident in Heather's ability, but her legs were unsteady as she walked from her car on Peachtree Street to the gallery door.

She was on time for her appointment, and he was late of course. *Artists.* Lauren shrugged as she sat as delicately as she could on the uncomfortable Le Corbusier chair. No matter their intrinsic design value, she hated those things! Finally, after what seemed like forever, his assistant indicated that the owner was ready for her. Lauren made a mental note to tell the owner that his assistant didn't even offer her something to drink—rude little thing. But only after he agreed to buy, or better yet, show Heather's work. She needed to be sure that she positioned herself to maximize the return on her investment.

Lauren tentatively removed the pieces, one by one, from the portfolio and clipped them onto the blank poster boards that were set up on easels around the large office. The owner studied each one carefully, moving slowly from canvas to canvas, not saying a word. Lauren shifted in her seat and waited for his critique.

"These are fabulous! I must share this wonderful work. No wonder you have such impeccable taste! You were an artist as well as a collector—what a well-kept secret," the owner said.

"Oh, I'm not. The artist is ... a dear friend of mine, who, um, lives in California, and ..." Lauren thought, briefly, about just lying about the whole thing and saying that they were hers, but she knew that would be heaping worse on top of wrong. *I should have gotten my story together before. I can't believe I didn't anticipate these questions!* she thought to herself.

"I can't believe there's not a gallery closer to home that wouldn't die to get their hands on these," the owner commented.

"Well, to be honest, the artist is very reclusive and prefers to remain as anonymous as possible, so a gallery far away is just perfect for her."

"Well, I'm sure she won't want to be anonymous once the checks start coming in," the owner laughed. "And I hope that she will at least show the courtesy of attending her own opening. And you have the authority to act on her behalf? You are her representative?"

"Representative? Yes, I am her representative." *That's the word I was looking for,* she thought. "Do you really see promise in her work?" Lauren tried to feign indifference.

"Well, of course, I have to study them a little longer and keep them with me for a while to determine how many and which pieces exactly, but yes, there is definitely great promise here, and I am going to show them. There's nothing more rewarding than discovering a new great talent and being the one to share that talent with the world. I will have my assistant send over the standard agreements. Once you have reviewed them, we can have another meeting to discuss the particulars. Oh, I have to look at my calendar to see how soon I can squeeze it in, because I don't want to wait too long. I feel there is an urgency in these pieces, and I want to capitalize on that energy."

"Thank you so much. I'm so excited! And please know that I will be more than willing to partner with you on marketing and public relations; I have extensive contacts among individuals who would be most interested in these works and your gallery. This will be a mutually beneficial opportunity, I assure you."

Lauren's heartbeat steadied, and the moisture in her hands evaporated. She held her head a little straighter as she walked out of the office, and her shoulders seemed more square as she made her way through the gallery, past the rude assistant, and out the door to her car, empty-handed.

Heather

MY MOTHER BOUGHT ME A new outfit and everything. I didn't wear dresses much, so a new pair of jeans and shirt worked just fine. I was a little embarrassed about having an "art show," but my mother insisted, and they were all her friends anyway, so I knew they'd be nice. Still, it was my heart on the canvases that she spread around the living room.

The special breakfast of blueberry buckwheat pancakes my mother prepared was left untouched on the kitchen table. My mother just shook her head and laughed as she watched me sitting there—a bundle of nerves.

I finally left the table and kept walking around the living room, rearranging the pictures we had set up on easels. Which order looked best? Should the purple one go before the yellow or after the red? Did it even matter? My mother stopped my pacing, took me by both shoulders, looked me in the eyes, and told me how proud she was of me before anyone saw one picture or said one thing, good or bad. I think she wanted me to know that I was wonderful all by myself. I only wish I had heard her.

Neva

THE STILLNESS OF THE NIGHTS in the hills at Bayside could not quiet Neva's thoughts. She tossed and turned most nights. She was becoming awake to so many new things in less than two weeks. Her therapist, Dr. Hughes, was helping her to press into what she was feeling instead of pressing her feelings down. She heard his words reverberating in her head.

> *"Allow yourself to feel what you feel when you are feeling it, good or bad. Trust yourself to be able to handle it. It is all about developing the courage to be fully present.... I know it's hard," he would say, "but you are stronger than you know, and whatever pain you may feel at any given moment is still less than the inevitable pain of denial."*

Therapy was hard work, and Neva was exhausted. The large Kohler tub next to the expansive shower stall in the bathroom had been inviting her since her arrival, so instead of fighting sleep another night, she decided to give it a try. The stocked bathroom, full of all kinds of bath salts and oils, provided many tempting options. She chose lavender.

As she gently placed one foot into the water, then the other, she winced a little because the water was almost scalding, but for some reason, it felt good. She closed her eyes and leaned back against the wall of the tub. There was something about the hot hot water and the cold hard tile that opened her up somehow. The heaviness of all the hurt she had been carrying rose through her body, seeped through her pores, and went out into the water. She was literally practicing Dr. Hughes's admonition to "sit with it a while." *Let's see if it will pass.*

Guilt, regret, disappointment, and shame swirled around in the soft water until Neva's body had to make water of its own. Neva looked down at her shriveled hands and through her tears started to see herself for the first time in a long time.

I know I have to tell him. I can't keep it a secret forever. The silence of the secret is already killing me. I have already stood up to him once. I can do it again. No matter what happens, I have to tell him the truth. I just need to summon the courage somehow.

No matter if he leaves me, I will make it somehow. I don't know who would even hire me or how I would ever juggle Ellington and work, but I will figure it out. I just have to.

Tamara

TAMARA COLLAPSED ONTO THE WHITE living room couch after successfully putting Ellington to bed one more night. The sink was full of dishes. The stove still had remnants of several attempts to please Ellington's difficult palate; there was one pot with a little bit of dried spaghetti, an attempted grilled cheese sandwich in a skillet, a cookie sheet with the crumbs from the coating of chicken nuggets, and an empty pizza box. She hadn't even bothered with the vegetable. Too little return on that investment of time and energy.

She needed to refer to the list of what was on tap for tomorrow. *It can wait.* She just needed a minute to rest. She had forgotten to call Neva tonight. Ellington forgot too. *Hopefully, Neva will be okay. There was really nothing new to report: Ellington was fine, wearing her out, but fine. Heather was stable, no change. Still no word from Lauren.* She sat up a little to look around when she realized she didn't even know where her cell phone was; getting off the couch to get Neva's landline was out of the question. *I'll call her first thing in the morning,* she thought as she gave in to the heaviness of her eyelids and dreamed about what she was going to do once Annette came in a few days.

Annette

ANNETTE LOWERED HER MOUTH ONTO his with an urgency that reflected the short time they had to be together. It was Tuesday afternoon, he was only in for one day, and Annette was leaving on Friday to go back to California. He pulled his head back, caressed her hair, and whispered, "Slow down."

She just laughed and proceeded to unbutton her blouse as she urged him to hurry. He simply shook his head and unfastened his pants, while Annette, already down to her black Hanky Panky thong and matching camisole, rid him of his shirt and tie.

She had told her assistant she was at lunch. Annette suggested they "eat" in his hotel room. She was ravenous, although clearly not for food. It wasn't like she hadn't been sleeping with Thomas, because they had been more active than ever now that he fixed his little mechanical problem. *Thank God for Viagra!* Still, there was no fire. It was frequent, but perfunctory. Faking it was getting old as well. *The sooner it's over with, the better. Just make your deposit and be gone,* she usually thought when they were in the midst of the act. She missed the passion she used to have with her husband. She thought it was gone from her forever. For a moment, she almost started to believe that something was wrong with her, that her body had ceased to be a vehicle for desire, and instead had become just a defective tool, a failed piece of equipment. That's why DC was so compelling. With him, she felt a desire that she had never known. Right or wrong, it was good to feel good again.

He was a little surprised, she could tell, at her suggestion of a lunch quickie, but *a girl's gotta eat,* she thought as she removed his plaid boxers, pulled him to the edge of the bed, got down on her knees, and took him delicately into her mouth.

Lauren

LAUREN DECIDED TO INVITE PRESCOTT to her bed in part to see what his reaction would be but also because she missed him, even if he was having an affair, which she was almost certain of now. Annette was right, it had been too long since they had been together. She was sure he had been with other women. She was determined to give it the good old college try one last time. Maybe that would bring him back to her. She was extra flirty last night and sent him a very suggestive text early that morning.

She took the afternoon off, endured the pain and humiliation of a bikini wax, bought a new nightgown, got a mani-pedi, and was going to try to seduce her husband once and for all. She checked her phone to see if he had responded. Nothing. *Hmmm. Maybe I wasn't clear enough. How can I make it plain?* she wondered as she pulled into her driveway, got out of the car with her lingerie bag, and went upstairs.

She rehearsed the evening as she went: Zoe was going to take the children out for dinner, so they would be alone in the house when he returned from work. She would greet him at the door in the negligee with the bottle of champagne and the chocolate-covered strawberries she bought at Whole Foods. The rest was up to him.

She couldn't stop her hands from shaking a little as she slipped on the black silk nightgown. She examined herself in the full-length mirror in her dressing room and decided that she was still beautiful and her body didn't look that bad in a nightgown that draped to the floor. Prescott never complained or commented one way or another. *Does he even see me?* She thought as she ran her hands over her silk-covered hips. She looked down at her ample bosom, and thought of a way to make sure her husband was clear about her intentions for the evening.

She grabbed her phone, pointed it downward, and snapped a photo. She looked at it, thought it was okay, and pushed "send." *There should be no doubt now what I'm thinking.*

She ran her fingers through her short wavy hair and wished she could do something different to it, to make it look extra-special for tonight. She just wanted him to notice her. He had to.

As soon as Zoe left for dinner, she went downstairs to set everything up.

After about an hour, Lauren thought she heard the car pull into the circular driveway. She peeked out of the window and thought she saw the lights of her husband's car. She scurried to her practiced position reclining on the couch in his library just off the foyer. She waited. And waited. She lay there, looking her most seductive, perfectly still, anticipating hearing her husband's key in the door. It never turned. She lay there for as long as she could. *I thought he was right outside. I could have sworn I saw the lights and heard his car. Maybe I was wrong. Maybe I didn't see him at all.* She got up slowly and headed toward the window just in time to see her husband's car continuing around the half-circle drive and headed who knows where.

Lauren hung her shoulders and went back into the library, retrieved the bottle of champagne, and proceeded to drink—first out of the crystal flutes, and after a few glasses, straight from the bottle.

～ᴧ ᴧ～

"Mommy." Kyle gently shook his mother's shoulder.

Lauren's right leg hit the floor and she bolted upright from her reclined position on the couch, where she had drifted to sleep. She shook her head to get the fuzziness out of her mind and smacked her tongue against the roof of her mouth to get rid of the imaginary cotton that had grown during her rest.

"What are you doing with all this stuff?" her daughter Katherine asked, pointing to the half-burned candles, the bowl of untouched chocolate-covered strawberries, and the bottle of champagne.

"Oh, my ... I, uh ..." she stammered, mortified. Lauren reached for a robe or a blanket or anything, but there was nothing to cover herself with.

"These look yummy, Mommy. Can I have one?" Kyle asked while reaching for a strawberry.

"It's late; time for bed, little ones," Zoe said as she shooed the kids up the stairs.

"I want Mommy to take us!" Kyle screamed, refusing to move.

Lauren turned her back, shook her head, and covered her face, requiring Zoe to pick him up and carry him up the winding staircase.

Neva

FOR SO LONG, SLEEP HAD been Neva's only safe harbor. She would come home from taking Ellington to school and climb back into bed until it was time for pickup. After the abortion, sleep became an elusive lover evading her embrace. She would toss and turn all night—waking up often with a wet pillow, and she didn't even know she had been crying. Finally, here at Bayside, it seemed that she had found him again, and it felt so good to neither pursue nor serve him but to simply welcome deep rest. She considered getting out of bed but decided she would stay there a little longer. Her body started to stir with the condemnation of guilt for being lazy, but she quickly dismissed it and allowed the peace of being in the moment settle her.

Another session with Dr. Hughes today. At first she dreaded the sessions, the probing, the questions. It wasn't easy, but now, two weeks later, she found herself looking forward to her time with him. Despite her initial reticence, it was actually kind of nice having someone give you 100 percent of his attention for a fifty-minute hour—not judging, not criticizing; just listening and understanding, or at least pretending to understand. She thought she would have preferred a female counselor, but she soon discovered that Dr. Hughes's male perspective offered unique insights and particular opportunities for healing. She was not accustomed to a kind male voice in her life. She needed that, and as unfamiliar as it was, it gave her great comfort.

Tamara

TAMARA NEVER THOUGHT SHE WOULD be so happy to see 8:00—a.m. or p.m. Eight o'clock at night was Ellington's bedtime, and at the glorious hour of 8:00 a.m., he was in school, safe, and accounted for for seven hours. Tamara never realized how short the school day was until now. It seemed that as soon as she dropped him off, made it to the hospital, and stayed with Heather for a bit, it was time for her to drive back to wait in the pickup line. She had already made the mistake of thinking she could roll up at three o'clock sharp. *What a disaster.*

There were cars lined up, double-parked around the block. No one would let her in, of course, so she had to circle until the cars moved—and by then, she was late. Ellington was in tears, and the last one waiting. He only calmed down after an ice cream bribe. She didn't want to go through that again; still she thought it was a colossal waste of time to sit in your car doing nothing for twenty minutes. Waiting.

Tamara knew how to wait, but that didn't mean she liked it one bit. She preferred to make things happen instead of standing idle. But the older she got, the more she realized that control was just an illusion at best, and at worst, a cruel hoax. As she pulled into the hospital parking lot, she shrugged her shoulders in resignation.

By now, nearly four weeks since they first got the horrible phone call from Neva and two weeks into her solo stay, she was a familiar face to the nurses in the ICU, who greeted her with a warm wave. Usually, she would check in with Dr. Chandra first thing; he always seemed to be in Heather's room by the time she got there. He was really the only adult she had in-person communication with. Neva's husband, when he was around, barely said a word to her. *Asshole.*

Her conversations with Dr. Chandra often extended beyond Heather. He seemed really concerned (or was it intrigued) by all of them. He asked a lot of questions and really seemed interested in their lives before they intersected with his in this horrible way. Whatever his motivation, it was good to have him around. He was instrumental in helping them convince Neva to go to Bayside and even recommended a doctor for her treatment. *I'm not sure she would have believed she really needed to go without his "push."* He had become a bright spot in her long days in the hospital and a welcome break from her tiresome mornings and nights at Neva's house.

As she turned the corner into Heather's room, he was already there, as usual, his back toward the door. He was facing Heather, making notations in her chart. Tamara's feet stopped in the doorway for a moment, and she noticed the way his neck bent slightly to the side as his nimble hand scribbled away. His dark hair was a little long in the back and brushed over the collar of his white coat. She was noticing his strong back when, as if he instinctively felt her gaze, he turned toward her. Tamara's face turned crimson with embarrassment. *Busted!*

"Tamara, good morning, how was everything with Ellington today?" he asked as he put down the chart and walked closer to her.

Tamara cleared her throat in an effort to collect herself before answering, "Better. I think I'm getting the hang of it. Of course, now that I've said that, I've probably jinxed myself, but thanks for asking. How's our girl?"

Dr. Chandra shook his head, folded his hands, and reported grimly, "The same." They both stood there for a moment in silence. Tamara stood in front of him, her eyes wandering. She couldn't for some reason look directly at him, so she looked about the room, looked past him out the window, looked all around the room, looked at Heather, and then looked back to him. She didn't know why she felt so awkward today. Usually, they had a professional banter that came quickly. Something was different.

As she brushed past him to take up her regular post at Heather's bedside, Dr. Chandra gently held on to her arm and quietly said her name, "Tamara."

Her feet stopped still, and his grip on her arm forced her to look into those dark, warm eyes. It was like he was pulling her in. She wanted to avert her gaze but found herself unable to do so.

"Would you like to join me for a cup of coffee later on today?"

Tamara sighed in relief. "Oh, sure, Dr. Chandra. I can grab some in the caf, and we can have it when you stop by later this afternoon."

"First of all, when are you going to start calling me Aman?"

"I'm sorry, it's just a habit."

Aman shook his head, chuckled, and gently squeezed her arm. "One that we clearly need to break. And I guess my attempt at asking you for a simple date was so subtle, it was undetectable. I'm not talking about having coffee in here," he said as he gestured about the room. "I was thinking of a less sterile environment, outside the hospital."

"Oh, I …"

"You can leave Heather for an hour or two," he urged with a smile.

"Well, ummm …" Tamara wasn't sure what to say.

Aman was not dissuaded by her reticence and pulled her a little closer as he continued. "I just want to sit across a table from you, with something warm in my hands, while I look into your eyes and try to uncover what you work so hard to hide."

Tamara shouldn't have been surprised by his directness by now, but she found herself completely paralyzed by his statement. Her feet seemed cemented to the floor, her arm glued to his hand. She stopped trying to resist him in her mind and simply released herself to his gaze and his hold.

"What do you think?" he asked.

Somehow a "yes" escaped from her lips before she could stop herself.

Satisfied with her response, he let her go and said, "Good. I'll be by around one thirty. Will that give you enough time to pick up Ellington from school?"

"Um, yes, it should give me about an hour or so." She would have to speed to get in the pickup line, but there was no more room for excuses.

"See you then," Aman shouted over his shoulder as he walked out of the room.

Tamara still couldn't move.

Neva

NEVA TRIED TO FOCUS ON her breathing as she sat half-lotus (her legs were way too stiff to bend into a full lotus position) on her yoga mat in the Meditation Garden at Bayside. More of trying to learn how to be still, which was so hard for Neva. Her mind raced, and she seemed unable to focus. *What am I supposed to focus on?* she wondered as she tried to quiet herself.

She took a deep breath and tried to look inside herself. She saw herself in a beautiful, mountainous locale. It could have been the Grand Canyon or someplace equally amazing. The sandy-colored rocks around her were tinged with shades of red, yellow, and orange, and the sky was this amazing color of blue. When Annette helped drive her car to school the summer after their sophomore year, they stopped at the Canyon. Just for one night. She wanted to take a tour, ride a mule, or something, since they had come all that way, but Annette was in a hurry to get back to campus. There was a man waiting, and so they left without seeing a thing. She shrugged her shoulders, a signal that she had let her mind wander. *Focus,* she told herself, *and breathe.*

She returned to the plateau. She could see herself standing there. Alone. *Always alone.* Her arms were spread, her head tilted back, and her eyes were closed. She felt free—more free than she had in a long time. She walked to the edge of the precipice. *Be careful. Why are my eyes still closed? Open up! I'm going to fall!* She kept walking, arms open like wings, neck arched in surrender, eyes still closed. *What am I doing?* Neva wondered as she forced herself to keep "looking" at the scene that was unfolding in her mind. *Isn't meditation supposed to be peaceful and relaxing?*

Her feet moved forward until the tips of her toes reached just beyond the edge and were supported by nothing but air. Then she stopped. *How did I know how far to go?* Neva exhaled in response to her own question. Her eyes opened; she dropped her arms and looked around. She smiled broadly at the scenery that surrounded her in the garden. *What a beautiful place*, she thought as she breathed in deeply. She shut her eyes once more, opened her arms wide, and started to lean forward ever so slightly until she left the edge safely behind.

$\mathcal{T}$amara

HE CAME BY HEATHER'S ROOM at 1:30 sharp. He was on time, of course, and Tamara was surprised to find him wearing street clothes. It was the first time she had seen him in anything other than scrubs. *He looks nice in his jeans*, she thought, and suddenly found herself wishing she had on something decent. It was amazing how quickly she had adopted the unofficial uniform of a stay-at-home mom, workout pants and gym shoes. *It's just coffee after all.*

He greeted her with a broad smile.

"There's this great little coffee shop that I think is on your way to Ellington's school. How about I bring my car around, and you can follow me so that you can leave straight from there?"

That was thoughtful, she thought to herself.

"Sounds like a plan," Tamara replied.

Once he left, she ducked into the bathroom and quickly pulled her long hair into a perky ponytail and dug around in her purse for some lipstick, lip gloss, or something. Finding none, she smiled into the mirror, sighed, and hurried to Neva's car to meet Aman. He was waiting as promised. He waved as she passed him and climbed into the truck.

She followed his careful driving along the winding road that led from the hospital to the coffee shop. It was only about ten minutes away, and he was right, it was on her way to Ellington's school. She had never noticed it before. As she pulled into the parking lot and turned off her car, she pulled down the mirror from the visor and gave herself another once-over. *Nothing I can do about it now*, she resigned herself as she flipped up the visor, turned her head, and jumped a little because Aman was standing there just outside her window. Tamara's cheeks flushed pink as she hoped that he hadn't seen her primp.

She opened the door and smiled.

"It never fails to amaze me why some women want to tamper with perfection," he said.

She blushed as she stepped down from Neva's large truck and followed Aman into the coffee shop.

She ordered a doppio espresso and he, a chai.

As they took their seats, he commented, "Wow, you really like the hard stuff, huh?"

"I've been so tired lately, I need something to help me stay awake. I tell you, I don't know how Neva does it."

"That is why it is so good that she is getting the help she needs. You are being a good friend."

"I'm trying. This experience has helped me realize that I need to do more to help my patients prepare for what comes after the babies they are so desperate to have. They don't have a clue what they are in for."

"I'm sure you're right. Goals are usually good things, but sometimes we can be so fixated on them that we miss the whole point."

Tamara wasn't sure if he was still talking about her patients or her, so she didn't say anything in response.

"So tell me more about your patients, your practice. What is your best day at work?"

"You really want to know?"

Aman nodded for Tamara to continue, so she did, reluctantly. "Well, okay. For me, the best days are usually the most challenging ones. I guess I just like solving problems. Not too long ago, I had three of my patients go into labor at once."

"Wow."

"The first two went like clockwork. I delivered a set of twins around seven o'clock, and then I delivered the other patient, whom I had known for a long time. It was her fourth, so she was an old pro and everything went off without a hitch. But what made the day interesting was the fact that in between those two deliveries, another couple came in. The mother had preeclampsia, which was why she was referred to me, and from the beginning, these people had been so high-maintenance and stubborn. I was not looking forward to this one."

Tamara paused for a moment to check to see if he really wanted her to continue. Her mother was always telling her not to talk so much about her work, that it would turn men off. He didn't seem turned off at all; in fact, he seemed completely engaged. As he leaned in closer, she kept going.

"My exam revealed that the baby was breech. I thought I was going to have to do a C-section. The parents were very attached to their birth plan, although I had already told them that those plans were only guidelines, not a contract or something. I consistently informed them that if there was a complication or something unexpected, they would have to trust me to do what was best for Mom and the baby. Apparently none of my warnings had registered. It was in one ear and out the other. They had written their plan and wanted to stick to it. So, there we were, having at it in the delivery room."

"I bet you didn't back down," he inserted.

"I didn't, and I couldn't. But wouldn't you know, at the last possible moment, the baby turned all by herself, so everyone was happy and safe. They got their vaginal delivery, and I got a healthy mom and baby."

"It's amazing what miracles can happen when people get out of the way," Aman offered. "Without interference, the world most often rights itself."

"Do you really believe that?" Tamara questioned.

"Of course I do, don't you?"

"I guess there have been a lot of wrong things happening lately. It's hard for me to believe that they can ever be made right."

"You have to be patient, Tamara," he said with a smile. "Just wait and see."

Tamara blushed a little and returned his smile. *This is nice*, she thought to herself.

"I have always been in awe of OBs," Aman said, changing the subject. "I think having the regular privilege of ushering new life into the world, guiding all that potential into the earth … it's just amazing! I had this great opportunity after med school to work in Africa with the Peabody Fellowship. While I was there, I delivered a few babies, and I was a mess. I don't know who was crying more, me or the new parents."

Tamara laughed and then responded, "I used to approach it with that kind of reverence. In fact, that's one of the reasons I chose it as a specialty—the wonder of it all. I'm kind of embarrassed to admit that now it has all become so routine. It's like I'm on autopilot. Most of the time, I just find that I am going through the motions."

"Tamara." His tone became very serious as he took her hand in his and asked, "Don't you think you deserve more than that?"

Heather

THE FIRST TIME I PICKED up a brush, it felt so heavy. My hands were tiny, and it seemed so big. But as I moved it around and over the canvas, it became light as a feather. It was as if with each dabbing of paint on the brush and sweeping the colors over the canvas, I was less in touch with how I felt and became more consumed with how I was. I could have stayed in my studio all night, but soon, my mother would call for dinner or I had homework to do or some chore to complete, and I had to leave my haven to return to the world outside of it. It seemed that as soon as I opened the door, my heart would sigh.

Once I left for college, my mother turned my studio into an office for her political activities. A giant calendar hung where my canvases once rested. Campaign buttons replaced my brushes. Old-school posters leaned against the walls instead of paint.

My world started getting darker once I put my brush down. Painting never should have been optional for me, but somehow it became something I could take or leave. It was something that I felt embarrassed and unsure about. Painting made me different, and I hated being different. I wanted to be like everyone else. I couldn't see the colors in my head anymore.

When my mother got sick, some colors came back, but it was only shades of black, deep blues, and gray. I had to let them out of my head somehow. But I had to keep it to myself. No one could know. When I would steal away, making up some excuse so Tamara wouldn't suspect anything, the colors would flow quicker than I could put them on the canvas. I should have figured out way back then that painting was God's gift to me to help me navigate my world, that somehow He knew what my life would be like and what I would need and He gave me all I needed to make it from the beginning. You would have thought that I would have figured out that I didn't paint because I wanted to but because I had to.

I didn't have the nerve to show anyone. I just didn't think it was good enough, that I was good enough. It seemed that the more I learned about the great masters and spent afternoons wandering through the Rodin sculpture garden, I was more intimidated than inspired. I was certain I could never measure up, despising myself for not being great. Step-by-step, I walked away from my very center to find myself at the periphery of my very core and detested the only map that would return me safely home. So I walked further away—until I no longer knew the way back to myself.

Lauren

LAUREN COULDN'T BELIEVE HE DIDN'T even have the nerve to come in the house after she forced herself to send those racy texts. She felt like a fool. Busted by her children and his likely mistress. His response cemented her suspicions about the affair, but she had too many other things to focus on now. She really needed to get in touch with Neva.

She and Neva hadn't spoken in over two weeks, when she first left. For a while, she would get updates via voice mail, but those had stopped too. Neva's phone rang and rang, both cell and home. *Damn, was she still that mad? That's not like her.* Lauren thought as she hung up the phone without success again. She had two motivations for calling: one, to find out how Heather was doing, and two, to share her good news that Heather was going to have a gallery showing. Certainly that would temper their anger at her for taking the paintings. They would see she had been right all along. Besides, she couldn't think of a better get-well present. She did hope that Heather was getting better. But she was sure that if Heather had awakened from the coma, someone would have called her. *How long has it been now? Three weeks? Four?* The days seemed to run together since she'd been back. *How long are they going to leave her that way?* she couldn't help but wonder.

She decided to stop thinking about that and go to the gym, for the second time that day. It had only been a few weeks, but she swore her thighs weren't rubbing together quite as much anymore. Besides, Zoe was home, and it was becoming awkward, suspicions lurking behind every request and distrust in every response. She was almost certain that something had gone on between them, whether it was a full-blown affair or just stolen glances, intimate conversations, maybe a stolen kiss when she wasn't around. There was something there, she just knew it, but the less she focused on it and occupied herself with her new exercise program and Heather's show, she was surprised to discover she was just fine.

For the first time in a long time, there hadn't been any late-night Oreo binges on the pantry floor. No Ben and Jerry's summits on the couch watching *Real Housewives*. No chip extravaganzas or Big Mac attacks. She really was fine without her food friends. Maybe she would be fine without him too.

Annette

ANNETTE'S LATEST STRATEGY WAS TO leave before Thomas woke up, which was a task because he usually left home by 7:00 a.m. to get to school before it started. She just moved her appointment with her trainer to 6:00 a.m. and started going every day. She was tired of trying to come up with excuses why she didn't want to have the perfunctory morning sex that Thomas favored now that he was able to function again. The sex had gone from routine and bland to almost violent, like he was mad at her or something. He pounded away as if to prove that the infertility was her fault. He was so aggressive—it was like with every thrust he was telling her, "I am still a man!" or worse, "What is wrong with you?" Maybe it was just her guilt getting the better of her, but still, she would take punishment at the gym any day over that.

Besides, was there such a thing as too much exercise? It helped reduce her stress level, and her body was getting even more sculpted, which made her feel like a whole woman again, sexy and fabulous—babies or not.

She smiled as she thought of yesterday's lunch "quickie" as she rolled out of bed. How long it would last, she didn't know. A decision was neither necessary nor imminent; she had more important things on her mind, like going back to Oakland to check on her girls. Heather was still holding on, Tamara seemed to be at her wits' end, and Neva was hopefully regaining some balance. *Shit, my little dalliance is the least of my concerns,* she thought as she sleepily put on her workout gear.

It was a good time to go back. The deal was back on stable footing, and she was curious to see how she could handle motherhood, if only for a long weekend. Just a few days away from Thomas's disappointing looks would be an extra bonus. *What kind of man judged a woman like that anyway?* More and more she was thinking that maybe it was best that they couldn't conceive. The way he handled this challenge showed Annette what kind of man he really was—insecure, needy, and immature. *What kind of father would he be?* At this point, a baby would probably fall into the chasm their infertility had created, instead of bringing them closer.

Neva

THE MORNING FOG THAT SURROUNDED Bayside with a faint, gray mist made everything look a little eerie. It also made it hard to see too far ahead, which was nice, because it forced her to focus on just the step in front of her. Neva had never walked a labyrinth before. Now, she did it almost every day. She never understood how it worked, but the simple practice of intentional walking, simply following the path, carefully watching her feet, being sure to stay on course, brought her to a surprising place of peace. She liked it much better than meditating. She had finally found a way to be still, like Dr. Hughes had been suggesting.

Even when the things that rose to the surface were painful. Even when being fully present in the moment hurt so much. She learned that truly the presence of the pain was relevant information that required a response, and until she responded, nothing was going to get better. Neva let out a sigh as the circle became smaller and smaller and she got closer to the center. She had done this so many times now that she could almost close her eyes and still not get off course.

Neva's sessions with Dr. Hughes continued daily, and she was starting to feel like she was coming back to herself, but she wasn't sure how it would last. She was safely cocooned at Bayside. *It's easy to feel better here. What's going to happen once I leave? I'm afraid the tightness in my chest and the heaviness in my heart will return.* Dr. Hughes often reminded her that her time at Bayside was just the beginning of her journey of rediscovery, that it was not an end unto itself. "*We are taking a huge leap down the path, but the journey is still yours to travel. Now you won't be alone, and you have more strength for the trip.*"

She looked down at her feet as they moved deliberately—one in front of the other around this bend and that turn. She took several deep breaths, letting the fragrant eucalyptus fill her nostrils, then her lungs, and then spread all the way to her fingertips and her toes, which continued to gently move around the labyrinth's circular path.

Heather

AT THE END, THE STEADY stream of friends and visitors drained me more than helped sometimes. I know they thought they were coming for my mother or me, but really it felt like they were there more for themselves, to feel better or fulfill some sort of obligation. Either way, I just put on a fake smile, and my eyes would glaze over as I nodded in response to the hollow but well-intentioned remarks, like, "She's a fighter, you know," or "Hang in there, honey," or "Just be strong." As if words could help.

The one thing that could have actually helped didn't happen, and I don't know why I expected it to. If only my father had come. Although he left when I was only one and I never really knew him, I was in so much pain when my mother got sick, it was the kind of hurt that I imagined only a father could have made better. In those moments, when it was just too much for me to bear and the well-meaning words of others rang hollow, I would close my eyes and picture him wrapping his big strong ebony arms around me and melting all of my fears and sadness and pain away.

$\mathcal{T}$amara

TAMARA AND AMAN MET AT the Seminary Coffee Shop every day after their first date, which made the last two days before Annette's visit go by quickly. She enjoyed the adult conversation (she hadn't anticipated she'd be so starved for it) and the break from the waiting. It also gave her a reason to wear something other than sweats.

Usually they would follow each other, but today he wanted to drive them both. She shifted uncomfortably in the tan leather seat of his 1973 red Mercedes 450SL. The car suited him, she thought. Luxurious but not pretentious. An elegant throwback, a classic. He was kind of retro anyway, she thought, so gentlemanly and courteous. It was nice, and she was beginning to realize that nice is nice.

With Parker, it was all smooth talk and flashy demonstrations of what love was supposed to be, but Tamara couldn't really say he was kind like Aman. Parker always said the right thing without ever meaning it, like he read it in a book somewhere. Aman said what he really felt, and it always turned out to be the right thing.

They decided to sit outside; it was unusually warm and sunny. "Some sun would be good for both of us," he said.

"Are you trying to say that I look pale?" Tamara teased.

"No, of course not, Tamara. You look beautiful as always."

His compliments were becoming more frequent in their conversations, and Tamara was finally starting to get used to hearing them. Believing them was something else altogether.

They both got chai lattes today. Tamara tried one at Aman's request, and found the warm sweetness was soothing and the spiciness gave her a nice little kick. It had just enough caffeine to keep her going through the afternoon, until she could indulge in her other new ritual, a daily glass of wine.

"Is Annette still coming to town?" he asked.

"Yeah, later on tonight. I can't wait. Why?"

"Well, I was thinking, and I hope you don't find this inappropriate, although if I'm honest, even I do a little, but still, I feel compelled to ask you if, well, maybe we could go out … on a real date."

Tamara almost choked on her drink when she heard the words "real date." She liked having coffee with him, but a date, at night? And what exactly did "real" mean?

"If you don't want to or have other plans, that's fine. I understand," he replied quickly.

"No, I—I'm sorry."

Tamara took a deep breath to collect herself. *What is wrong with me? What is it they always say about the definition of crazy—doing the same thing and expecting different results? I have gotten the same results doing things my way for almost forty years of being single. What would it hurt to try something different? Besides, he is so nice.* "I would like that," she finally said after a long pause.

She thought she heard a sigh of relief from him, which made her smile. It was nice to know that despite his outward calmness, he wasn't always so sure.

Lauren

AS THE DATE FOR THE opening drew nearer, Lauren barely had any time for her morning walks, but she was determined to keep this appointment with herself. She was starting to notice she wasn't as winded as she used to be, and walking helped clear her head so she could prioritize all the tasks that needed to get done on any given day. Her plate was already quite full and her schedule booked before she took on this extra project, so it only made her busier and crazier, but she liked it.

She had been compiling her guest list, making sure that only the most influential people in Atlanta would be there. She kept toying with whether she was going to invite Tamara, Annette, and Neva. *And what am I going to do about Heather?* She had hoped that by now either Heather would have regained consciousness or Neva would have made the decision to, well, do the humane thing. No such luck, so Lauren was plowing forward, proceeding with her plan to characterize Heather as a recluse. She was toying with the idea of coming up with a mysterious illness that would keep her away from the opening. *Hopefully, it will make her seem elusive and will increase her marketability.*

Thinking of marketing, where will the money go? I wouldn't keep it, of course. Maybe establish a trust or some other shelter that Heather can use, if or when or whatever. I have to remember to talk to my accountant about that. After I make a final selection of whether I am going to allow a showing of all the paintings, or just some, or what. I suppose I should hold something back. That way I will have more to give people if they want it. If, huh? I know they will love Heather's work. I only wish she could have been around to realize what talent she had.

Lauren quickened her pace as she checked her watch and realized that she had to stop by the printers on the way to work to proof the invitations.

Neva

NEVA HAD BEEN TRYING SO many different things at Bayside, things she never thought or knew she could enjoy. Labyrinth-walking, meditation, now yoga. Another of Dr. Hughes's brilliant recommendations. He thought it might help manage her stress, and it was something Neva could do at home.

Neva stretched awkwardly into the downward dog pose. *Yoga is so opposite from any other type of exercise I have ever done. I'm a cardio queen. From aerobics to step class to kickboxing, I've tried and loved them all. But yoga is different. It stretches me in different ways. Much like meditating, it is hard to quiet my mind and focus on just being present in whatever pose I'm trying to pretzel my body into. Once I get in the poses, I hate staying in them for a long time. I like to "flow" better. I am always anxious to move on to the next thing. But I am learning to be present in my practice and how to breathe into the difficult spaces, even to enjoy them, no matter if it is uncomfortable.*

Whatever pain I feel during the practice, the feeling after yoga is probably why I really like it. It feels like I am floating. Neva sailed across the lawn to her room and prepared to engage in another of her newly discovered self-care activities—the bath. It had become a sanctuary for her, something else she could continue once she returned home. Even if she had to lock the door to keep Ellington out or wake up an extra half hour early, she now understood that she had to take care of herself first.

As she took off her yoga pants and cami, she looked at her svelte body in the mirror. She was never fat, but curvy—always a little too curvy for her own taste. A lot of people thought she had a great body, but she never did. In school, Annette used to tease that she was anorexic. Nothing could have been further from the truth; she just gravitated toward a more slender aesthetic, although it consistently eluded her until now. She could finally admit that maybe she did have a few body-image issues, now that she had become decidedly thin. She just couldn't bring herself to eat since the abortion. Dante never noticed, never asked if she was okay or if anything was wrong, which was ironic, because after Ellington was born, she couldn't lose the weight fast enough for him. She had barely gone to her six-week checkup before he was signing her up for boot camp.

She would never forget that day, how he took her into the gym, met with the personal trainer, and in front of everyone, proceeded to dissect her body, piece by piece, asking if the trainer could "fix this" or "get rid of that." She just stood there, letting him raise her T-shirt to display her midsection, still full from the aftermath of bearing life, to show the trainer the source of his greatest concern. What made it worse was that he didn't think anything was wrong with his behavior or attitude. He had seen other women have a baby and look no worse for the wear right away. "Why can't you do that?" he wanted to know. Their stomachs seemed to return to the prepregnancy flatness with no effort at all. She kept trying to tell him that everyone was different, but he couldn't hear her. He wanted her prebaby body back immediately. He even offered to watch Ellington so she could go to the early morning boot camp sessions. He never offered to help with him. Now she was thinner than she had ever been. Still, it didn't seem good enough for him.

She tried to forget all of that as she looked at her naked body in the mirror. She tried to just consider herself in the moment, without criticism, absent judgment, with no regard for the hurtful experiences of her past. She tried to look at herself with gentleness and acceptance, receiving the good and the bad, firm and jiggly, stretch marks and all, because after all, that was how she could tell she had grown.

Annette

ANNETTE SANK DEEPLY INTO HER seat and sighed as she closed her eyes in preparation for the journey west. She knew she was going to be "on" once she landed. *I hope I'm ready for this,* she thought to herself as she looked briefly out the window as the plane taxied from the gate to wait in line on the O'Hare runway. *The expansion needs to hurry up,* she concluded as the pilot informed the passengers that they were sixth in line for takeoff. *Maybe I should try to get in on that deal.* Her chest expanded and contracted again with a heavy sigh as she imagined one more thing on her already-overflowing plate. She tried to forget about all that and focused on helping her girlfriends.

Tamara

AMAN SAID HE WANTED TO spend the entire day together. *It would be a very long first date,* Tamara thought as she stood in the guest room with the few clothes she had brought spread out on the bed. Nothing really seemed right. She had such a hard time deciding what to wear; she wanted to be sure she looked perfect, but it was hard because she still didn't know exactly what they would be doing. Thankfully Annette would be there soon to help her decide. In some ways, she wanted to keep the whole thing to herself, so it could just be hers, but she always ended up telling Annette everything anyway.

Aman said he needed the whole day because there were so many things he wanted to show her, so many things she had never seen, even though she spent four years in the Bay Area. When she was in school, she rarely left campus because she was so focused on her studies. She didn't realize where she had been until she was gone. So busy with her head in a book, she didn't look up long enough to realize her beautiful surroundings and all the area had to offer. He said he wanted to "get her out of the coffee shop."

The things he said. They had the most wonderful, rich, and complex conversations at those coffee dates. Tamara enjoyed hearing his interesting perspective on everything, and she often marveled at his uncanny ability to pierce to the very core of what she was feeling, even if she couldn't, or didn't, want to articulate it. He challenged her, but in a compassionate way. He wasn't confrontational at all. And he asked so many questions. He seemed genuinely interested in her life, her thoughts, her work, her everything. It took some getting used to—a man who didn't talk about himself incessantly, like Parker used to do.

Maybe some simple black pants would work; can't go wrong there, she thought as she realized that Aman and Parker couldn't have been more different. She tried not to compare but couldn't help it. She hadn't let any man get close to her since Parker. If anything, Aman was the anti-Parker. In fact, Aman was unlike any man she had ever known, and that scared her because she didn't know what that meant. Especially when she considered their racial differences. She thought about what Lauren said and wondered if someone who wasn't black could ever really know her, but when she and Aman talked, it seemed as if he had always known her, whether he was black or not.

Even if she cleared the race hurdle, there was always the matter of distance. Chicago was a long way from California. *Why even venture down this path?* she questioned herself again as she took off a pair of jeans; *too casual,* she had concluded. *Maybe Annette will have something I can borrow.*

I can't believe I am so concerned about what I am going to wear. What's the big deal? It's just a casual date. It doesn't really matter. But the knot in Tamara's stomach told her otherwise.

Just when she had given up completely, resigned to be alone forever, he came along, completely unexpected but conclusively what she needed.

Tamara and Annette

TAMARA WAS SURPRISED TO FIND Annette sitting quietly on one of the metal benches outside SFO with her Prada sunglasses on, her head tilted ever so slightly, giving her face full exposure to the sun, instead of talking on her phone or feverishly texting away on the BlackBerry.

"Hey, girl, you're still alive!" Annette teased, lifting her head as Tamara approached.

"Barely. It took a summit meeting practically to get Neva's husband to take over this morning so I could come and get you. It's like he treats Ellington as a prop in the theater that is his world. He doesn't seem to understand that Ellington is a living, breathing human being and it takes adult intervention for him to get up, eat food, and get to school. It doesn't just happen automatically."

"I could have taken a cab," Annette offered as they piled the luggage, then themselves into Neva's truck.

"No, he needed to do something. I mean, I know I volunteered to stay, but he has been totally MIA for over two weeks! He hasn't done one damn thing to help. I don't know if he spends any time with his son at all."

"That's sad."

"I tell you, Annette, I can understand how Neva got to the point of feeling like an abortion was her only option. Motherhood is no joke, and I've been at it, what, only a couple weeks? I hope you're ready," Tamara half-joked as she pulled away from the airport and merged into the traffic on the 580.

"Having a baby is all Thomas can talk about, and I'm quite confident that he will be a very involved father—too involved, if there is such a thing. He really wants a child."

"What about what you want?"

"I don't know anymore, T, I really don't," Annette replied while looking out the window, avoiding Tamara's face but not her insight.

They went straight to the hospital. Annette was shocked to see Heather thinner and paler than she had been only two weeks before. She didn't know what she was expecting. Maybe she had let herself create an idealized picture of Heather, or maybe she hadn't allowed herself to picture her at all.

"Tamara, she … she …" Annette stumbled to find the words to describe how wasted she now looked.

"I know; she's not a sleeping angel anymore."

"She looks like she's …" Tears replaced the words that couldn't find voice even in the mouth of bold Annette.

"Dying. I know. She's not, though. I mean, she is being kept alive, so she's not dying, but still, she looks a lot different than two weeks ago. I like to think that she's still waiting."

"Yeah, but for what?" Annette asked no one in particular.

"I wish I knew. Aman, I mean Dr. Chandra, I mean … he says that some things are a great mystery that we are not supposed to understand."

"Well, can you give me a minute with her, alone? Maybe I can try."

"Of course." Tamara went to the waiting room and started reading *The Essential Rumi*, a collection of poems by the mystical Sufi poet that Aman had given her. He wanted to fill her thoughts with something beautiful, he told her. *I guess I have been complaining about Ellington and worrying about Neva and Heather too much during our coffee dates.* She wasn't much for reading poetry but considered it a thoughtful gesture. *Besides, I want to be prepared in case he wants to discuss it tomorrow.*

He had started bringing her little gifts now and then. First it was the Rumi, or a to-go cup from their regular coffee shop, so she could take coffee with her when she went to pick up Ellington. They were thoughtful and simple gifts, so different from the elaborate and expensive ones that Parker used to give—rare perfume, the latest designer purses and shoes, or spa days. In a few short days, she and Aman seemed to have spanned a lifetime of knowing each other.

Aman was giving her little pieces of himself, things he liked that he wanted to share with her, or things that would make her life more comfortable. Parker, she supposed, gave her all those fancy things because he couldn't give her who he really was.

As she contemplated the question, he appeared as if on cue, and observed, "Ahhh, you're reading the Rumi. So, what do you think?"

She jumped at first, startled by his presence, and then suddenly nervous as she could barely bring her eyes to meet his as he stood over her. She closed the book suddenly and replied, "They are really beautiful. I'm not sure I get all of them, but they are really nice."

"There's nothing to get or not get; they simply are," he smiled. "I am glad you like them."

"I do. They are different from anything I've ever read before. I was a human biology major, you know. Not much time for poetry reading."

"So, we have to make the time," Aman chuckled as he sat down beside her. "So, have you thought any further about what you would like to do tomorrow?"

"Oh, well, no, not really. I mean, whatever you decide would be fine, I'm sure."

"I can't believe you have no preference at all and are just going to allow yourself to yield to my plans. I've not known you to frequently lack an opinion," he added.

"Honestly, I just haven't had time to think about it. All I've been doing for the past two weeks is coming to the hospital and running Ellington around, so anything other than that will seem fun to me, I'm sure. Besides, I think I can trust you to figure out what I would like."

"Okay then, I will do that. I will pick you up early if that's okay, around nine-ish? Or did you want to meet here?"

Tamara hadn't thought about the logistics. "We can meet here. That way I can see Heather before we go."

"That's fine. I will see you here tomorrow at nine." He gently squeezed her hand as he left.

Annette walked up just in time to see him leaving. "Making plans for tomorrow, are we?"

"Girl, I can't even figure out what I'm giving Ellington for dinner from one day to the next, so trying to imagine what to do for an entire day seems beyond me at this point. I decided to let him work it out."

"Letting him be the man. I like that," Annette joked. "Hey, where did all those flowers come from in Heather's room?"

"Lauren. She sends them every few days."

"You are kidding me! If I were you, I would give them all away. She's a trip. She hasn't called anybody, but she's sending flowers. Some things never change."

"Who knows what her motivation is at this point?"

"She's up to something, I just know it. And what's that you're reading? I've never seen you with a book that thin before. Let me see it."

Annette snatched the book from Tamara's hands as she sat down and started reading the back cover. "'Rumi, the Sufi poet of love, is one of the most revered mystical poets of all time …' You are reading ancient love poetry? Girl, what has happened to you?" she asked jokingly, but before Tamara could respond, she answered her own question, "Or should I say who has happened to you? I leave you alone out here in California, and see what happens? You get all hippified, fall in love with a fine doctor …"

"Shhh, Annette, not so loud!" Tamara admonished, and took her by the arm and led her back toward Heather's room. "I told you, we've had a few cups of coffee, that's all. We have really good conversations, and he mentioned this poet to me and shared a book—no big deal."

"And what about this daylong date tomorrow? Is that 'no big deal' either?"

"Well, now that you mention it, I am starting to get a little nervous. I don't know what to wear. I don't even know exactly what we're doing, and I don't think I have anything date-worthy," Tamara rambled.

"Girl, just slow down and relax. Help has arrived. If I know anything, I know about how to prepare for a date. So, first things first, what do you have going on in your 'area'?" Annette moved her hand in a circular motion near Tamara's pelvic region.

"Annette!"

"What? I'm just saying you should be prepared, just in case."

"In case what?"

"In case you decided to, you know, 'open the box.'"

"Annette, really, I don't think—"

"You don't think what? C'mon now! You're grown; he's grown. God knows how long it's been for you. You might not be able to think tomorrow night after he puts it on you all day long!"

"What are you talking about? He's not trying to put anything 'on' me. He just wants to show me around, that's all."

"Look, no man—especially not a busy man—spends a whole day with someone if he's not interested in her. And I mean sexually interested."

"I don't think it's like that at all—" But before Tamara could finish, Annette jumped in.

"I'm not saying that you have to do anything, although he will definitely want to. All I'm saying is that you should just be ready in case. You know, you don't want to 'open the box' and find out it hasn't been properly gift-wrapped. That would not be good at all." Annette raised her eyebrows, looked at Tamara's hands, and then added, "And a mani-pedi wouldn't kill you, either. Your hands are through; I can only imagine what your feet look like."

"Annette, please, now you're being ridiculous. He's not into all that. Besides, I have barely had time to take a shower every day, much less get my nails done. I have been a little busy," Tamara responded.

"Number one, that's no excuse, that child is in school all day; and number two, I don't know what 'Doctor Fine' is 'into,' but no man likes to go on a treasure hunt through the jungle or likes getting cut up by some crusty feet. All men appreciate good grooming. After all, it's just polite. We've got time. I can call my old place. I wonder if they're still in business," Annette commented as she started searching her BlackBerry.

Annette had been getting bikini waxes since college—long before any of the others had even heard of them. She was always light-years ahead of everyone else. Before Neva got married, Annette took her for her first one. She remembered that Neva's legs were shaking so much that Annette practically had to hold them down so the aesthetician could work. That is not a place where you want someone to make a mistake. The thought of misplaced hot wax was enough to make Annette shudder.

"Well, maybe you're right. Did you find the number?" Tamara asked.

Annette smiled. "Just in case?"

Lauren

I THOUGHT THAT NEVA WOULD at least call to thank me for the flowers I've been sending. She won't take my calls, won't return my messages. It doesn't seem that anything I do will get her attention. They leave me no choice but to forge ahead, Lauren thought as she reviewed the menu for the opening. She made the gallery owner agree to allow her to be involved in every aspect of the event. Everything had to be just right. She had a lot riding on this.

The seeming reality of Prescott's infidelity gave Lauren more impetus to focus all of her attention on Heather's opening. She hadn't decided what she was going to do about the infidelity, but for now, she didn't have time to think about it. This art show was many things, but a convenient diversion was among the most unexpected—and welcome. But no more "Ms. Nice Guy." She was careful to make innuendos and drop hints to let Prescott know that she knew he was up to no good, which was slowly shifting the power dynamic in the relationship in her favor, which she liked. He didn't know how much or what she knew, but he definitely understood that she had him over the barrel, and anytime she wanted to, she could drop the blade and send him into financial and professional ruin.

I have time to figure this out. But first things first.

Tamara and Annette

ALL WAXED AND READY, NOW Tamara just had to figure out what to wear on her big date. Ellington was safely away, watching *The Backyardigans* on television. *Thank God for TV,* Tamara thought. She didn't know how she would have made it thus far without the electronic babysitter. She knew she should have been engaging him or something, but she just needed a minute or two of quiet.

Annette's overbearing and opinionated presence, which sometimes got on Tamara's nerves, was welcome today because she needed help. She didn't want to be too dressed up or not dressed up enough. She wanted to be cute, but she didn't want to look like she tried too hard.

Annette opened her suitcase and said, "You can pick out whatever you want; go ahead."

Tamara started going through the things while Annette kept talking. "Now what time are you all going out again?" she asked.

"Early, like nine o'clock, and he said I should plan to be gone all day, unless I get tired of him."

"Nine o'clock in the morning? That is early. And you have no idea what you all are going to do?"

"He said we could do whatever I wanted."

"I like him even more," Annette teased. "Well, then, what do you want to do?"

"I don't know. It doesn't really matter to me. Honestly, Annette, it's been so long since I've been on a date, I don't know what to do or where to go. I hope I remember how to act."

"Just act the same way you've been acting at coffee. Just think of it as an extended coffee date. Be yourself. Girl, he has already seen you at your worst, so anything else, he'll think is awesome. I think you should go to Napa for the day. That would be sufficiently activity-driven, while still giving you guys time to talk, and it's so romantic."

"Now, I don't know how romantic I am ready to be."

"Oh, Tamara, just jump in! Let yourself live a little."

"I did that once, remember?" Tamara reminded Annette as she picked up a black short-sleeved turtleneck sweater and held up to her chest.

Annette shook her head no and patted the bed for Tamara to sit next to her. "Look, Tamara, I don't think I've ever said this to you before because I felt somehow responsible for what Parker did to you, I guess because I introduced you. But here's the thing: you have got to let Parker go. You have got to leave him and what he did in the past and move forward with your life. You have been nursing that hurt and feeding that pain for a long time. I'm tired of you wasting opportunity after opportunity, shutting down nice guy after nice guy just because you fear they are going to be another Parker. Yes, he lied to you. Yes, you suffered humiliation and rejection because of what he did. And I can only imagine the imprint that experience left on you, but, Tamara, you are bigger than that one very horrible experience. You are better than the way he treated you. It's time you acted like it. Give yourself a chance to be happy. Open up that crusty heart and see if you can believe in love again."

Uncharacteristic tears started flowing from Tamara's eyes at Annette's unusually keen observation and sensitive words.

"Honestly, Annette, I don't know if I can."

"Bitch, you better try," Annette laughed as she pulled out a casual colorful sleeveless dress, a cardigan, and a belt. "It's going to be cool in the morning, so wear the sweater first, and then when things, I mean it heats up, take the sweater off and just be cute in the little casual dress. I would wear flats during the day, but bring some heels in case you go out for dinner at night."

"Thanks, 'Nette. I don't know what I would do without you."

"I know. Now, what are we going to do about this hair?" Annette asked with a raised eyebrow.

Tamara

TAMARA DROVE FASTER THAN EVER to the hospital. Her anxiety mixed with her curiosity and created a happy jitteriness that Tamara hadn't felt in a long time. *Will we get along? Will we argue? What will he have planned? Am I wearing the right thing?* They had only been together about an hour at a time up to now.

She had already decided that she was not going to have sex with him, but that was the only rule she established. She figured it was best to work it out in advance; it lessened the possibility for irrational responses on her part. She didn't want him to think less of her. Somehow, though, she was certain that regardless of whether she slept with him or not, he would still respect her.

Annette and Tamara went in and sat with Heather for a moment.

"You have everything you need? I gave you Neva's car keys, right? And you have the schedule for the weekend?"

"I've got it, I've got it. Stop stalling and let's go meet your 'Mr. Wonderful.'"

"You're staying here with Heather, right?"

"And miss this? Oh no. C'mon. This I want to see."

Tamara groaned as they left Heather's room and exited the hospital. As the sliding glass doors opened, Tamara didn't see him initially. She looked to her left as she went out, then to her right without seeing him anywhere. Finally, she fixed her gaze straight ahead. There he was, handsome as ever, leaning against the passenger door of his car, looking down at his phone.

"Aman!" Tamara was surprised that her voice quivered a little as she called out to him. He looked up from the phone and smiled broadly. As

Tamara approached him, he greeted her with a warm hug, then turned to Annette and said, "Annette, it is good to see you. You look well."

"Thank you. Now, you take care of my girl. Stay gone as long as you like. I've got Ellington covered," Annette responded maternally, which embarrassed Tamara a little bit.

"Now, don't forget he has soccer at ten and a birthday party at noon, the present is in the closet, and he likes—" Tamara replied.

Annette cut her off before she could finish. "Girl, you have already told me this once before. I've got it. Go on and have a good time. God knows, you deserve it. Bye." Annette waved and went back in to sit with Heather.

"Are you ready?" Aman asked as he opened the car door for Tamara. She climbed in delicately. As he got in beside her, he asked, "So, I have a few different ideas on what we can do today, and you can pick. We could go to Napa, then come back to the City for dinner. Or we could just do a bunch of touristy stuff in the City. Or I didn't know if you would want to go down to visit your alma mater."

"Wow, they all sound good, but I think Napa would be fun. I've never been."

"Perfect. That was my first choice, too. Okay then. By the way, you look amazing. That color is beautiful on you," Aman commented as he started the car and pulled off.

⌒⌒

Tamara couldn't believe how beautiful Napa was and that she had never been before when it was so close. The rolling hills of lush green were organized in rows and rows of grapevines, which were neatly parted and arranged, almost like cornrows. She and Aman chatted easily as they drove along. She didn't even mind when he asked if he could put the top down. She normally didn't even like the windows down, because she didn't like her hair to blow. But today, she broke out a ponytail holder to contain her flowing dark hair and decided to let go.

Aman quickly put any of Tamara's uneasiness about the activities to rest. He was completely disarming. As they went from winery to winery, he remained the perfect gentleman—opening every door, deferring to her preferences, and making sure she was comfortable and having fun at every stop. He had put a lot of thought into making the day special—like the way he carefully mapped out the order of the wineries they would visit so they would end up at Sequoia Grove at lunchtime for a picnic he had stashed in the trunk. They opened one of the bottles they purchased earlier and enjoyed what was certainly the best grilled vegetable sandwich Tamara had ever eaten, along with a Greek salad and enormous chocolaty brownies. Brownies were her favorite. *Did I tell him that, or did he just know?* she wondered as they ate, nestled among the giant sequoia trees. He seemed to know so many things.

They stopped at one more winery after lunch, and then they headed back to the City. Tamara closed her eyes on the way back. The wine and the food relaxed her, and it had been a long few weeks. Aman reached over and gently moved a piece of hair from the side of her face. Tamara shifted in her seat but did not wake up.

He whispered her name to wake her once they arrived back in the City. "Tamara, we're back."

She slowly opened her eyes. "I can't believe I fell asleep. The wine, I guess."

Aman chuckled and started to lean in to give her a kiss, but she stretched her arms and yawned widely, so he retracted before she even noticed.

"It was a good day, no?" Aman asked.

"Oh, it was a great day. I had such a good time. I can't believe I never took the time to go before."

"You need to start enjoying life."

"I have a feeling you can help me with that."

"I certainly hope so." Aman replied. "So, we have dinner reservations tonight. I hope you like the place. It's supposed to be great." Gary Danko was one of San Francisco's hottest restaurants.

"Do you want to come up for a bit to freshen up before we go out? Not that you need to."

"Uh, sure. I guess."

Once inside his apartment, he excused himself to the bedroom, where he quickly took the tags off the new black pants he bought for dinner. His wardrobe predominantly consisted of scrubs and running clothes. And for this occasion, he wanted something new.

After he changed, he gave himself the once-over in the mirror and determined that saleswoman was right; he could never go wrong with black pants. She also suggested a steel-blue shirt to go with it. He would have never made the combination, but he guessed it worked. He sprayed on a bit of cologne before heading out to the living room.

Tamara had added higher heels and removed her sweater, which revealed her strong, well-defined arms. Her regal neck was accented by a new hairstyle. Her long, dark hair was up in some sort of twist. She looked even more beautiful than she had earlier, Aman thought. He liked that she didn't make a lot of fuss or require an entire production team to look so amazing. As he opened his mouth to tell her so, she rose tentatively from her seat on his beige suede sectional and gave him a measured but warm hug as she said quietly, "Thank you for the perfect day."

He wanted to hold her longer but found the strength to let her go. He was lost for a moment inside the union of her body pressed against his, but finally he found the simple words, "You are most welcome."

Before they both knew it, it was time to go to dinner. The night was so beautiful, they decided to walk to the restaurant. Their table was perfect, the food was delicious, but neither one of them seemed to have much of an appetite. The latent sexual tension that clung beneath the surface of their interaction all day had risen to the top with Tamara's hug. It lingered throughout dinner, and by the time they got to dessert, it was almost palpable.

Aman offered her several options for the balance of the evening. "What would you like to do next? We can listen to some music, go dancing, or take a walk by the water …"

"You know, it's been such a full day, do you think we can just go back to your place and hang out for a bit?" Aman paused before responding, and immediately Tamara started to backpedal, "Or maybe you could just take me back to Neva's house …"

Aman took a deep breath and simply responded, "I think you should come home with me."

The cab they took back seemed to crawl along. They could not get home fast enough. He held the door open, remaining a gentleman. Tamara now looked furtively around the room, unsure of where to sit or whether she should stand. She wrung her hands around and around, not knowing where to put them. Aman proceeded cautiously, careful not to push too hard.

"Tamara, are you okay?"

"Huh? Oh, yeah. I'm fine," she replied awkwardly as she moved to the sectional and sat down on the edge as if she wanted to be able to jump up quickly if needed.

"Please, Tamara, relax. Make yourself at home," Aman said as he turned on Sade. "I want you to feel comfortable," he said as he walked over to where she was sitting, knelt down, and took off her shoes. He wanted to run his hands up her taut legs but restrained himself. She was obviously not at ease, and he had to prove to her that she was safe with him. "Now, something to drink. Champagne?" he offered. Tamara just nodded. Aman was immediately glad that he put in some of the champagne they bought earlier in the day to chill before they left for dinner.

Aman expertly popped the bottle and poured some champagne into two slender flutes. As Tamara took a long sip and looked up at the open metal staircase, which led presumably to his bedroom, he sat down beside her. Tamara couldn't help but giggle as the fizzy bubbles of the champagne mimicked the fluttering of her insides. They sipped quietly for a while and listened to the slow melodies and sensual rhythms of "Secret Taboo," a Sade classic.

Finally, Aman could wait no longer. He reached over to Tamara and gently stroked her face, looking intently into her eyes. He took the glass of champagne out of her hand and placed it on the glass coffee table, took her face in both of his hands, brought it closer to his, and kissed her, deeply and passionately. For a long time. He paused when he thought he tasted the salt of a runaway tear that escaped from her eyes and trickled down her cheek into the corner of his mouth.

Tamara blushed and pulled back from Aman. She wiped her eyes with the back of her hands. Her hands shook as she reached for her glass of champagne, which she downed. "I'm sorry; I don't know what's wrong with me. I feel so stupid."

"Tamara, why are you apologizing? You can no more control your tears than you can control the beating of your heart," he said as he placed his hand carefully over her heart, "or the quickness of your breath," he whispered as he moved his hands to still her quickly rising and falling chest. "You feel what you feel," he said as he moved closer and put his arms around her. He told her in the most gentle of voices, "It's okay. We don't have to do anything you don't want to do. I'm in no hurry."

The warmth of his embrace, along with the perfection of his words, reached around Tamara's heart and encircled all of the hurt and pain that she had carried for so long; she couldn't stop the tears from flowing.

Although she hated crying around people, Tamara couldn't muster up any more embarrassment or shame for doing so. She just received the safe harbor that Aman so generously offered.

He quietly and patiently held her like that for a long, long time. As quickly and feverishly as the tears came, they stopped just as fast. His new blue shirt was damp, and mascara ran down her face. She pulled away from him and chuckled as she said, "We are a mess!"

"A beautiful mess you are."

"I've ruined your shirt. I'm so sorry."

"Stop apologizing. It's just a shirt."

"You should take it off. We don't want you to get sick, Dr. Chandra," Tamara teased.

"When are you going to start calling me Aman?" he teased back, and then stood up and responded with a kiss.

He took her hand in his and led her upstairs, where she deftly removed his shirt, revealing his chiseled chest and abs.

As he undressed her, his hands moved with intentional admiration. He felt her body stiffen, as if she were traveling down this road for the first time. He kissed and caressed her breasts gingerly, giving each one equal attention. He looked up at her and saw that her eyes were closed in ecstatic revelry.

"Tamara, are you okay?" Aman asked tenderly, bringing his face beside hers. "We can stop anytime. I want you to be sure."

"I'm fine, and I have never been more sure," Tamara smiled as she opened her eyes. "Thank you," she whispered as she held his face in her hands and the tears started to well up in her eyes again.

He kissed each of her eyes as she closed them, and then he teased, "Don't thank me yet," as he worked his way down her body with his mouth, slowly planting kisses in all the right places as he went.

Annette

ANNETTE WAS SO TIRED FROM her busy weekend, she was still sleeping. Between soccer, the birthday party, and getting lost in between, coupled with a bit of jet lag, she was wiped. Annette felt someone's presence and hoped it was not Dante. She hadn't seen him all weekend. *I don't even know if he realizes that I'm here. Whatever.*

Ellington tugged at the bottom of the sheet. Annette turned over and tried to keep sleeping. Ellington was persistent.

"Aunt Annette, you gotta get up."

Annette groaned, turned, and stretched.

"You gotta take me to school. Did you forget?"

Oh shit, it's Monday. Annette sat straight up in the bed. *Tamara will kill me if he's late. What time is it?* Annette turned and looked at the clock. It was 7:30 a.m. *We're going to be late for sure.*

"C'mon, we have to hurry. Go run and put your clothes on. I'm going to jump in the shower."

"I need your help. I don't know what to wear."

Annette's eyes grew big. "Just wear whatever. It doesn't matter."

"But I can't do it myself," Ellington whined.

"Are you serious?"

Ellington just stood in place.

"Okay, okay. Let's go to your room and find something cute."

Annette followed Ellington into his room and found some jeans and a T-shirt, along with underwear and socks. *Why can't he do that by himself?*

"Okay, let's go get some cereal for breakfast while I get dressed."

"I don't like cereal," Ellington said while walking down the stairs.

"Are you kidding me? Well, what do you like?"

"Oatmeal."

"We don't have time for oatmeal. What else do you like?"

"Nothing. But I eat peanut butter and jelly."

"That'll work."

Ellington sat at the kitchen counter and started kicking his feet against the wood while Annette looked for the makings of the sandwich.

"Ooh, Ellington, you've gotta stop doing that. It's driving me crazy."

"Sorry," Ellington whimpered as if he were about to start crying.

"That's okay, baby. Auntie Annette just isn't used to doing this."

"I can tell."

Annette placed the sandwich in front of him and started up the stairs to the guest room to get dressed. Just as she was halfway up the stairs, Ellington called out in a voice muffled by a mouthful of peanut butter, "You forgot my drink!"

Annette sighed, "Wait until I get dressed. Keep eating."

"I can't! The peanut butter is sticking to the roof of my mouth. I can't eat anymore."

"Ugh!" Annette released a loud grunt as she stomped back down the stairs, still in her pajamas, opened the refrigerator abruptly, found some orange juice, slammed a glass onto the marble countertop, filled it quickly, spilling most of it on the counter, and then slammed the glass in front of Ellington.

"Thank you, Aunt Annette."

"Ugh," Annette sighed before heading upstairs.

Tamara

TAMARA AND AMAN LINGERED AT his house all day on Sunday, neither one was anxious for their date to end. Tamara and Aman rode to Alta Vista Hospital together the next morning. Tamara was going to meet Annette and then take her to the airport later that afternoon. Tamara's cell phone rang.

"Where are you?"

"Who is this?"

"It's Annette. I'm here at the hospital waiting for you. You're not still at Aman's house, are you?"

Tamara chuckled.

"Who is it?" Aman asked.

Tamara mouthed "Annette" before answering her. "Don't worry, Annette, I am on my way. We are on our way."

"Good."

"Why do you sound like that? You still have plenty of time to get to the airport."

"Girl, I've got to go back to Neva's house first and change. I didn't get a shower, haven't had a bite to eat. I can't get on a plane like this. You never know who you are going to see."

Tamara chuckled again.

"You are certainly in good spirits."

"The best."

"Well, you'll have to tell me all about it when you get here. Hurry up!" Annette hung up the phone.

"What's up? Is everything okay?" Aman asked.

"She just got a good dose of Ellington, I think."

"Oh, I see."

"She'll be fine once she gets back to work."

"When are you going to go back to work?"

"I promised my partners four weeks, no more."

Aman looked sad at that news.

"But I can always come back."

"Or maybe I can come to Chicago to visit you. I've never been. I'm due some time off."

"But who will take care of Heather if you're gone?"

"Well, we don't have to figure all that out right now. Let's just enjoy the time we have."

Annette

"GIRL, YOU ARE FLOATING," ANNETTE commented as Tamara walked into Heather's room.

Tamara blushed.

"And you are wearing the same clothes." Annette shook her head and threw Tamara a pair of jeans and a T-shirt. "Girl, don't you realize how many of these nurses and orderlies saw you leave here with Dr. Fine in that same dress? Go and change. Good thing one of us is thinking."

"Annette, thank you so much for loaning me this dress. He loved it," Tamara shouted from the bathroom.

"Well, I want details."

"All I'll say is that it was perfect." Tamara smiled broadly as she returned to the room in the clothes Annette had brought.

Annette examined her face, smiled, and commented, "You did it. I can tell. You're all glowy and shit."

Tamara blushed and smiled.

"You don't have to say anything. I can tell. I'm glad. Now take me home so I can get out of here. Two days of motherhood is enough for me!"

Neva

AT ABOUT THE THREE-WEEK MARK, there was a special visiting day for family and friends. Tamara was bringing Ellington. Dante opted not to come. Neva nervously dressed that morning, unsure of how Ellington would respond. Although they had spoken every day, he could be so unpredictable.

"Mommy!"

"Ellington!" She was so happy that she cried, although she wasn't sure why. She was learning now to let the tears flow when they came.

"Mommy, why are you crying? Aren't you happy to see me?"

"Of course I am. Of course. These are happy tears."

"Yay!" Ellington jumped up and down.

"So tell me all about what I missed for the past few weeks," Neva said to Ellington while taking his hand and walking around the grounds.

"Well, I went to school. I went to soccer practice. I had fun with Aunt T. We played games."

"You did?" Neva turned to Tamara, who was walking behind them, and raised an eyebrow.

"Yep."

"I am so glad you've been having fun. Mommy missed you so much."

"I missed you too, Mommy."

"I can't wait to come back home and be with you."

"Me too, Mommy. Are you all better now?"

Neva chuckled. "I'm better but not 'all better.' I'm getting there."

"Well, I want you to be all better!"

"Me too. Mommy is going to need your help when I get back home, okay?"

"Me, and Daddy too?"

Neva smiled awkwardly in response to his question.

"You are being such a big boy, and I'm so proud of you!" Neva reached down and gave him a big hug. He ran out ahead and left the two friends walking slowly behind.

"You look good, girl," Tamara noticed. "I can tell they've been making you eat."

Neva smiled. "I'm doing better. How are you holding up? Is everything okay? Is Dante helping at all? Is Ellington being too much?"

"It is an adjustment, but I think I'm getting the hang of it. He has a lot of preferences, but I'm getting them down," Tamara smiled. "It's really not that bad, Neva. Dante has been steering clear of the house and us for the most part, which is probably better for me anyway." Tamara took Neva's hand as they slowed down and watched Ellington spin himself around in circles until he fell down, dizzy.

"I am glad to have been able to do this for you. It's an honor," Tamara said in a serious voice.

"Oh, T, I can't ever begin to thank you. I wouldn't be here if it weren't for you," Neva said as she embraced Tamara. "And Ellington, he looks so happy. I was so worried about him—and you. And I missed him so much. That has been an unexpected gift. I am usually just so worn-out with him, I have barely had a chance to love him."

"Girl, kids really are resilient and intuitive. He was geared up to be a big boy for you. I can tell. We've been getting along okay. And I haven't lost my cool. Well, maybe only once, but I apologized right away," Tamara giggled. "I think the daily phone calls helped a lot. You are a good mom, Neva. He just wants you to be better."

"I really do feel better. I wasn't sure I ever would, but I do, thanks to you. I guess I needed some way to clear some space in my head and my heart. It's like finally I have room for something other than fear."

"I know; me too."

Annette

THE CLICK-CLACK OF ANNETTE'S BLACK Louboutin pumps echoed in the hallway of the doctor's office. She was so tired the whole time during her California visit and still exhausted once she got home. *That boy really wore me out.* She was sure that was all it was, but Tamara made her promise to go for a checkup once she got back home—a regular old internist, not an ob-gyn. Tamara was always saying how too many women, especially those over forty, use their ob-gyn as their primary care physician, when every woman needed to see a regular doctor at least every two years, even if she was healthy. Annette hated going to the doctor; it was such a waste of time. She was always fine, and she wasted a whole afternoon because she couldn't even use her BlackBerry while she was waiting.

There had been way too much waiting in her world lately, and it just didn't suit her. She wanted what she wanted when she wanted it, which was always right now—and yesterday was even better. But what could she do but wait for Heather to wake up? And wait to conceive? Her lover said he would wait for her. He would not accept Annette's attempts to cut things off. He was convinced that she was his soul mate, but she was married and she was not ready to leave Thomas; she just needed to be reminded that she was still captivating. Nothing more. She still loved him, affair or not.

She sighed as she considered the whole thing, and then she heard the nurse call her name. *Finally*, she thought as she followed the nurse into the exam room. They did the usual—weight, blood pressure, both fine, of course. Then the nurse suggested that she give a urine sample. Annette complied, then gave some blood and had a brief chat with the doctor about how she had been feeling—tired, but given her workload, the stress of Heather's situation, and spending a weekend with Ellington, it was definitely explainable.

The nurse called the doctor out, and he excused himself for a moment, leaving Annette shivering in the thin hospital gown sitting on the examining table. *I really don't have time for these interruptions; I have things to do.* Annette's frustration began to rise as she swung her legs against the table's edge and folded her arms across her chest defiantly.

Before her frustration reached the next level, the doctor burst back into the room.

"Well, I think I know why you have been so tired. I suspected it but didn't want to say anything until I had confirmation," he said excitedly.

"So?"

"You're pregnant. My guess is about four weeks, but you should make an appointment with your ob-gyn right away. Congratulations. I know you have been trying for a long time."

Annette's feet stopped swinging, her eyes opened wide, and she felt her heart stop beating, just for a second.

Heather

MY HEART USED TO SKIP a beat whenever I saw a black man who I thought looked like me. Every time I saw one, I would look into his eyes to see if he recognized me. I thought we would both just know, that there would be a connection that was undeniable. Most of the time, my mother would apologize and pull me away. Other times, I would get a smile or a look of pity, but never the warm embrace I was looking for. So, I kept looking, always thinking maybe he was just around the next corner.

Lauren

HEATHER'S SHOWING IS COMING TOGETHER nicely, Lauren thought. The framing, nearly finished, looked fabulous. She finalized the guest list. The gallery owner was still dogging her about Heather's whereabouts, and Lauren had worn out the reclusive artist routine. She would have to come up with something. Technically, since Neva had Lauren's power of attorney, she supposed that Neva could give the official authorization. *I'm sure I could talk her into it, if I could get her away from those other two*, Lauren thought to herself. *Maybe I'll just do it myself.* She wondered what the penalties could be for forging something like that, as if anyone would ever find out. Then she thought about the repercussions when, not if, Heather's art career blew up: the whole thing could come crashing down. *All my hard work is not going to be for nothing again.*

She resigned herself to talk to Neva. She would get her permission, and they would move forward as planned. *I know I am doing the right thing.*

Neva and Tamara

As she arrived home, Neva silently surveyed the house and thought that Tamara had done a good job of keeping it all together. *I'm surprised, thankful, but shocked.*

"Everything's still here. Nothing's broken," Tamara assured her.

"I can see that, I'm just …" Neva stood in the kitchen and looked around, and tears started to fall.

"What is it? Too much being back? Did you need to stay another week?" Tamara rushed to her side and wrapped her arms around her.

Neva shook her head and herself from Tamara's embrace. "No, I didn't need to stay another week, not that I wouldn't have loved to, but it was time for me to come back. I am just so overwhelmed by what you have done for me. Tamara, I don't know if I can ever repay you."

"Neva, don't be silly. We aren't keeping score. I am glad I was able to help. Don't get me wrong: it wasn't easy, but I had help. Carmen kept things clean, which helped. Annette came out and gave me a break. And honestly, I think I learned a lot about myself in the past four weeks being here, as you did at Bayside."

Neva sniffed and sat down on one of the stools in the kitchen. "What do you mean?"

"You know, I'm on the go, go, go all the time. I never stop and slow down even for a minute to consider my life or my choices. Being here, being you for this time, watching Heather just lie there day after day, it taught me a lot."

"Like what?"

"Well, I learned that being a mother is no joke," Tamara laughed as Neva reached for a tissue. "But, seriously, I think that maybe the fact that I don't have kids is right for me, you know? I'm not sure that I would ever be cut out for this."

"Humph, I'm not so sure that I'm cut out for this either."

"You are a wonderful mother. The fact that Ellington is so happy is proof of that. And he's not an easy kid. I mean, managing him and your husband, you should get even more points because you have been mothering under duress."

Neva chuckled at Tamara's remarks.

"I'm serious. I don't see how you do it. Dante was pretty much out of sight while I was here, but, girl, I can tell he is a trip. I'm glad that I don't have one of those either if husbands are like that. I don't know, I suppose that I am starting to see that maybe where I am is exactly where I'm supposed to be, even when I don't want to be there," Tamara finished.

"You sound like someone else I know. So, how is Dr. Chandra, or Aman as we now call him?" Neva teased.

"He's fine," Tamara blushed. "You know, not that I am at all glad that Heather did what she did and is in a coma or anything, but if she hadn't and if she weren't and if you didn't need to go to Bayside and if I didn't stay here, we would have never discovered each other—is that wrong?" Tamara gushed.

"No, it's not wrong at all. Heather would be happy for you. Oh, my God, I don't believe it. Tamara, are you in love?"

"I'm not saying all that—yet. But, Neva, I have never met a man like him before. I don't know how to describe it; he's extraordinary," Tamara beamed.

"Wow," Neva's eyes widened. "I am so happy for you."

"Thanks, but I do feel a little guilty."

"Why?"

"I was supposed to be taking care of Ellington and watching over Heather, and instead, I'm falling in love."

"Ha! So you admit it. Ta-ma-ra's in love! Ta-ma-ra's in love!" Neva continued her lighthearted teasing until she felt what had become the unfamiliar internal girding, the unconscious constriction of her insides, as if preparing for an anticipated blow, which could only mean that Dante was near, home from his weekly Saturday morning golf game. He stood in the foyer with his golfing gear still on and paused when he saw her in the kitchen. Both Neva and Tamara stood frozen for a moment, unsure of what his reaction would be.

He took off his hat and exhaled loudly before stating, "I see you finally found your way back home, but then, we've managed to make it fine without you, haven't we?" As he walked upstairs to shower, he added sarcastically, "Welcome back."

As soon as he cleared their hearing, Tamara asked, "Okay, so what are you going to do about that? You can't keep living with him, or you'll never get completely well."

Neva's familiar uncomfortable smile turned to a grimace filled with resolve as she said carefully and quietly, "Tamara, I have to leave him. I am going to tell him about the abortion, and then Ellington and I are going to leave."

"Wow!" Now it was Tamara's turn to open her eyes wide.

"I mean, I'm not saying I'm getting a divorce, but you're right. I cannot live like this anymore. It's not healthy for me or Ellington. I thought I was going to talk all about me in therapy, and instead, we spent most of our time talking about him. How his heart was closed to my needs. How he abandoned me over and over again with his silence. How his demands left me diminished. How his criticisms stole my esteem. How his verbal jabs and constant humiliations beat me down as sure as any fist. I'm certain that I've been emotionally abused for almost my entire marriage, and I now know that that's domestic violence too.

"If he wants to change and wants to get some help, then maybe we can work through this, but until he does, I am saving my own life."

"Well, all right then," Tamara straightened up with pride. "Now that's the girl I used to know."

Neva chuckled as she continued, "The reality is, once I tell him about the abortion, he'll probably leave me before we can go anywhere."

"I want to say I'm sorry and I am for Ellington, but for you—I'm glad. And I'm sorry for feeling happy, but I could tell that you were withering away in this marriage, in this life, and I don't want to lose another friend."

"You're right, I would have been lost if it weren't for you. Will you come back when I tell him? I just ... I just don't want to be here by myself."

"Of course. Do you want me to ask Aman to come over too? I think it would be good to have a man around, just in case."

Lauren

HER HANDS WERE SHAKING AS she dialed Neva's number. Lauren hoped that Neva wouldn't answer as much as she wished she would. *I have to face her eventually; it might as well be now,* she sighed to herself while the phone rang. And rang. And rang. Finally, Lauren heard Neva's voice sounding stronger than ever on the line.

"Hello?"

"Um, Neva … this is Lauren."

"I know."

"Well, I—"

"How've you been?"

"Who, oh, me? Well, I've been okay. Hey, listen, I'm sorry to have rushed off that way; I just couldn't—"

"You don't have to explain to me, Lauren. You did what you had to do. What's up?"

Lauren wasn't prepared for Neva's directness. *She must really be mad. This is going to be harder than I thought.*

"Well, I guess you figured out that I have the paintings with me. I wanted to show them to an expert to see really what we were dealing with, you know, so that we could make the best possible decision for Heather."

"Lauren, it looks like you made the decision for all of us."

"Well, okay, I kind of did, but for all the right reasons. I knew you all would disagree and try to stop me, and I knew what I was doing was right. I can't explain it, but I had to try. I had to see. And guess what?"

"What?"

"He loved them."

"Who are you talking about?"

"I took the pictures to a gallery owner, and he loved them. He wants to do a show."

"Wow."

"I know; it's amazing, right?"

"That's a word for it."

"So, how is Heather doing?"

"I was wondering when you were going to ask."

"Well, I just got so caught up with the art ... and trying to explain."

"She's the same. Still in a coma."

"Well, how long are you going to let her stay like that? It's been over six weeks, for God's sake."

"I'm not even going to answer that. So, you know how Heather is doing. You confirmed that you stole her artwork, and now have gotten someone else interested without Heather's permission. Are you going to send them back? Because if not, I'm not sure we really have anything else to talk about."

"Well, actually, um, I want to talk to you about actually doing the show. This guy is really charged about it, and I think it could be a great thing. I could really use your help."

"Lauren, I can't think about something like that right now. I have too much going on in my life right now. A little art show is the least of my concerns at the moment. I'm glad you're doing okay, but I really have to go now. Oh, and I will be informing Annette so that we can take whatever legal action is required."

Neva abruptly hung up the phone.

Lauren was not going to be dissuaded by Neva's obstinacy. She was determined to continue moving forward with the show whether Neva agreed or not.

Neva

INTEGRATING WHAT SHE LEARNED AT Bayside into her daily life was proving to be more difficult than Neva had imagined, and it had not even been a week. She had only seen Dr. Hughes once since she left Bayside, and now that Tamara was gone, she never felt more alone. The decision to leave Dante was swirling around in her head—what to say, how to say it, when to say it ... Dr. Hughes said, "Don't rush. You'll know when the time is right."

Would the time ever be right to destroy a family? she thought as she climbed out of the corner of the bed where she relegated herself to sleeping since she'd gotten back and headed to the bathroom. She had been waking up a half hour earlier so she could have some time before she started giving herself to everyone else. She thought it would have made her more tired, but she actually found herself less drained than before. She shuffled into the bathroom and turned on the water. She sat on the side of the tub while it filled with hot water and closed her eyes for a moment. Before long, she felt water touching the sleeve of her pajamas, and she jumped awake in time to turn off the water before it overflowed. She let some of the water out while she yawned and reached for some bath salts.

Her pajamas hung loosely on her increasingly slender frame. She slid them off easily and stepped into the hot water gingerly, wincing a little as her cool skin made contact with the steaming water. As she leaned back in the tub and let the aroma of eucalyptus and rosemary fill her nostrils, Neva closed her eyes and thought about how she would tell him. The oversize tub nearly swallowed her. She ran different scenarios through her mind, letting choice words float to the surface and then submerge themselves again.

The news about the abortion should definitely be the first thing I say, and then I can talk about why I had it, why I kept it a secret, and why we need time apart. Or I could talk about how his treatment of me and the environment he created caused me to feel like I couldn't endure another child, and why I was too afraid to tell him and why all of that adds up to the fact that our marriage is in trouble. She closed her eyes and wondered, *Where will I find the strength to actually do it? I have never really confronted him before, and I'm not sure if I can do it now. I'm stronger than ever, but somehow I'm not sure I'm as strong as I need to be. One thing is for sure: I cannot continue living in his shadow.*

Tamara

TAMARA WAS BACK ON THE lakefront doing her post-delivery run and feeling thankful that spring had finally decided to make an appearance in Chicago. Typically there were two seasons, steaming and freezing. Crisp fall days and hopeful spring days were rare. She was trying to let her mind be more still as she ran and let the water calm her. Aman wanted her to stop wearing her iPod too; he said it would help her be more in the moment, but she wasn't giving that up. *I hope I don't have to give him up either.* She smiled to herself as she thought about her upcoming trip back to the Bay Area.

The nature of the journey was most grim. Neva was finally going to confront Dante, and they were going to discuss options for Heather. But she could not contain her excitement about seeing Aman again. He invited her to stay at his place instead of Neva's but completely understood when she told him that she didn't want to leave Neva alone. Before she could even ask, he volunteered to come over, in case they needed a nonhostile male presence in the house. *He is so wonderfully intuitive,* she thought in amazement as she neared Oak Street Beach.

The conflicting emotions she felt—anticipation and trepidation, and then guilt about the anticipation—were difficult for her to navigate, but he was right there, helping her remain engaged in whatever she was feeling and convincing her that no matter how challenging it was to experience, having the experience was better than being so hardened that she felt nothing. These days, she was feeling all sorts of wonderful things.

As she turned around at Fullerton Avenue, Tamara shrugged and wondered how Annette was doing. They hadn't really talked since she came back from Neva's house. Things had been really busy for both of them, but they promised they were not going to fall into this trap again—their relationship, all of their relationships, had to become a priority. At North Avenue, she considered running over to Annette's house, since she was so close. She looked at her watch, 6:00 a.m. *Pretty early, but Annette might be awake and on her way to the gym,* she thought to herself before continuing down the lakefront path to the hospital. *I'll see her soon enough.*

Annette

ANNETTE HAD BEEN AVOIDING EVERYONE since she learned the news. She hadn't spoken to Tamara in at least two weeks. *She would know the minute she saw me. How could I be so stupid?* she thought to herself as she boarded the plane to go back to the Bay Area. *I knew better.* It had been her third trip in as many months—so much had changed in such a short time—and Thomas wanted to come. *Thank goodness I was able to convince him to stay put. I do not need him here.*

She was sure they were going to notice, although she had managed to hide her newly discovered pregnancy from Thomas so far. After all, her face had gotten fuller, her breasts a little juicier, and she could barely keep her eyes open, but she was still doing "on demand" performances of sex. She had to keep up the pretense that they were still "trying."

She was not looking forward to this flight, and she didn't even have the benefit of alcohol. Hopefully the exhaustion would kick in and she could sleep the whole way. As if she could. The noise from the debating voices in her head were hard to ignore. Should she keep the ambiguity of her baby's father a secret and proceed as if she were sure that it was her husband's child, or should she tell the truth? Then there was also the possibility of informing Thomas while keeping her paramour in the dark. *He would never leave me alone if he even thought there was the smallest chance that I was carrying his child. No, he must never know.* Annette sighed as she looked out the window as the plane jetted down the O'Hare runway and lifted off the ground. She wasn't sure if the sinking feeling in her stomach was from the plane taking off or her own suspicion that something was going to go terribly wrong with this pregnancy. *It would serve me right, I suppose.*

Lauren

THE CREAMY COMPLEXION OF THE three invitation envelopes contrasted sharply with the dark mahogany stain of Prescott's ample desk. Lauren lined them up like dominoes, deciding whether she was going to let them fall. She took a long sip of the earthy scotch as she considered her options. *Should I go ahead and gloat, or would I end up tipping my hand?* A preview for local art critics went extremely well. Press coverage was confirmed. RSVPs were pouring in. People who weren't invited were angling for a spot on the coveted guest list. Her marketing skills were finally being put to good use.

I am going to make Heather a lot of money, she thought to herself. *I hope she's around to enjoy it. They would have told me if she came out of the coma, wouldn't they?* she wondered as she swirled the remnant dark brown liquid spirit around in the crystal highball glass and finished it in one gulp, enjoying the smoky taste as it glided down her throat. She stood up from the high-back black leather chair, picked up the invitations, and threw them in the garbage can.

Neva

"WHERE IS TAMARA?" ANNETTE ASKED as she got out of the car and walked into Neva's kitchen.

"She came in a little earlier to spend some time with Aman, I mean Dr. Chandra, I mean, well, you know what I mean," Neva responded.

"At least one good thing has come from all of this," Annette suggested as she set her own bags in the foyer and took a familiar seat at the kitchen counter. Neva stood on the other side of the island, wiping down the granite countertop.

"And what's that?"

"Tamara is finally getting some!" Annette giggled and then yawned.

"Girl, that flight really got to you, huh? You haven't stopped yawning since I picked you up."

"Yeah, I guess." Annette wanted to distract the attention from her unending first trimester fatigue. "When is T going to grace us with her presence? We've got a lot to discuss."

"Later, I guess. There's really no rush, is there? They really are cute together, aren't they? I am so happy for her. Who'da thought after all this time. He seems perfect for her. She so deserves it."

"You do too, Neva."

"One step at a time, Annette. I haven't even said anything to him yet."

"Which is another reason why we're here. I can't wait. 'Let's get ready to rum-ble!'" Annette said, imitating the famous boxing announcer.

"You always did like to fight."

"That's why I'm such a damn good lawyer. I welcome confrontation, even thrive on it. I'm always ready to throw down. I know you're a lover, not a fighter, which is why your husband's bullshit pisses me off even more. You're too damn nice."

"Oh, Annette."

"What? I'm serious. Do you know what you're going to say yet? Do we need to practice? Let me be him," Annette said as she stood up and pulled down her tunic, one of the few tops that hid the growing baby inside her.

Neva chuckled at Annette's enthusiasm. "Sit down. I'm good."

She had been going over different scenarios with Dr. Hughes. Preparation was important, but he convinced her that honesty and authenticity were key.

"I'm sorry, I'm being rude. I haven't even offered you anything to drink. Want some wine?" Neva asked, turning to open a cabinet door.

"No, I'm good."

"Are you sure?" Neva prodded with a puzzled look on her face. Annette didn't often turn down a glass of wine.

Annette didn't know how much longer she would be able to not drink without suspicion. She heard a key in the door and knew it was Dante. She never thought she would be glad to see him, but she was not ready to tell Neva, not yet. She looked at Neva as Dante's footsteps entered the foyer and saw her entire body freeze, full of tension. It was like he came in the room and the entire atmosphere shifted. *Poor Neva.* Annette shook her head.

Dante started to walk upstairs without even saying hello, but once he noticed the back of Annette's auburn head, it was as if someone flipped a switch, and his countenance instantly glowed. He beamed as he walked into the kitchen and greeted her with a warm kiss on the check. "Annette, always good to see you."

"Hey," Annette responded blandly. She was past done with him. He didn't seem to register her lukewarm response and squeezed her shoulder briefly before turning to Neva to ask, "What's for dinner?"

Neva took a deep breath before responding, "I don't know. I haven't really had time to think about it yet."

"Humph," was his only response as he took a towel to wipe down the handle of the refrigerator door before opening it to get a beer. "You should really try to keep this clean. It only takes a minute."

Annette opened her mouth to respond, but Neva placed a hand on her arm to quiet her. Dante took his beer and went quietly upstairs. Annette rolled her eyes before commenting, "Girl, you are a saint, I swear. I don't know how you dealt with him all these years."

"I dealt with it because I guess, deep down, I didn't realize it was wrong. He wrapped his control in the right words, and his demands of perfectionism were masked by beautiful gifts and beautiful things, so I thought everything was my fault. I thought something was wrong with me. Everything I said was denounced and whatever I did didn't measure up until I couldn't find anything else to say and only could do what he wanted. I spent the last ten years on my tiptoes, walking around on eggshells, making sure they didn't break; instead, I did. But now ..."

"Now you are standing flat-footed with your head held high. I know it hasn't been easy, and I am so proud of you."

"I haven't done anything yet," Neva replied shyly.

"Are you kidding me? Finding the courage to tell the truth, taking the initiative to heal yourself, that's major. You have got to start giving yourself more credit."

Neva looked away, trying to avoid Annette's penetrating gaze. Annette put her hand on Neva's arm and forced their eyes to meet. "I know you've been through a lot and you feel all broken down, but believe me, you won't be broken forever. In fact, I can already see what's beyond the broken; and I tell you, it looks beautiful to me."

Tears welled up in Neva's eyes, and before she could release them, Tamara burst through the door. She kept the key she used when she was staying with Ellington.

"Hey!" Tamara shouted into the kitchen as she put her bags down in the foyer. Despite the tragedy that was imminent, she couldn't contain her joy.

"I was just wondering when you were going to be able to pull yourself away from Doctor Fine." Annette rose to hug Tamara but suddenly put her hand to her mouth and ran to the bathroom instead.

"What do you think that's all about?" Neva asked Tamara. As she finished the question, they both looked at each other knowingly, took off running down the hallway to the bathroom, and started banging on the door.

"Annette, you're pregnant!" Tamara shouted.

"Oh my God, I can't believe you didn't tell us!" Neva added.

"Woo-hoo!" Tamara shouted and raised her fist to bang the door once more, only Annette opened the door and walked out of the bathroom, wiping her mouth.

"Neva, can I have some water?" Annette quietly asked.

"Of course," Neva responded after giving her a big hug. "I'm so happy for you!"

"Me too!" Tamara echoed and gave her own hug. "I can't believe your ass didn't say anything. What were you waiting for? I'm a little hurt. What about you, Neva?"

"Oh, I'm definitely hurt—and highly offended," Neva teased as she brought the glass of water into the living room, where they all sat down.

"I guess we know how you're feeling," Tamara stated, rubbing Annette's back. Annette turned her head and shot her a look of surprise.

"Has the morning sickness been really bad?" Neva asked. "I never got sick with Ellington, thank goodness."

"It's been okay, not too bad, I guess," Annette responded. "It's been harder to keep it all a secret."

"Why would you need to do that? You and Thomas have been trying for so long. I know he's thrilled," Neva replied.

"He doesn't know."

"Why, Annette, what's wrong?" Tamara asked.

"I didn't want to do this here, not now, not when we have to deal with Heather and Neva."

"Annette, it's okay; just tell us," Neva prodded.

Annette drew in a deep breath before sharing the embarrassing truth: "I haven't told Thomas or either of you, or anyone else, because I'm not 100 percent certain who the father is."

Tamara withdrew her hand from Annette's back. Wringing her hands, she said, "Oh, Annette, not DC …"

"Yes."

"How could you do that? How could you be so careless? I mean, you knew you were trying to get pregnant, and you didn't make him wear a condom?" Tamara inquired pointedly.

"Condoms break, you know," Annette responded.

"And it only takes one time," Neva remembered. "Oh, Annette, what are you going to do?"

"I don't know. I am having this baby, no matter what—that much I do know."

"Of course," Neva answered. "You tried so hard."

"Yeah, and for it to happen like this, it just seems so unfair," Annette replied.

"Well, unfair or not, it's a blessing. A new life is a blessing," Neva said deliberately.

"I know," Annette replied.

"So, are you going to pretend it's Thomas's, or tell him the truth? And what about DC? You have to stop seeing him, right?" Neva asked.

"Of course. I've already cooled things off with him. I don't want him to see me and suspect anything. But how can I tell Thomas? He'll be devastated."

"But the secret, the secret will destroy you," Neva shared.

"I know, but I don't know if I can handle it if he leaves me. I do love my husband. I know it may seem strange to you all, given my indiscretion, but I do," Annette admitted.

"It's complicated," Tamara encouraged, "but you'll make the right decision, and whatever that is, we're right here for you."

"No matter what," Neva echoed.

Neva, Annette, Tamara, and Heather

ANNETTE AND TAMARA AND NEVA gathered at Heather's bedside after saying their individual good-byes. Carmen was there as well. She had been stopping by every so often to pray with Heather. They thought her prayers would be good to have today. They struggled long and hard with the decision to disconnect Heather from life support. *How long is long enough to wait?*

Heather's brain activity had decreased significantly over the past weeks, and Dr. Chandra was certain that the Heather they knew and loved was no longer there. He had been a tremendous help, trying his best to assuage any guilt that might prevent the right decision from manifesting.

"There comes a moment when waiting without action can become like trying to force the hand of God," he told them. "You have to know when to loosen the grip on what you want and open your hands to receive what God wants to give you."

Neva found it hard to believe that God wanted to give her good things. Dr. Chandra even said, "What God wants for us always surpasses the things we want for ourselves." *Then why so much pain?* Neva wondered. Dr. Chandra and Dr. Hughes tried to help her comprehend that sometimes the hard places are necessary to get you to where you are supposed to be. Neva would have preferred to skip the bad stuff altogether but knew too well that life doesn't work that way. And, like Dr. Chandra asked, "Would joy be as recognizable if there was no discomfort or pain?"

She hated to admit that he was probably right, but still she would have preferred a life where all her girlfriends were happily married, with beautiful, healthy children and fulfilling careers (or not, whichever they truly preferred). No abortions, suicides, affairs, guilt, or betrayals allowed. Neva knew she was being naïve but couldn't change her desires for more peace for herself and all of her friends, even now, when the only one who really seemed at peace was Heather.

The room was so still, almost hushed. They could feel Heather's presence, as if she herself confirmed that they were doing the right thing. As they stood around her, hand in Kleenexed hand, eyes red and swollen, but hearts open, she encircled their gathering and affirmed their actions, giving them courage to do the right thing.

They all stood still and watched intently as Dr. Chandra turned off the respirator. Usually he wouldn't have done it himself. Such an ordinary action. He told them they didn't have to be there, but they wanted to be— had to be—there for this moment, which was not ordinary at all. It was indeed sacred, and they had to be present to bear witness. Although they knew it would never happen, for just a moment, they held their collective breath with the unlikely hope that Heather might somehow start inhaling and exhaling on her own, that once again her eyes might flutter with life again, but as Dr. Chandra gently removed the tube from her mouth, after a final rise and fall of her thin, frail chest, she was still.

Lauren

As Lauren walked around the gallery, the noise of the caterers clanging glasses upon silver trays and the clank of highboy table legs falling into place faded to a subtle din. It was as if she were in a trance and Heather herself was giving her a guided tour, piece by piece. No matter that she had become so intimate with the paintings over the past few weeks; tonight it was as if she were seeing them for the first time.

The countless mornings she had spent in her husband's library poring over each detail made the work seem like old friends, like the friends she left behind, or who left her—*which was it, exactly?* Either way, she was there, with Heather, in a way. It was like Heather knew, that somehow she understood that Lauren needed this. This was as much for herself as it was for Heather.

She took a deep breath and smoothed the skirt of her new black dress, one dress size smaller, as she went to open the door to let some of the people in. Not everyone, not all at once.

She didn't feel nervous at all. She didn't know how, but deep inside, she felt sure. She knew she was doing the right thing.

Heather

I FEEL SO WARM, AND I don't know why. It's like someone lit a candle at the top of my head and the flame has slowly burned all the way down to the soles of my feet, leaving everything melted inside. The warmth is drawing me inside of itself, and as I wrap my arms around it, I can no longer tell which part is the warm feeling and which part is me. It is wonderful. I close my eyes and soak it in for a nice long time.

When I finally open them, my mother is standing so close, I think I can touch her. She is radiant and beautiful as ever. Beside her is someone I have never seen before. He is tall and dark. His eyes are like an infinity pool of gentleness that keeps spilling over when he looks at her. It never runs out but keeps overflowing with love. She is smiling and looks like she would dive right into those eyes if she could. Then they both turn toward me, holding their hands and extending them to me, inviting me to join them with smiles so brilliant and white.

I have to go.

Open Book Editions
A Berrett-Koehler Partner

Open Book Editions is a joint venture between Berrett-Koehler Publishers and Author Solutions, the market leader in self-publishing. There are many more aspiring authors who share Berrett-Koehler's mission than we can sustainably publish. To serve these authors, Open Book Editions offers a comprehensive self-publishing opportunity.

A Shared Mission

Open Book Editions welcomes authors who share the Berrett-Koehler mission—Creating a World That Works for All. We believe that to truly create a better world, action is needed at all levels—individual, organizational, and societal. At the individual level, our publications help people align their lives with their values and with their aspirations for a better world. At the organizational level, we promote progressive leadership and management practices, socially responsible approaches to business, and humane and effective organizations. At the societal level, we publish content that advances social and economic justice, shared prosperity, sustainability, and new solutions to national and global issues.

Open Book Editions represents a new way to further the BK mission and expand our community. We look forward to helping more authors challenge conventional thinking, introduce new ideas, and foster positive change.

For more information, see the Open Book Editions website:
http://www.iuniverse.com/Packages/OpenBookEditions.aspx

Join the BK Community! See exclusive author videos, join discussion groups, find out about upcoming events, read author blogs, and much more! http://bkcommunity.com/